Spectres and Darkness

Selected Works

JOE NASSISE
DREW WILLIAMS

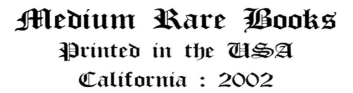

Medium Rare Books
Printed in the USA
California : 2002

These stories are works of fiction. Names, characters, places and incidents are either the product of the author's imagination or are used fictiously. Any resemblance to actual events or locales or persons, living or dead, is entirely coincidental.

Published by Medium Rare Books
Anaheim, CA 92804
www.MediumRareBooks.com
Cover Art John Turi
All Design Work (c) MMII

Word Count: 74,000

International Serial Book Number
ISBN 0-9711162-3-7 softcover

Manufactured in the United States of America and distributed to the book trade by www.MEDIUMRAREBOOKS.com

1 3 5 7 9 10 8 6 4 2

First Edition

Acknowledgements

Drew would like to buy the world a Coke, but since that's a bit out of his price range, he'd like to say thanks to his wife, Cathi, for allowing him to use the computer.

Joe (who thinks Drew is nuts because everyone knows that Pepsi is the One) would like to thank his wife and children for giving Daddy time to finish his "scary stories." He'd also like to thank Drew for agreeing to this crazy idea in the first place.

Both authors would like to thank Brian Keene for writing the introduction and the publisher of Medium Rare Books, John Turi, for bringing this collection to the unsuspecting public.

"Funky Chickens"
first appeared in The Rare Anthology. Disc-Us Books, 2001.
"Twilight at The Cairo"
first appeared in Deviant Minds, January 2001.
Portions of Art and Becoming were serialized
at The Art of Horror, October 2001.

The Truth of Lies
An Introduction
By Brian Keene

NOTE: The following is a true story—a recounting of actual events. If you are a wife, friend, family member, or employer of Joseph Nassise or Drew Williams, stop reading now!

Eleven P.M. in Seattle, Washington. The World Horror Convention 2001.

I was backstage, having just passed an empty cup around to the audience to collectively spit in, and then consuming the contents. I did this as a contestant in the annual Gross-Out Contest, a beat séance of repulsive fiction and performance art.

The crowd dug it. I won.

(Don't worry. I'd had six-months worth of shots in preparation).

So I was busy puking other people's spit when the police started beating on the door. These weren't friendly "can we come in?" knocks. These were frame-rattling blows, followed by some rather unfriendly and angry voices.

The Seattle City Council had suggested to me that I not do the act. Something about decency laws. I was supposed to consider it a warning.

Before I could even stand up, I was being led to a police car. They put me in the back, next to a guy who reminded me a bit of a shorter Michael Gross (circa *Family Ties* and *Tremors*). At first, I thought the cops must have had their own distillery in the back of the vehicle. Then I figured out that the tequila and bourbon was wafting off of my fellow passenger.

"I'm Drew," he happily slurred. "What's your name?"

"Hi, Drew. I'm Brian Keene."

He drooled gleefully and asked me to sign a book for him. I politely declined, pointing out that my hands were busy being handcuffed behind my back at the moment, and he'd left his book inside the hotel, along with his other belongings.

It turned out that Drew Williams had been doing a lot of that on this particular evening. So much, in fact, that the authorities had to be called. I've never learned the complete details, but apparently he followed a certain best-selling horror author into the bathroom and tried to get his autograph while the man was sitting in a stall.

Drew was in the stall with him at the time.

They put us in the holding tank, along with a gentleman named Bubba, who told Drew "you're my little puppy dog now." Drew asked him if he was a writer too.

After a few hours, he sobered up enough to comprehend our predicament. He was worried, and rightfully so. Turns out Drew Williams held a Ph.D. and taught Creative Writing.

I promised Drew that I'd get us out of this before his school found out, but in return he had to promise to leave Bubba alone. He agreed.

Before I could hatch a plan, however, the cops told us we had a visitor. On the other side of the bars stood a kind-faced, soft-spoken man.

Drew introduced him as Joe Nassise.

It turned out that the two of them knew each other already. Joe witnessed the police loading us into the car, and had come down to offer his assistance. He couldn't post our bail, as he had no money (something I've never believed, since he seems to fly all over the country for free). He was there to offer us some spiritual stamina; a light against the darkness, and that sounded all right by me.

He began to quote a passage from Psalms, chapter one forty-two, verse seven. "Bring my soul out of prison, that I may praise thy name."

At this point, the guard jumped as if somebody had jolted him with a cattle prod.

"Wait a minute," he snarled. "I heard these boys say you was a *horror writer.*" He said that the same way somebody says 'phlegm' when asked what that is floating in their soup.

"I am," Joe beamed. "I'm also a church bishop."

The guard proceeded to lock Joe up with us, again quoting the city's decency laws.

"You ought not to be writing that devil crap," he muttered, slamming the cell door. "A man of God should be writing stuff like the *Left Behind* series."

"But the *Left Behind* books *are* horror, you jerk!" Joe shouted, waking Bubba.

We sat there for another hour, before my agent finally bailed us all out.

And that is how I met Joe Nassise and Drew Williams.

True story, and one they didn't want me to tell.

Well, okay, maybe you thought it was true. Maybe you knew it was a lie, knew it was fiction, but wanted to believe it anyway.

That's because that is what writers do. We tell lies, and make you want to believe them. Occasionally, a writer comes along that not only tells believable lies, but can also show you some hidden truths within them.

Joe Nassise and Drew Williams do that exceedingly well. They are, in fact, two of the most talented and exciting authors to hit the horror genre in quite some time. There's a buzz about these guys, the kind of buzz that only comes along once in a decade.

If you've read Drew's novel, *NIGHT TERRORS*, or Joe's novel, *RIVERWATCH*, then you know what I'm talking about. These guys don't just tell one hell of a good horror story (which they do). They force you to examine some things that you'd probably rather not think about. They've done it again with this collection.

I hate introductions where the author tells you all about the stories you are going to read, so I'm not going to do that here. These stories are meant to be discovered and enjoyed solely by you. I've read them already, and what I read chilled me to the bone—and made me think.

There are truths hidden within these pages, my friends. Dark truths that have been put there only for you. Other readers won't notice them, but you will. You won't be able to help yourself.

The cell door has been opened, and you won't be able to shut it again.

You are about to embark on a journey through honest-to-goodness horror, brought to you by two of the best new voices in the genre.

And that is no lie…

Brian Keene
Baltimore, Maryland
February 2002

BRIAN KEENE is the author of the short story collections *No Rest For The Wicked*, and *4X4* (co-written with Cooper, Huyck, and Oliveri), and the novel *Love And Worms*. He is the former editor of *Jobs In Hell*, a popular and irreverent newsletter for horror professionals, and the fiction editor of Horrorfind.com. He also edited the *Best of Horrorfind* anthology. For some of his favorite recipes and home decorating tips, visit his website at www.briankeene.com

~ Contents ~

Art and Becoming

Drew Williams

The dead guy's name was Henry Wallace. He was five-foot-nine, weighed a hundred and seventy four pounds, had brown eyes, brown hair, and was an organ donor. Of course his vital statistics lost their relevancy at 12:09 in the morning, right after Henry put a shotgun inside his mouth. Too short to reach the trigger with the barrel in his mouth, Henry had ingeniously tied one end of a string around the trigger and the other end around the big toe of his right foot. That done, all it took was a three count and a thrust of his foot for the double-barreled gun to blow off three fourths of the back of Henry's head and splatter bloody chunks of gray matter and bone in a the shape of a question mark on the kitchen wall behind where Henry sat.

Officer Lance Jacobs glanced down at Henry's driver's license and frowned. "Not even forty," he muttered, uncomfortably aware of the closeness in his age to that of the deceased. Jacobs held the license closer, comparing the unsmiling face to the lump of flesh that remained above Henry's neck. *Same jaw*, Lance thought. Everything else was pulp.

"Morning officer."

Jacobs stole a quick glance behind and grunted at the tall, thin man wearing white scrubs and holding a clipboard. "Hey, Phil, you got here quick."

Phil Luxor shrugged and pushed his fist into the loose pockets of his labcoat. "We were in the neighborhood," he said, looking past Jacobs at the remains of Mr. Wallace. "Same old, same old. Huh, Lance."

Jacobs looked at the bloodstained floor and the nearly headless corpse. "Yeah," he sighed. "Same old, same old."

* * * * *

Phil Luxor was the senior driver on the graveyard shift and the man who had christened the twenty-year-old ambulance that had been converted into a pickup vehicle for the county morgue the Bony Express. By his own estimation, Phil had picked up over a thousand corpses during his career as a driver for the Allegheny County Morgue, about a third of them, like Henry Wallace, bloody aftermaths of suicide or murder. Phil knew the business of corpse retrieval better than anyone, and as was the case with the particularly messy bodies, there was usually a lot of waiting around. Another ten or fifteen minutes, Jacobs told him soon after his arrival. Then the cops would be through and the body would be ready for the Bony Express.

Phil popped a stick of gum into his mouth and glanced at his new partner, Jeff French. All of Phil's previous partners had been losers in some way or another. Some, like his first partner, Stu Fendler, were incapable of holding down any job that required the use of the cerebrum. They usually got bored within a few weeks and quit to pursue some other meaningless career. Or there were those like his last partner, Gail Yakota, who couldn't stomach the often-gruesome pickups. She quit her third night on the job after she and Phil went to pick up the body of a man who had been electrocuted a week earlier. One look at the purpling lump of fried flesh that used to be a plumber named Izzy Stewart and Miss Yakota hurled chunks all over the corpse's bare feet.

Phil could usually size up how long a driver was going to last within a two or three shifts, but with Jeff French it was different. To Phil, Jeff definitely did not look like someone who would be working nights loading corpses into a broken down ambulance. Jeff looked like someone who should be on the cover of a magazine. He was tall, muscular, and had the kind of cool, wavy black hair that Phil secretly always wished he had. And Jeff had a pair of the deepest blue eyes Phil had ever seen. And though Jeff didn't say much, Phil could tell he was no dummy. There was no doubt about it; Jeff French was not the typical loser who Phil usually found riding shotgun with him in the Bony Express. He was different.

"Pretty gruesome, huh?" Phil said, pointing to the corpse.

It was only Jeff's fourth week on the graveyard shift and, so far, this was about the worst pickup he and Phil had made.

Jeff never took his eyes off the body. It reminded him of someone waiting in a dentist's chair. Except, of course, that most of Henry's teeth were stuck in the drywall above the kitchen sink. "What do we do with all the brains and stuff on the walls?" Jeff whispered, not sure why he didn't want the cops to hear him.

"Blood we don't worry about. Solid matter, we got to clean up."

Jeff turned to Phil and asked through pursed lips, "How?"

Phil opened up the small, red toolbox he always took with him on calls and fished out a pair of tweezers and a thin silver spatula. He slipped them into the oversized pocket of his labcoat before extracting a clear plastic bag from the box. Snapping the lid shut on the toolbox, he flipped the baggie to Jeff. "You hold, I'll scoop."

Jeff nodded and looked at the bloody mess that was the kitchen. Mixed with the blood on the floor and walls, broken teeth and fragments of bone were visible like tiny pebbles peeking through a thin covering of mud. The more eye-catching examples of solid matter, however, were the hunks of brain and scalp that clung to the wall above the sink like globs of gray snot. Absently, Jeff began to twist the baggie around his fingers.

"You okay?" Phil asked.

"Yeah," Jeff said, then adding. "I'm getting used to it."

* * * * *

Considering the amount of Henry Wallace's brains that was no longer inside his skull, the clean up went smoothly. First, Phil took a second, larger see-through bag from his toolbox and placed it over Henry's head so that no more of the man's brains would spill out onto the floor. Then, with one hand beneath Henry's ass cheek and the other hooked under his armpits, Jeff and Phil gingerly lifted the corpse off the chair and onto the gurney. A thumb-sized glob of blood and brains got dislodged in the transfer, but the bag caught it before it could add to the mess that was the kitchen. After the body was secured, Phil knelt on the floor and started to pick up the bits of Henry's brains with his tweezers. Humming softly to himself, Phil plucked up anything that looked as if it was once housed inside Henry's head, gave it a quick sniff, and then flicked it into Jeff's baggie. Once Phil was satisfied that the floor was picked clean, he turned his attention to the wall. Using the spatula, Phil expertly scraped the brains off the wall. There was only one time that Jeff thought he might lose it. That was when a particularly tacky chunk of gray matter flipped off Phil's spatula and struck Jeff in the cheek. Jeff jumped back and batted at his face as if a wasp was buzzing around his nose, but he quickly regained his composure after hearing Phil laugh.

"It's only brains." Phil said, picking the blob off the floor with his fingers. "It doesn't bite." Phil motioned for Jeff to hold out his baggie. "Just relax, we're almost done." Phil dropped the dime size bit of brain into the plastic bag.

Jeff looked down at the pulp he was holding, surprised that the sight of a half-pound of matted brain, scalp, and hair didn't make him want to puke. It reminded him of some small animal that got turned inside out, like some mouse that got stuck inside a microwave for too long.

Brushing his spatula across his thigh, Phil announced the job completed. "You see any more goop?"

Staring at the faint pink stain on his partner's khakis, Jeff said no and handed Phil the baggie. Phil held it up to his face and eyed the contents. "Weird, isn't it? These chunks in here used to be part of this guy's whole personality. His thoughts, who he was." Phil took a black pen from the same pocket that hid the spatula and wrote the date and time on the baggie. "Ever wonder where thoughts go when there's no more brains to hold them?" he asked as he wrote.

"Nope," Jeff said dryly. He glanced at the gurney that held Henry Wallace's body. It was covered with a stiff white sheet. "Never thought about it."

"They go out into the air," Phil said, snapping the cap on the pen and slipping it into his pocket. "Just like radio waves. They stay out there, just floating around. You can hear them too. You just have to have the right antenna to pick them up." Phil tossed the baggie onto Wallace's chest. "I'm going to sign out with Lance. You want heads or tails?"

Without a word, Jeff walked to the end of the gurney where Henry Wallace's big toe peaked out of the stiff, white sheet.

* * * * *

After the body was loaded and the pair was on their way to the morgue, Jeff asked Phil what he had slipped into his labcoat pocket when the two were cleaning the brains off the kitchen wall. "What are you talking about?" Phil asked. He was in the passenger seat smoking a cigarette, his feet planted on the dash.

Jeff didn't take his eyes off the road. "When we first started scraping off the wall, you bent down like you were tying your shoe and picked something off the floor and slipped into your pocket. What was it?"

A few seconds of silence followed, then shifting his ass so he could face Jeff, Phil stuck his hand into his left coat pocket and brought out a small piece of plastic. "Souvenir," he said.

Jeff glanced at the object in his partner's hand. It was a blood-coated ball the size of a dime. "What is it?"

Gripping the object between his thumb and forefinger, Phil held it up to Jeff's face. "Hearing aid."

Upon closer inspection, Jeff could see that what looked like a small ball was really cone shaped. Tiny pinholes dotted the larger of the two ends. "That's the kind that goes into the ear, right?"

Phil nodded and slipped the hearing aid back into his pocket. "Yup," he said." Goes right into the ear canal. When old Henry blew his brains out, it went flying." Phil patted his pocket before resuming his previous position. Staring at the passing street lights, Phil asked, "You gonna tell?"

Jeff shrugged and turned his attention back to the road. The thought hadn't crossed his mind. "As long as you're not doing weird shit to their bodies, I don't care what you do."

"Thanks," Phil said, again patting his pocket. "It's for my collection."

Jeff expected the man to elaborate, but he didn't.

The two drove the last three miles to the morgue in silence.

* * * * *

The rest of the shift was relatively easy, only two pickups and both of them were at local retirement homes. No gore, no mess, just two old men who went to sleep and didn't wake up. Though he didn't say any more about the hearing aid, Jeff kept an eye on his partner as they made their remaining pickups. But either because Phil knew Jeff was watching him, or that the pair of dead seniors didn't prove interesting enough, Phil didn't pocket any more souvenirs. When the Graveyard Shift ended an hour before sun up, neither man had mentioned the hearing aid.

After they brought in their last delivery, Jeff signed out with Kenny Sessoms, one of the morgue supervisors who never seemed to have any work to do. Jeff and Phil usually signed out together, but by the time Jeff had changed his clothes and went to the supervisor's desk, Phil was already gone. "Your partner was in quite a hurry,"

Sessoms said, pushing his clipboard toward Jeff. "He didn't even change out of his uniform."

Jeff scribbled his name beneath Phil's, then marking the time, slid his timecard into the punch clock. All the while, Kenny was bitching about the uniform being morgue property and that Phil had better not try steal it. Once punched-out, Jeff put his timecard back into its place on the wall and slid the clipboard back to Kenny. "See ya," he said, then turned and headed to the delivery entrance in the back of the building.

By the time Jeff left work at a little after five, a slight drizzle was blowing from the east. Standing on the rear steps of the morgue, Jeff turned his face into the rain and closed his eyes. He stood like that for almost a minute before continuing on his way down Pirl Street. His apartment was ten blocks to the west, an easy walk for the twenty-four year old ambulance driver. But per his custom, Jeff traveled only four blocks before stopping in front of The Strand, a 24-hour diner and bar hidden between a donut shop and a woman's hat factory. Jeff plucked a cigarette from the breast pocket of his work shirt and lit it before stepping into the diner.

Not quite 5:30 in the morning and already a dozen men were milling about the small diner. A few of them were chomping on grease burgers, but most were lined up at the long bar sucking down draft beer. Like Jeff, most of the guys were just getting off the late shift, though a few of the men were trying to catch a quick buzz before they went to work. When Jeff entered the diner, nearly every head turned to watch him come in. Jeff scanned their hard faces and felt their gaze upon him. It was a feeling Jeff had grown accustomed to.

The men returned to their beers as soon as Jeff slid his butt onto a stool at the end of the bar. The bartender, a slight woman with reddish-blonde hair and the hardened look of someone who had spent the last forty years behind a bar came up to him. "What'll it be, hon?"

"Budweiser," Jeff said. "And a shot of Jack."

The woman nodded and headed to the far end of the bar where she kept the whiskey. Jeff pulled two twenty-dollar bills out of his jeans and laid them on the bar. When the bartender came back, she offered a quick, appreciative smile toward the bills before putting the shot glass on top of them. "You want to run a tab, hon?"

Jeff nodded through a cloud of cigarette smoke.

The woman pulled a crumpled notepad from an invisible fold in her dirty apron and wrote 'shot and beer' on the top sheet. Before ripping the paper out of the pad and sticking it on top of the antique cash register with the other tabs, she asked Jeff if he wanted any food.

"Not today," Jeff said

"Sure thing, hon."

After the bartender left, Jeff poured half of the beer into a seven ounce glass then placed the glass directly in front of him. He took the bottle and put it to his left. Then he slid the shot glass with the bills still beneath it to his right. "Father, Son, and Holy Ghost," he said humorlessly. He rested his folded hands within the triangle of booze and wondered who the hell he was.

＊ ＊ ＊ ＊ ＊

Phil Luxor lived in an expensive, open-loft apartment that he bastardized by erecting a series of plywood walls that created a disjointed maze effect of small rooms. Phil liked things compartmentalized. Living area on the Westside of the apartment; sleeping area on the north. His gallery and studio faced the east, so he could feel the sun as he worked. Phil fancied himself one of the last great beatnik artists, but at thirty-one years old, he was too young to have been part of the beat generation.

However, that didn't deter Phil Luxor from enjoying the role of the bohemian artist. A product of affluence, he didn't have to work if he didn't want to; a trust fund set up by his grandparents kept him financially secure. His becoming an ambulance driver for the city morgue was done on a whim, an act of impulse that allowed him to discover the gift that had lain dormant within him for his entire life. Like most artists, Phil Luxor had an insatiable desire to experience all that life had to offer. And to an artist, he reasoned, death was one of the most interesting parts of life. So when he saw the want ad in the newspaper for ambulance drivers at the morgue, "no experience required," Phil applied. Since he wasn't a convicted felon or had any blemishes on his driving record, and he was willing to work nights, he was hired on the spot.

He soon discovered that the work was simple, almost mindless. He drove through the city streets at night and picked up dead people. Sometimes Phil would take them to the county hospital, most of the times, they were brought back to the city morgue where he would drop them off to one of the attendants who would sign off on his slip then give him the address for another pickup.

But after three months on the job, Phil started to get bored. Handling a steady stream of corpses hardly proved to be the inspiration he imagined it would be. During the first two weeks on the job he completed a trio of paintings he called the "Going, Going, Gone" trilogy, but other than that, his artistic production was nil. Death just stopped being interesting.

Then Phil met Grace Finster.

It wasn't a formal meeting. Grace was dead, murdered in her apartment. She had been dead two or three days before the police found her on the dining room floor with a kitchen knife sticking out of her throat. Following procedure, Phil and his then partner, an obese Iranian named Turok who smelled of sausage, waited until the police told them they could take the body. While waiting for the go-ahead, Phil was drawn to the collection of framed pictures atop the sideboard in the living room. Most of photographs were of Grace and a chubby, middle-age man with a baldhead and a sour expression. There was also a silver bowl on the sideboard that held Grace's keys, some spare change and a thin pair of bifocal glasses. Though he knew better than to touch anything at a crime scene, Phil plucked the glasses out of the bowl and held them to his face. Peering through their thick lenses, Phil could barely make out the photographs in front of him. He was about to return the glasses to the bowl when Turok called his name, telling him it was time to get the body.

Phil turned toward his partner, and without thinking, slipped the glasses into his pocket.

That night he found out that he could hear the dead.

* * * * *

"Hey, I know you. You drive the Bony Express."

Jeff's head nap-jerked up. Directly in front of him the blurry image of his own face stared vacant-eyed back at him from the dirty mirror that hung the length of the bar. An empty shot glass and a half-filled bottle of Budweiser sat inches from his fingertips. Jeff squinted and strained to get a better look at the face staring at him, his own face.

No, a woman's face. A flat mound of smooth flesh beneath a main of auburn hair. No eyes, no ears, no mouth. But she was screaming, a burning switchblade of a scream jabbing through his eyeballs into his brain. She had no eyes but she saw. She had no...

"You drive the 10:00 to 5:00 with Phil Luxor, dontcha?

Jeff swiveled on his wobbly seat to face a skinny, pockmarked man with a greasy, blonde mullet who hardly looked old enough to be in a bar. "You know me?" Jeff asked, his fingers instinctively stretching for his warming bottle of beer.

"Yeah, you're the new guy at the morgue, aren't you?" The

pimply-faced man swung a long skinny leg over the stool next to Jeff and sank his rear-end onto it. Seeing the pack of smokes in front of Jeff, the man reached into his left jacket pocket and pulled out a lighter. "I got flame," he said. "But ran out of sticks. You mind?"

Jeff shook his head. "No, help yourself."

Needing no further encouragement, the man snatched the pack of cigarettes off the bar and tapped one free. He plucked it out with his teeth, and then made an elaborate show of flicking open his Zippo and lighting the smoke. As the man sucked in his first lungfull, the bartender took the opportunity to ask him what he wanted. "Rock-n-Rye," he said, blowing a thick trail of smoke out the side of his mouth. Realizing that he'd just exhaled on Jeff, the man quickly added. "And get my man here another one of whatever he's drinking."

Jeff offered the bartender a half-smile and gave the Budweiser a slight wiggle. "You're an attendant at the morgue." Jeff turned to the man. "On the night shift. That's where I know you."

"Yup. Harry Kane," the man said, extending a finely manicured hand toward Jeff. "But folks call me Candy." He took Jeff's hand before Jeff could properly extend it and gave it a quick but powerful squeeze. "And you're that French guy, right?" Candy asked, his hand still wrapped around Jeff's.

"Yeah, Jeff French. Nice to meet you."

The drinks arrived, allowing Jeff to retrieve his hand. There was something odd about Harry Kane's touch, as if the man's hand was too soft, too smooth. Jeff shuddered and polished off what was left in his beer. Harry Kane's hand had felt like a slug.

Candy shot back his Rock-n-Rye and ordered another. "So how do you like riding the Bony Express? I know it gets crazy as shit sometimes at night."

Jeff shrugged. "It's not too bad. It can be kind of ugly though."

Candy snorted twin streams of smoke from his nostrils "Yeah, you don't have to tell me about it. I've been tagging stiffs on the night shift for almost four years now. Ain't much in the way people croak that I haven't seen." He eyed Jeff a moment. "So, you planning on becoming a doctor or something?"

The question took Jeff by surprise. "A doctor. No. Why would you think that?"

The bartender brought a second Rock-n-Rye and a shot for Jeff that he couldn't remember ordering. Candy grabbed his shot but didn't drink it. "Well, a lot of times, college guys get jobs running ambulances or filing stiffs while they're in pre-med. They think that will give them some kind of bullshit experience when they get to med. school. Those guys are always pricks." Candy sucked in another lungfull of smoke then crushed the half good cigarette atop the bar. "You look like you could be one of those college guys."

Candy said college guys as if he was chewing on a turd. "Not me," Jeff said with a laugh, which Candy interpreted as an invitation to pluck another smoke from Jeff's pack. "So, you think I look like the college type."

Candy lit the cigarette, this time without the dramatic flair. "Well, it's not so much that you look like a college guy. It's just that you don't look like the usual kind of guy who drives the night shift. They're mostly burnouts or freaks." Candy paused for an almost imperceptible moment, but Jeff noticed it. "Like your partner."

* * * * *

The first night, Grace sang to him in his sleep. It was a soft, gentle song about a forgotten love whose memory had surfaced after a hundred years. Though Phil heard the song in a dream, he knew Grace Finster was speaking to him from the grave. She told him to wake up and put on the glasses he had stolen.

Phil did as he was instructed, and when he peered through the ill-fitting bifocals he saw the twin fates of heaven and hell. One in each lens. All he had to do was adjust his focus or tilt his head and he would go from indescribable paradise to an inferno of the damned.

The sight was enough to drive him mad, but Grace Finster's voice came to him just as he was about to rip his eyeballs from his socket *You have been chosen*, she whispered. *Chosen to save our souls.*

Phil ripped the glasses off his face, but the voice of Grace echoed inside his head. *To save our souls, Phil. Can you do it?*

Weeping, Phil fell to his knees "I don't know," he cried out. "Whose souls am I supposed to save?"

Mine, came the answer. *And more, many more.*

* * * * *

"My partner?" Jeff asked surprised. "What's wrong with Phil?"

Candy laughed and swiveled on his stool to face Jeff. "You ever notice anything odd about Phil? He ever say anything weird?"

The image of Phil Luxor slipping the hearing aid into the pocket of his labcoat jumped into Jeff's mind. "He doesn't really say much," Jeff said. "Not much at all"

A smug grin stretched across Candy's face as if the skinny man knew Jeff was lying. "Is that so? Well, you just wait. Most of the guys who've ridden with him say he's nuts. Always talking about weird shit like art and where people go after they die. One guy, Chet, told me that Luxor told him how he liked to visit the graves of the people he picked up, just to see how they were doing in the afterlife. I'm telling you man, it's weird."

Jeff nodded, and for a moment considered asking Candy if he knew about Phil's collection, but decided against it. Instead, he asked Candy why everyone at the morgue called the ambulance he drove on the night shift the Bony Express.

"Don't know," Candy said. "Phil Luxor started calling it that when he took over the night shift. Maybe its because he thinks it's the fastest way to get to the bone yard."

Jeff accepted the answer and turned back to his drinks. The glass and the bottle, both empty now, still formed a triangle with the small pile of ones that was all that remained of Jeff's twenties. Father, Son, and Holy Ghost. Jeff was getting tired. He'd have to go home soon, but he couldn't sleep. He couldn't risk that.

Jeff closed his eyes and allowed his chin to drop to his chest. From far away, he heard Candy asking him if he was all right. Jeff didn't reply. He just closed his eyes so tight that they started to burn behind his lids.

Staring back at him from the mirror was a woman with auburn hair and no face.

She was screaming.

* * * * *

Phil stared out the window of his twelfth-story apartment at the empty street beneath him and sighed. He was still pretty buzzed from the four bong hits he took when he first got home, but unlike most mornings, the dope didn't prove to be the inspiration he needed in order to get to work. Absently, Phil rolled the hearing aid he collected that morning between his fingers. It felt warm to his touch, vibrating softly. Henry Wallace had something to say, Phil was sure of that. But right now, he wasn't interested in listening.

Phil turned from the window and stared at the enormous blank canvas in front of him. For once, he thought, he wanted to paint something without their help. Just take the brush and let his own creative genius explode upon the canvas.

The thought made him laugh out loud. He was no way near stoned enough to convince himself he had a modicum of creative genius. He knew the limits of his talent; genius was for others.

But there was something holding him back today. Something that wouldn't let him work. He held the hearing aid to his face and frowned. The humming continued which made Phil think of his new partner on the Bony Express. He was testing Jeff when he told him that the hearing aid was for his collection. Testing the new guy to see how curious he was.

But Jeff didn't take the bait. He pretended not to be interested. But the indifference was an act, of that, Phil was certain. He could see it in Jeff's perfect blue eyes. Deep within their beauty and intelligence, they burned with curiosity. Yes, there was something different, something special about Jeff French.

Smiling, Phil set his coffee mug on his sofa and picked up a thick, used paintbrush off the floor. *This painting is for Jeff*, he thought, slipping Henry Wallace's hearing aid into his left ear. As soon as it came in contact with Phil's flesh, the hearing aid stopped vibrating and grew cold.

And Phil was inspired.

* * * * *

It was nearly 11:00 am when Jeff left Candy at the bar and started back to his apartment. He drank up the two twenties he originally laid on the bar plus another five dollars worth of booze, yet he still didn't feel drunk. His new drinking partner, however, had downed half a bottle's worth of Rock-N-Rye. And since Candy had the evening off, he decided to remain at The Strand and get royally shit-faced. He suggested that Jeff call in sick and join him for an afternoon of drinking, but Jeff shrugged off the offer telling Candy that he was too new on the job to do that. "If you say so, man," Candy said. He plucked a pen out of his jacket pocket and scribbled on a spent pack of matches. "Home number's on top," he said, handing the pack to Jeff. "Cell phone is on the bottom. Call me if you change your mind."

"Thanks," Jeff said, slipping the pack into the ass pocket of his jeans. "I might do that."

But as he strolled down Pirl Street, past the boarded up dry cleaners and the camera repair shop, Jeff knew he wouldn't call Candy. The last thing he needed now were friends, even a casual drinking buddy could prove dangerous. He was alone now, and there was safety in isolation.

Hello my pretty one.

Jeff shook her voice from his memory and took the matchbook out of his jeans. Looking down at the pack, Jeff chuckled to himself. Candy had written *Call me* above the numbers, a two word message Jeff had received hundreds of times before from an equal number of women and men who wanted a hell of a lot more out of Jeff than polite conversation. As Jeff stared at the message, memories of the life he abandoned just a few months ago came flooding back. Memories of faces and bodies that he had held and kissed. But these memories brought no nostalgic longing for the old days; no hunger to head back west to his old life.

Call me

"If only you knew what a mistake that would be, Candy," Jeff said, ripping the matchbook into shreds and letting the pieces fall at his feet.

Jeff resumed his walk homeward, and as he did every morning, said a prayer that in those few hours he slept before another night of picking up the dead, he wouldn't dream. It was always so much worse when he dreamt.

* * * **

For the next three days, the routine remained the same for Jeff. He and Phil drove the Bony Express and picked up the late-night dead, and in the early morning just before sunrise, Jeff would go to The Strand to drink. Before Jeff could finish his second beer, Candy would show up and bum a few cigarettes and do everything possible, short of coming out and saying it, to convey the fact that he wanted to take Jeff home and screw his brains out. Jeff felt bad for Candy. Maybe at another time in another place he would have let Candy take him home. Like untold times before, he would have just closed his eyes and allowed himself to be devoured. Man, woman, it didn't matter. Sex was all the same. And for Jeff, it had never been a hassle.

But those days were gone; gone like her face.

"I don't know why you want to talk about him," Candy snapped when Jeff asked for more information about Phil Luxor. It was the third time the two men drank together, and Jeff could tell that Candy was growing possessive of his company. "I told you, he's supposed to be some kind of artist. Probably not a good one." The jealousy in Candy's voice was so thick Jeff nearly laughed.

"Why do you say that?" Jeff asked. "Have you ever seen his work?"

Candy shook his head. "No. But he used to talk about this big project he was doing called Metamorpho. He said it was going to make him famous. A star in the firmament of heaven." Candy started laughing. "I swear to Christ, that's what he said. A star in the firmament of heaven."

Jeff nodded and pushed his cigarettes closer to Candy. The gesture was met by quick smile. "So what ever happened to Metamorpho? Did he finish it?"

"Don't know," Candy said. "Last time he mentioned it was last year." He took up the pack and tapped out a fresh smoke. "And he sure as shit ain't no star in no fucking firmament of heaven."

Jeff looked into the mirror behind the bar and saw the faceless woman where his reflection should have been. Her head was whipping back and forth across the glass, struggling to free herself. "None of us are."

* * * * *

Three days later, Phil added to his collection.

It was a hairpin taken off of a 57-year-old widow named Stella Linkletter who had been murdered in her kitchen while doing the dishes. Being mostly deaf, Stella didn't hear the intruder enter her three-room apartment. She had her transistor radio in the kitchen turned up full blast and was singing along with Bobby Goldsboro when she was impaled from behind. Dressed in her bathrobe and with her hair in curlers, Stella died clutching at her chest in a desperate attempt to hold in the blood that spurted into her sink turning the white, soapy bubbles an odd brown. As her life poured out like the dishwater flowing down the drain, Stella's last mortal thought was not of herself, but of whoever might find her. Always a woman who took pride in the meticulous care she gave her home, she died sorry that she wouldn't have an opportunity to tidy things up a bit. Though small, it would have been a consolation to her to know that the mess would be much less than she imagined.

Stella had been dead for over forty-eight hours when Phil and Jeff were called in to take her none-too-fresh-corpse to the morgue. Once again, it was Officer Lance Jacobs who greeted them at the door.

"Long time no see," Phil said when Lance ushered them

inside. "I hear you got another one for me." Phil grinned and cocked his head toward his partner. "I mean us."

Lance cast Jeff a sideways glance and frowned. "It's ugly, alright. Poor lady got it while she was doing the dishes. Been dead for a few days, it seems."

"A ripe one," Phil said, but Officer Jacobs didn't seem to notice the joke. He just took the clipboard from Phil and scribbled his name at the bottom.

"This one's different, Phil. When you see her you'll know this one ain't right." For a second it appeared that Lance was going to say more, but he stopped and handed the clipboard back to Phil. "We're all done in there, so you can take her now." He paused, then added. "You know the routine."

Taking back the clipboard, Phil motioned for Jeff to pull the gurney closer to the kitchen. "All too well," he told Officer Jacobs.

This time the cop cracked a slight but sad smile and shook his head. "I'm gonna go into the hallway and get some fresh air," he said. "This one's giving me a real bad feeling." Jacobs cast a quick glance toward the kitchen. "It just stinks too much."

And for the first time, Jeff noticed it too. Beneath the smell of decaying flesh; beneath the scent of mold and three day old Lemon Pledge, was another smell. A subtle undercurrent that permeated the smell of death with its own unique perfume.

It was hatred.

Hello my pretty one.

Jeff turned to Phil and sniffed. "I know what he means," he said. "I can smell something too." Jeff inhaled again and shuddered. The odor was painfully familiar.

"Probably one of Lance's guys farted," Phil replied, slipping his hands into a pair of latex gloves. "Let's go. The dearly departed awaits."

With the scent of hatred still fresh in his nostrils, Jeff followed his partner into the kitchen. Stella hadn't been moved from the spot where she died face down on the kitchen floor. A thick, dirty chalk outline was crudely traced around the woman's body like a cheap, white aura. "Look at that," Phil said, pointing to what was left of the woman's back. The tone of his voice was low and oddly subdued. "Lance is right. This ain't normal".

Phil stepped to the side, allowing Jeff an unobstructed view of Stella's corpse. She was on her stomach, the right side of her face flat against the tiled floor. Though her arms were tight against her sides, Stella's bare legs were spread wide as if they were swept out from beneath her. Her left foot, still in a fuzzy, purple slipper that looked like a dog, was twisted inward as if the ankle had been broken. Rolled up in a ball near her right shoulder was what was left of Stella's flannel housecoat. A ragged sleeve dangled over the side of Stella's face, covering her chin and left cheek. But her eye was still open, like some white marble staring in Phil's direction. And for a brief moment, Jeff thought the woman looked familiar.

"Look at her back," Phil said, though his gaze was fixed on Stella's vacant face.

Jeff looked to where Phil was pointing. Stella's back had been flayed open as if she was a giant cod. Foot length husks of skin had been peeled from her back and draped over her rigid arms. Covering Stella's buttocks like a blanket were long strands of tissue-thin flesh. But being a small woman with a tiny ass, most of the extra skin spread off Stella's rear-end onto the floor barely concealing the faint square pattern of black grout. Jeff took another step closer to the body and swallowed hard. The smooth ridges of her spine were exposed, allowing Jeff to count each of her vertebrae.

"There ain't any blood," he said, turning to Phil. "There should be blood all over this place."

Phil pursed his lips and nodded. "Pull the gurney in, and let's get this over with."

Needing no further encouragement, Jeff pulled the gurney into the cramped kitchen. Tossing a clean, white sheet over Stella's body, Phil moved toward her head, while Jeff positioned himself at her feet. Grabbing her ankles with his right hand, and hooking his left arm under her knees, Jeff was ready to lift when he noticed Phil staring at the mound of hair peeking out the top of the sheet. Phil's left hand was fiddling with something beneath the sheet. "What the hell are you doing?" Jeff whispered as Phil plucked his hand free of Stella's hair. In it he held a thin, brown bobby pin.

Jeff's eyes bulged at what Phil had collected. "Are you nuts?"

Phil pocketed the souvenir and commenced to slide his arms beneath Stella's shoulders. "I need it," he said, not looking at Jeff. But even with his face downcast, Jeff could see Phil's expression. It was troubled, but excited. "I can't tell you now, but I will."

"You'll tell me when we're done."

Phil nodded. "Deal. Now let's get her on the gurney and get out of here."

* * * * *

"Have you ever heard of Ovid's Metamorphosis?" Phil asked Jeff as he passed him the tightly packed bong. The two were in Phil's apartment sitting on the overstuffed couch in the north-end cubicle that served as Phil's living room. Though Jeff insisted, Phil refused to tell him why he had to take the hairpin from Stella's corpse until, as Phil said, they were on his turf. "After our shift, we'll go back to my place, and I'll be able to show you what I'm talking about. But until then, I can't talk about it.

Okay?"

Jeff could tell the man was serious, so he didn't press the issue. "Okay, but if you blow me off, I'm going to tell Sessoms."

But true to his word, Phil didn't blow Jeff off. The pair had two more pickups that evening, and after dropping the last one off to Candy, Phil told Jeff it was time to go to his place. "You're not meeting me at the bar?" Candy asked, surprised. He glared at Phil, but the ambulance driver ignored him. "I thought we were going to meet."

"Not today," Jeff said. "Maybe tomorrow."

"When?" Candy began, but stopped when Phil started for the door. Leaving Candy's question unanswered, Jeff hurried to Phil's side.

"I think he likes you," Phil said when Jeff caught up to him.

"Yeah, but he doesn't like you."

Phil grunted. "No biggie."

The pair quickly signed out for the morning then gathered their personal belongings from the staff lounge and headed for Phil's car. The two spent the ten-minute drive in silence, but when Phil pulled into the parking lot of the Exeter Towers, Jeff let out a low whistle. "I've only been in town a few months," Jeff said. "But I know this is one pricey place. How do you afford it?"

Phil shrugged. "I'm rich," he said. "That's all."

"Must be nice," Jeff replied. In his mind's eye he pictured his own efficiency apartment that sucked up over half of his monthly paycheck in rent.

"Come on." Phil turned off the ignition and pushed open the driver's side door. "I live on the top floor."

When Phil opened the door to his apartment, Jeff was stunned by the enormity of the place. But instead of receiving a tour, Jeff was quickly ushered through the narrow maze of plywood walls to the living room. "Have a seat," Phil said, pointing to the sofa. "I'll go get us some beers."

Less than a minute later, Phil was back with a twelve pack of Corona and a silver-plated water bong. "I hope you don't object," Phil said, holding the bong aloft.

"Nope," Jeff replied, though it had been months since he last got high. "No objections at all."

"That's the spirit." Phil set the beer on the floor. As Phil sat on the couch and packed the bong, Jeff removed two beers from the package and opened them. He took a long swig, then seeing that Phil was finished packing the bong, handed him his beer. "It's good," he said. "Cold."

Exchanging the bong for the beer, Phil asked his question about Ovid's Metamorphosis.

"I think so," Jeff said before putting the bong to his lips. Phil produced a lighter and lit the bowl while Jeff inhaled.

"Really?"

Jeff nodded but kept his mouth shut. He let the sweet smoke fill his lungs until they began to burn, then slowly, he exhaled. Perhaps the dope-free months had lowered his resistance to pot, because no sooner had he exhaled the first bong hit then the hazy mellow feeling of an impending buzz surfaced. Either that, or Phil Luxor was in possession of the best damn weed he'd ever smoked. Phil noticed the look on Jeff's face. "Good shit, isn't it? I got it from some kid in town named Espy." Phil took the bong and did his own quick hit. But unlike Jeff, Phil was practiced enough that he could still speak with his lungs full of marijuana smoke. "So you know about The Metamorphosis."

"Yeah. When I was in high school, I had this one English teacher who made us read all these Greek and Roman myths. Most of the kids thought it was boring, but I kind of liked them. The Metamorphosis is some myth about the gods changing people into animals and things, right?"

"Something like that."

Jeff took a quick sip of his beer and eyed Phil sternly. "So what's that got to do with you taking that hairpin off that dead lady tonight?"

"Everything." Phil took the hairpin out of his shirt pocket and held it in the palm of his right hand. "Let me explain the Metamorphosis first, then I'll show you what this is all about." Phil wrapped his fingers tightly around the hairpin. "Okay."

"Fine with me." Jeff took the bong and stoked up another bowl. The buzz was starting to creep up on him. It was a pleasant feeling that he'd long missed.

"I know Harry Kane has told you that I'm an artist, and that I've been working on a piece called Metamorpho."

"Yeah. He said it was going to make you a star in the firmament of heaven."

The embarrassed look on Phil's face told Jeff that the artist wasn't expecting him to know that. "Anyway, Ovid's Metamorphosis is a lot more than just a collection of ancient stories; it's a kind of mythological blueprint for the evolution of man and the universe from the beginning when everything was chaos through creation, and then the four ages of man. "

"Sounds like heavy stuff," Jeff said before taking another bong hit.

"Very," Phil shot back. "And underlying the entire thing is

the idea of eternal and constant change. Everything in the universe is in a constant state of metamorphosis, changing from one state to another. And that includes people."

"So? Isn't that what Darwin was supposed to be all about?"

"Not exactly. I'm not talking about evolution." Phil started to drum his fingers across his near-empty beer bottle. "What I'm talking about is the metamorphosis of the individual as the changes of life continue on into death."

Passing the bong back to Phil, Jeff pushed himself deeper into the oversized couch. "I still don't know what any of this has to do with art, or, for that matter, the stuff you've been taking off the corpses."

"Fair enough," Phil said, placing the bong on the floor. He grabbed two beers from the container and motioned for Jeff to get up. "Maybe if I show you, you'll understand."

Reluctantly, Jeff stood up and followed Phil through the maze of his apartment to the gallery. The beer and bong hits coupled with the succession of quick turns Phil led him through made Jeff dizzy. By the time the two of them reached Phil's gallery, Jeff's head was spinning, and he needed to sit down. Noticing his friend's discomfort, Phil put his hand on his shoulder and guided him through the door. "Here we go," Phil said once the two were inside the ten by ten room. "Ta-da."

Jeff took a few uneasy steps into the room and glanced around. Nearly every inch of wall space was covered with Phil's art. But it wasn't art in any sense that Jeff was familiar with. The paintings, mostly portraits of various shapes and sizes, looked as if they had been done by a talent-deprived madman whose natural medium was black velvet canvas. The portraits all shared a disturbing commonality; regardless of the sex, the faces in all the paintings resembled effeminate versions of Phil Luxor.

Maybe it was the dizziness in his head or the lingering effects of the pot, but Jeff felt a sudden queasiness at the sight of Phil's collection. It was too disorganized, too much of a mixed match of obtuse colors and discordant styles that made Jeff feel as if he'd been sucked into an orgy of electric blues and purple. It was too many pairs of Phil Luxor's badly painted eyes staring at him from the walls.

"I know a lot of them are rather primitive," Phil said. "But I think I finally have found my style as a portraitist. Sort of a cross between neoclassicism, Picasso, and Norman Rockwell."

His eyes clamped shut, Jeff imagined Phil to be the bastard son of Rockwell and Picasso. A sickly love child with too much time and too little talent. The thought did little to ease his discomfort.

Phil tapped Jeff on his shoulder and motioned for him to look at a painting to Jeff's right. "That's the first piece I did after becoming an ambulance driver. It's a man named Gary Kenny, my first pick-up."

Jeff opened his eyes and glanced at the painting Phil was pointing at. Dressed in a plain black tuxedo, Gary Kenny was a thin, awkward looking man with the slightly elongated and pouty face of Phil Luxor. "Why is he in a tux?" Jeff asked.

Phil shrugged. "He had a heart attack while watching TV. in his underwear. I just thought it would be nice to dress him up a bit. But this is what I really wanted to show you," Phil said, pointing at the far end of the left-side wall. "These are the paintings I did based on Ovid's Metamorphosis."

Jeff turned, half expecting to be confronted with more of the same garishness, but what he saw was much different. It was a series of four paintings depicting a man undergoing a painful change from man to wolf. Unlike the clownish Phil-faced portraits that covered the rest of the gallery, these paintings demonstrated a mature handling of tone and color. Though he was no art critic, Jeff had been taken to more than his share of gallery openings, and these paintings were as good as anything he'd seen in a museum. Jeff took a step forward and whistled between his teeth. "Damn," he said impressed. "These are good."

Phil could tell that Jeff was sincere in his praise. "Thanks. These are the only things in the gallery that I'm actually proud of. The rest of this stuff," he said, waving his arm in a semicircle at the opposite wall. "Is just a lot of wall filler."

"Tell me about these," Jeff said, not taking his eyes of the first painting in the series. It was of a handsome brown-haired man in a tunic running through a plush, green meadow. The man is caught in mid-stride, his face partially turned as if looking over his shoulder for signs of a pursuer. His left arm is thrust in front of him, but instead of a hand, a vulpine paw extends from below the forearm. "Who is this?"

"It's Lycan," Phil replied. "In the Metamorphosis, Zeus grew angry at him and turned him into a wolf. It's where the word lycanthropy comes from."

"Lycanthropy?"

"Were-wolfs," Phil explained. "That's the technical term for turning into a werewolf."

Jeff nodded and examined the remaining paintings. In the second, Lycan has fallen to one knee, the left arm now fully transformed into a wolf's front leg. In the third painting, Lycan's limbs have all become that of a wolf, and the transformation has begun in his face. His hair is now longer and scraggly, and his nose and jaw have become elongated and more pointed. In the final painting, all traces of humanity have vanished from Lycan's form. He has been completely transformed into a wolf.

Not completely.

Jeff took another step forward and examined Lycan's wolfen face. Everything was perfect, except for the eyes. Lycan's eyes were still those of the man in the first painting. Only now they reflected an unimaginable fear. "He still has a man's eyes," Jeff said, pointing to the painting.

"Yes," Phil said. "In the story, Lycan's true punishment is that he knows that he is a man trapped in a wolf's body. He spends the rest of his life lamenting his lost youth and beauty. He has nothing left but to howl in misery because he cannot escape what he has become."

Jeff nodded and glanced again at Lycan's sad, terrified eyes.

"Come on," Phil said. "There's more I want to show you."

Jeff took another moment to admire the quartet of paintings before turning toward the door. "I always thought art was a type of metamorphosis, a way of changing one thing into another," Phil said as he ushered Jeff out of the gallery and back into the plywood maze. "An artist takes raw materials and transforms them into something new. And for the longest time, I thought that was enough. But then I realized that when my paintings or sculptures were done, they were no longer . . ." Phil stopped, struggling for the right word.

Jeff supplied it.

"Becoming."

"Exactly. They were no longer becoming something; they were finished. But don't you see, Jeff? If everything in the universe is going through a constant state of change, the very fact that my art was completed made it meaningless. Its very completeness made it foreign, something unnatural. Do you know what I mean?"

Jeff said he thought he did.

"Good." Phil had taken Jeff through three twists in the maze to a black door that opened to his studio. "So I was left with only one thing to do. Create a work of art that was in a continual state of metamorphosis."

"Metamorpho."

Phil opened the door. "Yes."

Jeff took one step into the room and stopped. "Good, God," he said when he saw the thing in front of him. Expecting another painting, Jeff was stunned to discover that Metamorpho was more machine than art. At least nine feet wide and seven feet high, Metamorpho was an intricate system of pulleys and wires surrounding a six-foot skeleton of a headless man. Made of metal pipe and chicken wire, the skeleton swayed slightly from side to side, a result of the counter balances attached to the pulley system. At the end of the skeleton's tubal arms, broken pairs of reading glasses had been attached to serve as fingers. Glued to the fingers of the left hand was a paintbrush sopping with Van Dyke Brown. Jeff watched, amazed, as the arm jerked back and forth sending bits of brown paint flying off the brush onto an enormous canvas just inches out of the skeleton's reach.

"It's a machine," Jeff said, his gaze still fixed on the automaton.

From behind him, Phil agreed. "That and more," Phil said, entering the room. "But it's a very special machine. It's also an artist." Phil pointed to the canvas. "Look," he said. "This is our work. His and mine."

Jeff moved forward to inspect the canvas. What appeared at first to be a collage of random splotches became more distinct. Dotting the canvas were hundreds of grimacing faces, each one projecting a moment of some intense private agony. Jeff moved as close to the canvas as he could. His gaze fell upon the face of a young woman painted in dark shades of red and violet. Two pinholes of black made up her eyes. As he stared, a drop of Van Dyke brown fell from the tip of Metamorpho's brush. When the paint touched her face, a subtle alteration came over it. Jeff inched closer. Another bit of paint hit the face making it seem to elongate, its features growing sharper, almost vulpine like the painting of Lycan.

"What is this?" Jeff stepped back from the canvas.

Phil stared at the picture, watching Metamorpho's brush pass over the other figures. "Like you said," Phil began. "They're becoming, changing from one thing to another."

"Who are they? What are they becoming?"

Phil turned to Jeff and shook his head. "You know who they are."

And Phil was right. As soon as he saw the tortured faces on the wall, Jeff knew he was looking at Phil's collection. "These are the people you've picked up in the Bony Express."

"Not all," Phil said. "Just some. Just the one's who talk to me."

"The one's who have talked to you?"

Phil shrugged, a slightly embarrassed grin coming to his face. "It's nothing, really. I just have this gift, I guess. But sometimes I can hear the dead."

Jeff wanted to laugh but the expression on Phil's face told Jeff that he was serious. "And what do the dead tell you? Paint my fucking picture."

Phil's grin grew wider. "Actually, yes." He motioned for Jeff to look at the bottom, right hand corner of the canvas. "This is a quote from Ovid's Metamorphosis. It sort of sums everything up."

Bending forward, Jeff noticed for the first time the soft hum of gears and a motor coming from the base of Metamorpho. Fucking thing has a battery, Jeff thought. He laughed softly to himself as he read the quote. *Our souls are deathless; always, when they leave our bodies, they find new dwelling-places.* "So, what does it mean?"

"It means that, like our bodies, every soul is in a permanent state of flux, always moving from one thing to another. But not everyone's soul is ready to move on. Sometimes bits of the soul get left behind. The souls who talk to me aren't prepared to undergo their metamorphosis, so I paint their souls onto this canvas and Metamorpho completes their . . ." Phil paused, smiling. "Becoming."

Jeff shook his head and wished he had brought the bong with him. "So you built this machine-thing so the souls you've painted can become something else, right?"

Phil crossed his arms over his chest and nodded. "Some become other people. Others become animals or trees. Even grass." Phil moved closer to the iron skeleton. "Look closely, Jeff. Melted into Metamorpho's frame are all the things I've collected from the dead. Eyeglasses, jewelry, watches. Anything where lost bits of their souls got trapped. Look here," Phil said, pointing to a small, brown lump near what would have been the right shoulder. "Henry Wallace's hearing aid."

"You see, Jeff. That hearing aid had a bit of Henry's soul in it, and it called to me. It asked for my help. I painted his face on the canvas, but it is Metamorpho that creates the becoming. Here," Phil said excitedly. "Look closer."

Reluctantly, Jeff moved within inches of the metal skeleton. What at first glance looked to be smooth metal piping, Jeff saw was pockmarked with dozens of ripples. Jeff could see soldered into the skeleton a number of coins and bits of glass. One shiny protrusion looked like half of a gold tooth. "The hairpin you took off the lady today," Jeff said, still examining the skeleton. "That will go on this too."

"Exactly. That hairpin has a bit of Stella's soul trapped in it. But once it becomes a part of Metamorpho, it adds to all the other bits of soul that are collected on him. That's the trade-off. Metamorpho helps them to become, and in turn, they give him a soul."

A wild urge to laugh gripped Jeff, but he swallowed it by pouring a half bottle of Carona down his throat. The uneasiness he felt in Phil's gallery was returning. Turning, he noticed an easel in the corner of the room opposite Metamorpho. A heavy black tarp covered it. "What's that?" Jeff asked, waving his bottle at the covering.

Without looking, Phil called it the work in progress. "I'll show it to you when it's done."

"I've seen enough," Jeff said. He couldn't explain the sudden sense of claustrophobia that gripped him, but he needed to get away from the headless metal man in front of him and back to the living room to smoke more dope. Not waiting for a reply, Jeff turned and headed out of the room.

Once he made it back to the overstuffed couch, Jeff immediately started to pack the bong. "So you really think you hear the dead?" Jeff asked, when Phil came into the room.

"I do hear the dead," Phil replied. He cracked open another Carona and eyed Jeff cooly. "That is the truth. Now I told you my story, you tell me yours."

The request took Jeff by surprise. "Why do you think I have a story?" he said, carelessly tapping the marijuana into the bowl. A healthy pinch of pot fell onto the couch. "Did the dead tell you that?" Jeff put the bong to his lips and stoked it up.

"Yes. At least Henry Wallace did. He said you're running."

Jeff laughed through a mouthful of marijuana smoke, but the sound that came from his throat was hollow and full of despair. "The corpse whose hearing aid you stole told you that I'm on the run. That's fucking rich. Did he tell you what I'm running from?"

Phil shook his head. "He only said you were scared."

Hello my pretty one.

"So tell me, Jeff. Are you scared?"

The question cut into Jeff's soul like a blunt ax. *Why not tell Phil?* Jeff thought. He did have a story that he'd been keeping to himself for nearly a year, letting it gnaw at him like a hungry rat that had gotten its teeth into a nice chunk of cancerous tissue. If anyone were crazy enough to believe why Jeff was on the run, it would be the bohemian artist who talked to the dead. After all, Henry Wallace sure nailed it when he said that Jeff was scared.

Jeff began. "Okay, you want my story? You got it. You ever hear of a guy named Scott South?"

Phil shook his head. "What is he, a rapper?"

"No. A porno actor."

Phil raised his eyebrows, a gesture that put Jeff in mind of Mr. Spock. "And I take it that you are this Scout South?" Phil asked, a thin smile creeping across his face. "A porno star with a past. What a world."

"I am Jeff French. Scout South was just my acting name."

Phil slapped his knee and burst out laughing. "Oh, tell me. You aren't one of those guys with a 14 inch schlong, are you? Some kind of John Holmes clone?"

"Nothing so dramatic," Jeff replied, casting a casual glance toward his crotch. "Nine inches, nothing special."

Phil snorted. "Yeah, maybe not for you. But for the rest of us mere mortals . . ."

This time Jeff did laugh. "Anyway, my story. You still want to hear it?"

Phil told him to proceed.

"Okay. I got into the porn business on the west coast about three years ago. I was never one of the really big porn names, but I had steady work doing three, maybe four pictures a week. Most of the directors I worked with liked me because I showed up to work on time, and I wasn't an ass hole. Anyway, a year ago I was doing a picture called *Hard Attack* with a friend of mine named Lenny Congreve. It was an easy shoot, my only scene was a three-way with Lenny and this new chick." Jeff paused and took a swig of his beer. "Her name was Cindy Hart, but in the films she was called Kissy Mantrap. Nice name, huh?"

"Anyway, Lenny and I are supposed to be T.V. repairmen who come over to Kissy's place and screw her in the living room. It was an easy scene, blocked out real simple. Nothing kinky, so Lenny and I would be out of there in about an hour with a grand apiece."

"A grand? You got paid a thousand dollars to have sex for an hour?"

Jeff shrugged his shoulders. "The money's good, but trust me, it's not as exciting as you think. It gets old real fast."

The look on Phil's face told Jeff that he didn't believe him

"Anyway, the director went over the scene with Lenny and me. Lenny was supposed to ring the doorbell and Kissy was going to let us in. Lenny and Kissy were supposed to have a few lines of dialogue before getting it on. I wasn't supposed to say anything; I was just supposed to stare at her. Kissy was going to be wearing nothing but a sundress, and she'd start by sucking face with Lenny. After they get started I was going to pay attention to her behind, and after about two minutes, Lenny would give me the sign to switch. Then she would do this little strip to get her dress off and we'd go to town. Like I said, the whole thing was pretty well-staged, but the

46

weird thing was that Kissy wasn't there when the director went over the scene."

Phil shook his head and placed his hands in front of him in a show of mock surrender. "Wait a second. Are you telling me that the sex scenes in pornos are . . . choreographed?"

"Of course they are," Jeff said. "Do you think we could just make that shit up?"

That was a good point. Phil wasn't a big fan of porn, but he'd seen enough porno movies to know that the degree of sexual variety could hardly be johnny-on-the-spot.

"So the first time Lenny and I see Kissy, the camera is rolling on a live take. We're standing in the exterior set in our repairman costumes, and I ring the doorbell." Jeff stopped and took another swig. "Kissy opens the door and tells us to come in. She wasn't the most gorgeous woman I'd done a scene with, but she was hot. About five foot six with long red hair and a face that looked like it was sculpted out of marble. There was something odd about her, exotic almost. I'm telling you she was as white as could be. Except for her eyes. They were green, but a weird green like they were on fire."

"Anyway, she invites us in and we start our scene. Lenny and her start things off, then she's doing me, and then she's doing Lenny. Back and forth like the director wanted, and she didn't miss a beat. Like a real pro, she just went between Lenny and me for about twenty minutes, then it was time for the money shots."

Phil held his hand up. "Money shot?"

"The cum shot, Phil." Jeff said patiently. "It's where we ejaculate on the girl."

"Oh," Phil said, slightly embarrassed that he wasn't familiar with that particular phrase.

"So Lenny and I are in what's called the double-dare. That's where one guy's screwing the chick from behind while the other guy's getting a blow job. Lenny was the one getting head and since he's the bigger name, he's supposed to come first. After he's done I'm supposed to do a ten count and blow my load."

"Jesus," Phil said visibly impressed. "You can do that on command? Just count to ten and ejaculate?"

"That's why we're professional, Phil. Anyway, this is where it gets weird. Lenny does his bit, but the whole time, Kissy is looking at me and smiling. Just looking at me like she's not even aware of what Lenny's doing. It was weird, but I'd been with enough chicks not to be too surprised. So when Lenny's done I start my count, but before I can get to three she starts laughing. Not that phony porno grunting shit; she was laughing, like she knew some big secret that the rest of us didn't."

"Then I noticed her eyes. They were black. Solid, like some kind of black stone. When I saw those I started screaming bloody murder. Then I ran. I mean I just ran like hell. Everyone was looking at me like I'd gone nuts, but I just grabbed my T.V. repairman duds and took off. I wasn't even worried about my money. I just knew if I didn't get away from that woman and her black eyes, I would go nuts."

"Did you?" Phil asked. "I mean, get away from her?"

Jeff shook his head. "Not really. The next day Lenny called me and wanted to know why I freaked out. He tells me that the director is royally pissed off at me and is saying that he'll never use me in any of his movies again. I told Lenny not to worry about it. That I just started feeling sick, and that I'd head over to the set that afternoon and apologize and straighten things up with the director. I was lying through my teeth, but Lenny didn't know that. He told me to come by his apartment before I headed over to the set. He said he had this big surprise for me. I thought he might have gotten my money, so I headed over to his place."

"Lenny lives in this first floor apartment in Belair. Real nice place, and he's one of the more popular guys in the business, so there's usually a party going on there. But when I got to his place, there wasn't anyone around. Thinking about it now, that's the first time I'd ever been to his place and there wasn't someone hanging out. But back then, I didn't think anything about it. His door was open, and I just walked inside."

Phil brought the tips of his fingers to his lips and nodded slightly. "What did you find?"

"Nothing at first. I mean, Lenny was always a clean freak and his apartment was spotless. And that's the way it was when I walked in. I called out for him, but he didn't answer so I looked around the apartment. Finally I went into the bedroom. That's where I found him."

"Let me guess," Phil interrupted. "He was dead."

Jeff grunted and shook his head. "More than dead. Lenny was on the bed, just lying on his back. For a second I thought he was asleep, but then I take another step into the room, and I can see that his chest is ripped open and his insides are gone. Just ripped out. His eyes, too, are gone. He's just got these two empty holes in his head. I nearly puked, and I'm scared shitless when I see this, but instead of getting the hell out of there, I go over to the bed for a closer look because I noticed something else."

"What was that?"

"Lenny's got a hard on," Jeff said blankly. "His guts are ripped out, yet his dick is standing up at attention."

"That's not possible," Phil said. "At least I don't think it is."

Jeff shook his head. "It's not possible, trust me, I know. But yet there's Lenny with no eyes and a fucking boner. It was the weirdest thing."

"What did you do then?"

"Well, I'm standing there just looking at Lenny's dick when I realize there's no blood anywhere. Lenny's chest is ripped open but there ain't a spot of blood in the entire bedroom. Nothing on the bed, nothing on the sheets. Everything was completely clean."

Jeff paused. From the brief, uncomfortable expression that passed over his face, Jeff knew that Phil was thinking the same thing he was. "Yeah, just like that lady we found tonight."

"Anyway, I decided I'd seen enough, so I start backing my way out of the room when Lenny's phone rings. I nearly shit myself when I heard it. I froze when Lenny's answering machine picked it up. I don't know why I didn't just get the hell out of there, but when I heard Lenny's voice telling the caller to leave a message after the beep, I just couldn't get my legs to move. Then I heard her."

"Who?"

"Who else? Kissy Mantrap. She was on the other end of the line, but she wasn't calling for Lenny. She was calling for me. She said that she was sorry our first encounter ended the way it did, and that she wanted to make it up to me. She said that she would come over to my place in an hour and we could talk."

"Shit," Phil said beneath his breath. "Was she watching the place? Waiting for you to show up?"

"That's what I thought at first, but I don't think so now. I mean, she knew I was there, but I don't think she needed to be watching Lenny's pad to know that. I think from the moment I met her, she's known everything I ever did. Everything I feel."

Cradling his head with his palms, Jeff sighed. "She's not a person, Phil. I found that out. She's some kind of thing. Some kind of creature that fucks and eats men."

"And you think she killed Lenny?"

"Oh, I know she did. Killed him and ate his insides."

Phil thought for moment then eased himself back further into his chair. "Succubus," he said.

Jeff took his hands from his face and shot Phil a confused look. "Huh?"

"Succubus," Phil repeated. "It's a female demon with an insatiable sexual appetite. She gets energy from sucking the life-energy out of men while she's screwing them. From what you've described of this Kissy Mantrap, she's a succubus."

Jeff shook his head. "I didn't know they had a name for what she is. But yeah, I guess so. Because I know she ripped open Lenny while he was screwing her"

"You know that for fact," Phil said.

Jeff wasn't sure if that was a question or a statement. "Yeah, I know for sure. She came to my apartment an hour later like she said she would and tried to do the same to me."

"Tell me," Phil said, eager for the story.

* * * * *

When Kissy Mantrap finished her message, a thousand impulses screamed in Jeff's brain telling him to run. Screaming at him to grab some cash and a toothbrush and make like a tree and leave. Every inch of skin on his body, every strand of hair and drop of blood told him that what gutted Lenny was on its way over to do the same thing to him. Rip his eyes out and eat his insides.

No doubt about it.

But a small sliver of his subconscious overruled the rest of his body and told him there wouldn't be any use in running. It wouldn't matter where he went, she would know. And she would find him. Whatever Kissy Mantrap was, Jeff was certain that was her nature. Cold, efficient, and hungry.

She would find him.

In fact, that same sliver of brain told Jeff that she fully expected him to run. Hoping that he would. It was the chase she loved. Tracking down her prey over weeks and miles, giving him just enough room to believe that he had actually escaped.

It was the part of the game she enjoyed most.

So Jeff stayed. It was the only chance to surprise her. To survive her.

But if he was to lay a trap for her, Jeff had to think fast. He had a gun back at his apartment, a big-ass Smith and Wesson he bought from a junkie for twenty bucks and three rocks of crack. Jeff wasn't into guns, but he had spent too many years on the street not to know the value of a little protection.

The first thing Jeff did when he got back to his apartment was to take the gun out of the footlocker he kept at the side of his bed. He slipped six bullets into the chamber and placed it on his bureau knowing that somewhere on the streets of Belair, Kissy Mantrap was just thirty hungry minutes away.

And that's when Jeff realized her weakness. She was a huntress, a creature of appetite who fed and fucked. Jeff pictured Lenny's erection, still poised in death as if bragging that it had been inside Kissy Mantrap. But, Jeff realized, it wouldn't have been enough for Kissy. No man could ever be enough for whatever Kissy Mantrap was, and that's why she devoured them. Because in the end they couldn't fulfill her, they couldn't satisfy her.

Not completely.

And that left her hungry.

Jeff grabbed the mattress off his bed and drug it into the living room. He knew what he had to do; it was so clear now. No man could ever fulfill the thing that was Kissy Mantrap, but unlike Lenny, at least Jeff knew he was playing with a stacked deck ahead of time. At least Jeff had time to prepare and maybe give her a little more than she expected. And maybe that little bit more would be just enough to catch her off guard.

Jeff flung the mattress in the middle of the living room, then brought out three pillows and arranged them at the head of the bed. He brought the gun from the bedroom and laid down on the mattress, his head square in the middle pillow. Letting his right hand dangle over the side of the mattress, Jeff stuffed the gun beneath it. The he got up, straightened the pillows and the lone sheet and went back to his bedroom. Sitting on the bare box spring, Jeff opened the middle drawer of his bureau and took out a thin plastic tube and a baggie containing four grams of cocaine. Glancing at the clock above his bed, he saw that he had twenty minutes before Kissy was to arrive. Just enough time, he thought, ripping open the plastic bag. He didn't bother with the formality of cutting up lines of coke on a mirror; he just dumped it onto his bureau and rolled up a ten-dollar bill and started snorting it into his nostrils.

The impact of the coke hit him right away, but Jeff's mind was racing too fast to appreciate the instant buzz that gripped him. Jeff did another massive line of coke then stripped off his clothes. When he was naked, he started snorting again. Almost immediately the euphoric feeling washed over him, and with that came the cocaine erection.

Anyone in the porn business can tell you that the myth of the cocaine erection is no myth at all. Just a few lines of coke can turn any man's erection into a slab of unfeeling iron capable of standing at attention for as long as the cocaine held out. For the next fifteen minutes Jeff inhaled coke as his penis bulged to almost epic proportions. It throbbed painfully, then grew numb, becoming a useless appendage. When the cocaine was gone, Jeff took the tube and squeezed its contents into his right palm. It was a colorless, odorless goo called Man-Da-Lay that promised, when, used properly, to maintain a man's erection for over an hour. Jeff used it on two occasions when he had to do scenes with hangovers, and in both cases Man-Da-Lay lived up to its billing. Jeff slathered a fistful of the goo onto his member and headed for the living room.

✳ ✳ ✳ ✳ ✳

"Sweet Jesus," Phil said as Jeff paused his story long enough to take another bong hit. "You just waited there for her with a hard-on in hand."

Jeff laughed, brushing aside reefer smoke. "Something like that. I laid down on the bed and waited. About a minute later the door opened. No knock, it just opened. I thought that seeing me naked with a hard on might take her by surprise, but it didn't. She just walked into the apartment wearing the same green sundress and said . . .

Hello my pretty one.

✳ ✳ ✳ ✳ ✳

. . . hello, my pretty one."

"I know what you did to Lenny," Jeff said when he saw her.

Kissy Mantrap nodded once, then without ceremony lifted her sundress over her thin shoulders. She was naked beneath the dress, and as she tossed it on the floor next to the mattress, Jeff was surprised to see just how unspectacular her body was. Except for the pale, whiteness of her skin, Kissy Mantrap's body was firm and curvaceous in all the right places, but in the porn business, it was hardly one that would have stood out. It was her face, Jeff realized. The cold, emotionless face of a statue that made her irresistible. Jeff stared at the fine, smooth contours of that beautiful face and longed to kiss it.

"And you didn't run. Why is that my pretty one?" Kissy asked, stepping onto the mattress. She positioned herself so that she straddled Jeff's knees then gazed down at him as if she expected an answer.

Jeff forced himself to look directly into her coal black eyes. "It wouldn't have done any good, would it?"

Kissy paused and rested her hands on her thin hips. "No, it wouldn't have. Wherever you would have gone, I would have found you. Sooner or later, I would have you."

Jeff swallowed hard before asking his next question. "What are you?"

Kissy's face remained emotionless, almost passive. "I'm a feeder," she said, her eyes fixed on Jeff's. "That is the only way I can describe what I am to you in terms you would understand. I do not know who made me or why, I just know that I am, and it is my nature to feed. We are not all that much different, your kind and mine. It is just that my kind is much older than you could ever imagine."

"We're nothing alike," Jeff said. "You feed on people, on men."

Kissy shrugged and the ghost of a smile came to her face. "I feed on men, I feed on women. It is all the same to me. But don't you see, that is where we are a lot alike. You are not particular who you fuck for money. Men, women. It is all the same to you."

"I don't murder people."

Kissy laughed. "No you don't do anything that dramatic. You just take women and slowly turn them into unfeeling lumps of flesh. And over time that eats up tiny bites out of their spirits until there's nothing left. I feed on flesh and you feed on the soul, and that, Mr. South, is much, much worse." As she spoke, Kissy's left leg brushed against Jeff's thigh. At the touch of her flesh, a surge of electricity shot up Jeff's leg as if he had stepped on a live wire. Jeff's hips arched upward, instinctively drawn toward the woman above him. And as the fire spread through his torso and burnt itself out in his brain, Jeff knew at that moment, he wanted Kissy Mantrap more than any other woman he'd ever known.

"Why," Jeff asked, his breath coming in short gasps. "Why me? Why Lenny?"

"Isn't that obvious," Kissy said, glancing down at Jeff's erection. "You have what I want. And besides." Kissy lowered herself onto her knees "You're so tasty."

Before Jeff realized what was happening, Kissy Mantrap thrust her torso forward and ground her hips against Jeff's. Though she looked as if she weighed no more than a hundred pounds, Jeff felt a crushing weight bearing down on his pelvis.

Once straddled across Jeff, a sound filtered out of Kissy's throat that was part moan and part growl. She threw her head back and dug her fingers into the slightly fleshy sides of Jeff's hips until five trails of blood seeped onto either side of the mattress. In a frenzy, she painfully bucked and ground her hips against Jeff's.

With every ounce of self-control he possessed, Jeff forced himself to remain rigid, staring at the plaster ceiling above him as Kissy Mantrap growled and humped him with an insane fury. He didn't dare look at her sculpted face for fear that seeing it would weaken his self-control. For nearly thirty minutes he was able to stave off ejaculation, and as each minute passed, Jeff could sense that Kissy Mantrap was both surprised and impressed. From the sound of her satisfied grunts that sounded more bestial than human, Jeff knew that he was taking her farther than any man had taken her before. But even for someone with over a thousand porn credits to his stage name, Jeff, unlike the thing banging the snot out of him, was still human and could only hold out for so long. After a half hour of insane grinding, the cocaine and prolonging gel started to lose their effects.

When a familiar tingling sensation began deep in his prostate, Jeff knew he was just seconds from orgasm. And if he came, he knew he would end up like Larry. If he was going to survive, he had to act.

As Kissy's hips continued their furious grinding, Jeff let his right hand slip off the mattress and onto the floor. As casually as a man in his position could, Jeff inched his fingers beneath the mattress until he was able to wrap his hand around the grip of the pistol. But as he was pulling the gun from out of its hiding place, Kissy's frenetic grinding slowed. Gripping the pistol, Jeff looked for the first time at the woman atop him, only now there was little about her that could be called human. Her thin body still resembled that of a woman, but it had lost its smooth whiteness and was now a pale, reptilian gray. The round, firm breasts that had first caught Jeff's notice on the set of *Hard Attack* were replaced by what looked like porous twin bricks with small trails of green veins snaking beneath twin black nipples.

Jeff's eyes traveled up the length of Kissy's torso to the hideous mask that was her face. Gone were the exotic, sculpted features, replaced by a twisted mass of gray misshapen flesh and angles. Small black bumps covered her taut skin like open sores, stretching from her forehead to the scaly lump that bore a passing resemblance to a nose. Kissy's lips were peeled back, stretched to where her ears met two bulbous cheeks. Two sharp rows of finger-length teeth filled the enormous cavity of her mouth. A thick purpled lump of flesh Jeff imagined to be a tongue hung out the right side of the gaping maw, a thick glob of drool dangling from its tip.

The pressure on the side of Jeff's hips subsided as Kissy flung her head back and spread her arms out in front of her. The nails that had been ripping Jeff's flesh now resembled serrated strips of bone jutting from the clawed tips of what used to be Kissy's hands. Her claws clacked together as a sound Jeff had heard countless times in his colorful career as a sex worker drifted out of Kissy's deformed mouth.

She was moaning in pleasure.

Good God, Jeff thought. *She's coming.*

Using the muscle control that had served him so well in the porn industry, Jeff staved off his own building orgasm until he was sure Kissy was about to climax. An agonizing minute later, the thing atop Jeff stopped its grinding and tossed about the wild mane of auburn hair that had been spared the transformation from woman to beast. Mouth agape, Kissy growled in ecstasy as the first waves of orgasm struck her. And as she came, Jeff swung the gun beneath Kissy's chin.

Then Kissy's eyes flew open, and despite their empty blackness, Jeff could see a mixture of pleasure and shock behind them. And, he imagined, some perverse version of love.

Which was enough to make Jeff climax.

And as he came, Jeff fired all six shots into the throat of the thing that was Kissy Mantrap, blasting her head off her shoulders even as he filled her with his seed.

* * * * *

"You killed her while you were having an orgasm," Phil said, both horrified and fascinated at what Jeff had just told him. "Sweet Jesus."

Jeff leaned forward on the couch and sighed. Telling his story had been an uncomfortably sobering experience. "I shouldn't have told you," he said, quickly adding. "But you don't believe me anyway, do you?"

Phil shook his head. "The exact opposite actually. I believe every word of it."

An uneasy silence followed where Phil struggled to find the words to tell Jeff what Henry Wallace had whispered to him. "You shouldn't," Jeff finally said. "Nobody should."

Instead of answering, Phil stood up and motioned for Jeff to follow him back to the cubicle that housed Metamorpho. When they got there, Phil headed for the draped canvas. "The work in progress," Jeff remarked as Phil went to remove the tarp.

"The first night you asked about my collection," Phil said, pointing to Metamorpho. "That was the night I took Henry Wallace's hearing aid. I put it in my ear and it told me to paint a picture for you."

"For me?"

"Yes," Phil said softly. "By special request."

Phil pulled the tarp off the canvas, revealing the work in progress, the surreal portrait of something with a twisted demonic grin on a woman's face; something with flowing auburn hair and a green sundress who stretched her arms outward as if waiting for an embrace. A painting that only moments before, Phil realized, was a not quite finished portrait of the thing that called herself Kissy Mantrap.

* * * * *

Ignoring the no smoking sign in the lobby of Jeff's apartment building, Phil lit a cigarette then tossed the spent match onto the floor. The action earned a disapproving look from an old lady waiting for the elevator, but Phil didn't care. He took a long drag then blew the smoke in the direction of the elevator before making his way out of the building.

Ever since Jeff told him about Kissy Mantrap, Phil's mind was consumed by a single thought. But before he could act on it, he had to make sure Jeff was all right. His reaction to the painting of Kissy Mantrap was not what Phil expected. Jeff simply gazed on the painting for a few moments then turned to Phil and said he wanted to go home.

"That's it," Phil shot back. "That's all you have to say?"

Jeff stood mute, not looking at the painting.

"I get messages from a dead guy to paint this monstrosity who you fucked and killed, and all you have to say is that you want to go home. Don't you think this is all a bit weird?"

Jeff lowered his head and looked at the floor. "You shouldn't have painted this, Phil," Jeff said. "I took her face away, and now you brought it back. You brought her back" A solitary tear fell from Jeff's eye onto the smooth, tiled floor. "Now take me home, Phil." Turning before Phil could answer, Jeff hurried out of the room. Dumbfounded Phil turned to the grinning horror trapped on the canvas.

"What did you do to him?"

But Kissy wasn't about to divulge any of her secrets.

"You bitch," Phil hissed at the painting, then hurried to catch up with Jeff.

* * * * *

Though Phil tried to get him to talk about the painting, Jeff remained silent. There really wasn't anything for him to say. The ugliness that he destroyed had been brought back. Not in form, but the image was enough to burn itself into the forefront of his mind. It stuck there like a scar, a deformity that once unmasked, could never be ignored. During the ride from Phil's place to his apartment, Jeff kept sneaking peaks of himself in the rearview mirror. The grinning, demon face of Kissy Mantrap stared back.

* * * * *

Phil's car was parked right outside of Jeff's building, but the artist hurried past it. Fortunately for him, Jeff lived dead center in the seediest part of town surrounded by dozens of dive bars, adult novelty shops, and a booming drug trade. Now that he knew of Jeff's past, Phil guessed that the red-light district probably felt like home for the ex-porn star.

Phil bypassed a pair of hookers looking for early trade and headed straight for the first adult bookstore he came to. It was in the third bookstore that he found what he was looking for. There he paid an overweight cashier named Bob twenty dollars for the store's lone copy of *Hard Attack*.

Hugging the videotape to his chest, Phil hurried to his car.

* * * * *

Jeff opened his eyes to find himself surrounded by darkness. Beneath his bare back and arms, Jeff felt the soft fabric of flannel sheets. *I'm home*, he thought. How he got there was a mystery, though. The last thing he could remember was Phil unveiling the portrait of Kissy Mantrap.

The work-in-progress.

Jeff took a long, slow breath. With the air came an odd mixture of gunpowder, cigarettes, and cheap perfume, a scent that made him think of Stella's apartment. It was definitely the smell of hatred, mixed with an undercurrent of desire.

Jeff pushed himself into a sitting position. In front of him came a rustling sound.

Jeff stared forward into the darkness and said, "You're here, aren't you?"

The rustling came closer.

"You found me."

Hello my pretty one.

The words came so low and soft that Jeff wasn't certain if he had heard them or only thought them. But it didn't matter. Kissy Mantrap had found him. Whatever she was, six bullets into the head wasn't enough to kill her. Oddly, Jeff felt a strange sense of relief knowing that his death was moments away. He calmly reached over to the nightstand on the right side of the bed and flicked on the light.

Perched at the end of his bed was Kissy Mantrap. Lacking only stone wings, she looked like an auburn-haired gargoyle. Behind her stood the skeletal frame of Metamorpho.

"You're here to kill me," Jeff said, staring into the black pools that were Kissy's eyes. "Just like you did Lenny."

Kissy shook her head slowly from side to side. "No, Scott South. I'm not here to kill you. Punish you, yes. Kill you, no."

"Don't call me that," Jeff shouted. "That's not my name."

"Maybe not," the thing replied. "But it is who you are. A petty whore who longs for the feeling of flesh against flesh. Don't you, Jeff? Miss the touching, the kissing, the licking? Don't you miss me?"

Jeff tossed the covers off his legs and sprung out of bed. "No! That's not true. I got away from all of that when I got away from you!"

"But you didn't," Kissy said. "The desire is still there. The never-ending hunger." Spreading her arms out to the side, Kissy offered Jeff a full view of her naked, upper body. Jeff stood transfixed at the sight, unable to take his eyes off her rough leaden breasts. He was seized with a sudden, powerful urge to caress them, to run his fingertips and tongue along their cracked surface. He took two steps toward Kissy then stopped. The succubus chuckled and folder her arms over her chest. "We're the same, Jeff. We've both fed on flesh, and we like it. We just have separate appetites. You fuck without emotion, I feed without emotion. What's the difference?"

"I killed you," Jeff said, his voice barely registering a whisper.

"No. You can't kill me, Jeff. Just like you can't kill the hunger that lives inside you. I am that hunger, Jeff. That darkness that lives in everyone like you who craves flesh. We are eternal. All you did was take away my pretty face. But you're going to help me find it again, aren't you? You're going to help me be pretty again." Kissy laughed and hopped off the bed. "Come, my new friend has something to show you." Kissy hooked a clawed hand around Jeff's left arm and pulled him toward Metamorpho. "I know you two have met."

With her free hand, Kissy snapped her claw like a castanet. At the sound, Metamorpho took a lumbering step forward. "Look, Jeff. No gears, no pulleys. Your artist friend has succeeded in creating a living statue."

"No," Jeff said. "It's a machine. It's not alive."

The grip tightened until Jeff thought his arm might snap in two. "But it is alive. Filled with all the shards of souls your friend collected." Kissy threw her head back and laughed. "That fool. He thought his masterpiece was saving the damned, helping their souls to become something else. Giving them new life. Well look at it, Jeff. This is the only thing those souls have evolved into. A private hell of metal. Now look!" Kissy shoved Jeff forward, sending him into the waiting arms of Metamorpho. "Look at his body," Kissy hissed. "Look at what has become of the souls your friend collected."

Realizing that he could not escape the statue's grip, Jeff

did as Kissy instructed. He bent his head forward and examined the souvenirs that Phil had stolen from the dead. When he first examined Metamorpho's frame at Phil's apartment, the bits of eyeglasses and coins soldered onto it appeared to be little more than oddly spaced raises and bumps along the statue's smooth metal surface. Now that smooth surface erupted in dozens of open sores that oozed a viscous substance that was too dark and oily for blood. Jeff moved his head forward and stared at one golf ball sized eruption on Metamorpho's chest where half of a quarter had been soldered. Only now the quarter was desperately trying to free itself. It quivered against the metal frame trapping it, the half visible face of George Washington writhing in agony. As Jeff stared, Washington's mouth opened, his lips peeled back in a silent, but agonizing scream.

Jeff shut his eyes.

"They are in hell," Kissy said. There was no malice or gloating in her tone. It was a statement of fact. "Your friend damned those people."

His eyes still closed, Jeff felt Kissy stroke the back of his head with one of her clawed hands. *At last*, he thought. Enough of the bullshit, Kissy was done playing and was ready to rip his head off.

But the expected decapitation didn't happen. Instead, Metamorpho let him go.

"Look," Kissy said when Jeff was released. "A little visit to yesterday."

Jeff opened his eyes to find himself in the living room of an unfamiliar apartment.

But it wasn't unfamiliar; he had been there once. Recently.

From behind a closed door at the point where the combination living room/dining room emptied into the kitchen, a high-pitched voice was singing an old Bobby Goldsboro song.

Instinctively, Jeff knew he was inside the apartment of the woman whose corpse he and Phil had removed earlier in the day. The lady named Stella.

Only now, she wasn't dead.

But she would be.

Jeff ran through the kitchen door as Stella's sing-along version of "Honey" came to a violent end. As Jeff flung himself into the kitchen, Metamorpho was hoisting Stella into the air, his metal arms shredding the terrycloth fabric of her housecoat, and ripping open her back. Jeff gasped as the tips of Metamorpho's eyeglass frame fingers poke through of the soft flesh of Stella's throat just above the collarbone.

"No!" Jeff wailed. He started toward the headless monstrosity that was skewering Stella, but a stone-like hand clamped itself on his shoulder and pulled him back. "Let him finish," Kissy's voice sounded in Jeff's ear.

Jeff struggled against Kissy's grasp but couldn't free himself. Though he couldn't see her, the scent of Kissy Mantrap filled the room. It was a dark fusion of cheep perfume and rotting flesh, the smell Jeff recognized as hatred.

No, not hatred.

Evil.

Helpless, Jeff watched as Stella writhed against the statue's metal frame, her frail arms and legs twitching wildly in the air. Thin geysers of blood squirted out of Stella's throat in time with her heartbeat spraying the walls and floor. *That's not right*, Jeff thought as the carnage continued. *There wasn't any blood when we picked her up.*

When life mercifully left Stella a minute later, Metamorpho tossed the woman's corpse to the floor and took a few steps back. "Time to feed," Kissy said, thrusting Jeff toward the bloodied carcass in front of him. "Yum, yum, yum."

His shoulders clamped in the vices that were Kissy's claws, Jeff shot a quick glance at Metamorpho. The blood that coated the lower half of the statue's arms was being sucked into the open wounds where the individual pieces of Phil's collection were soldered. "Yes," Kissy said. "He feeds."

Grabbing Jeff's collar with her left claw and his belt with her right, Kissy thrust Jeff into the air and held him over Stella's body. From the twin holes ripped into her back, the warm stench of shit and decay filtered upward. Jeff gagged from the smell, but he couldn't take his eyes off the fleshy pulp of Stella's back. And as he dangled over Stella, Jeff understood what had become of her blood and internal organs.

"We all must feed," Kissy said, dropping the former porn star.

* * * * *

Jeff screamed, the coppery taste of warm liver fresh in his mouth.

"Wake up, Jeff," a voice said at his side. "You're having a bad dream."

A soft hand gently pressed itself on Jeff's bare shoulder and carefully shook him. His head was pounding and his throat felt as if the devil had pissed in it. "Where am I?" Jeff asked, opening his eyes.

The hand on his shoulder slipped forward and cupped the hard roundness of Jeff's pectoral muscle. "You're at my place. Don't you remember? You came here yesterday afternoon."

Jeff shuddered. The voice belonged to Candy.

"I thought you were drunk," Candy continued. "With all

that raving about Phil Luxor and his statue." Candy lifted his long fingers and began to trace them up along the thin path of hair that ran down the middle of Jeff's chest. "I didn't think you were interested in me," Candy laughed. "You sure proved me wrong." The hand found its way back to Jeff's pec. "I think I'm going to be sore for days."

Brushing Candy's hand aside. Jeff pushed himself into a sitting position. He didn't have to remove the damp sheet from his lower body to know that he was naked. Beside him, Candy's too-thin frame stretched across the length of the bed. He too was naked, but unlike Jeff whose memory was a blank, Candy was smiling in anticipation of continuing their earlier sexual adventures.

"What did I say?"

Candy's grin faded, replaced by a confused pout. "When?" he asked.

"When I got here yesterday," Jeff shouted. "What did I tell you?"

Candy's pout slipped into a frown. "You were talking weird. You said that Phil Luxor made some statue and that it was alive, and it killed that old lady you picked up the other day. Like I said, I thought you were drunk."

"What about the woman? Did I tell you anything the succubus?"

"The what?" Candy raised himself on one elbow then slid his feet off the bed and sat up with his back to Jeff. "Were you with a woman before you came here?"

"Damn it, Candy. Did I say anything about a woman named Kissy Mantrap?"

With his back still to Jeff, Candy shook his head. "No. You

were just babbling about how some big metal statue ate some woman. I'm telling you, Jeff. You were freaking me out." Candy turned his head and smiled. "But I'll forgive you if you give me a kiss."

Candy puckered slightly and leaned forward quickly, catching Jeff by surprise. Before he could pull away, Candy pressed his lips against Jeff's. At the touch, the taste of Candy's lips burned through Jeff's mouth, down his parched throat and into his stomach. He could taste the blood and tissue beneath the thin top layers of flesh that covered Candy's thin lips.

Jeff closed his eyes and allowed his mouth to slip open.

But then the hot pressure of Candy's mouth was gone.

Jeff's eyes shot open in time to see Candy being yanked off the bed and onto the floor. For a split-second, Candy's face was caught in a clownish expression of bug eyes and an o-ringed mouth. Then the face, with the rest of the body, disappeared off the side of the bed.

Jeff started to move toward his friend but two distinct sounds coming from the floor stopped him. The first was Candy's scream, a high-pitched feminine wail, which quickly devolved into a weak gurgling whimper. The second sound was more sublime, but infinitely more disturbing. It was the sound of paper being ripped from a spiral-ring notebook, an innocuous sound Jeff had heard thousands of times when he was in school. But there were no notebooks stashed beneath Candy's bed to be ripped, no secret diaries to provide convenient fodder for shredding.

There was only Candy and the thing that yanked him off the bed.

Jeff froze, not daring to lean over and watch his most recent lover's flesh being ripped off his body. He didn't have to, he pictured Stella's corpse on the linoleum floor. Her skin neatly flayed in ribbon-like strips.

The ripping lasted much longer than the screaming. When it stopped Jeff breathed in deeply the scent of cigarettes and stale perfume. "Kissy," he whispered.

Beneath the bed came a shuffling. "Still haven't found my pretty face," her disembodied voice said from beneath Jeff's mattress.

Jeff stiffened at the sound.

"Metamorpho has been very thorough with your boyfriend, Jeff. Do you want to see?"

"No," Jeff said, but his body was already inching toward the side of the bed.

"Just a peeky-weeky before I'm finished."

Jeff leaned across the bed and looked over the side.

The floor was bare.

"What?" Candy's body should have been sprawled out beneath him, gutted like a fish. But there was nothing there. No body, no torn flesh. No blood.

Candy was gone.

But he wasn't.

Jeff snapped himself back into his seated position and looked down at his lower body. The mauve colored blanket was torn off the bed. Draped over his waist and legs in its place was an odd-shaped translucent sheet that reeked of sweat and blood. Jeff's face contorted into an oddly similar version of Candy's bug-eyed look when he saw a pair of hollow arms trailing from the sides of the sheet.

"Oh shit," Jeff wailed when he saw what had become of Candy. Somewhere from beneath the bed came the sound of Kissy's laughter.

Jeff screamed.

Then he shut his eyes.

Then screamed again.

And woke up.

* * * * *

He was in his own room, still dressed in the same jeans and t-shirt he wore from when he went to Phil Luxor's apartment.

Jeff greedily inhaled the familiar aroma of his efficiency apartment. The smell of pot wafting from his clothes was almost overpowering, but behind it Jeff could detect a hint of the bug spray he used the day before. He breathed in deeper. Yes, there it was. The smell of old feet that was permanently ground into the worn fabric of the carpet.

It was an unpleasant smell. Foul even.

But it wasn't the smell of warm blood and evil.

Hello my pretty one.

Jeff groaned, pushing himself out of bed. It was just a dream. Another total mind-fuck of a dream. It had been months since he'd had a nightmare that bad. But he'd had them before. He'd have them again. And as long as the memory of Kissy Mantrap liked to play hide'n'seek in his subconscious, the nightmares would come.

"No bout-a-doubt it," Jeff said, plucking a cigarette off the nightstand next to his bed. He lit the stick and ran his fingers across his scalp. He brushed back his greasy hair then sniffed his fingers and decided to forgo a shower. The clock on the nightstand burned the time in red numerals.

9:15 PM

Jeff allowed himself five minutes to finish his smoke before he started getting ready for work.

* * * * *

Jeff was reaching for his timecard to check in when someone grabbed his arm, sharply pinching his left tricep. "Where the hell have you been?"

Yanking his arm free, Jeff spun around to face Mort Nevin, the nightshift supervisor and Jeff's boss. A small overweight man with a bad prostate, Mort was wiggling a pudgy finger at Jeff, his face skewed in a tight-lipped frown that turned the scalp beneath his thinning white hair a light shade of puce. "I don't know what the hell you did at your last job, but you sure-as-shit aren't going to get away with just taking off and not getting someone to cover your shifts."

"What are you talking about?" Jeff said, pushing himself past Mort. "I got off at five this morning."

Mort laughed and pulled Jeff's time card off the wall. "What kind of idiot do you take me for, French?" Mort shoved the cardboard slip in Jeff's face. "Read it. You haven't been here in three days."

Jeff snatched the card out of Mort's hand. He scanned the column that marked the time he started work with a perfectly shaped hole. There were no holes for the last three days. "This is bullshit," Jeff said, slamming the card back into its slot on the wall. "I worked my shift, and afterwards I went over to Phil's house."

At the mention of Phil's name, the frown on Mort's face

deepened sending new traces of puce across his forehead. "Phil Luxor," he said. "That bastard hasn't been here either."

"Phil hasn't been to work?"

Nevin shook his head. "Nope. Now I don't know what kind of games you and Luxor are playing, but your little vacation left us up to our asses in stiffs. The graveyard shift has had twenty-seven pick-ups in the last 72 hours. Twenty-seven pickups and no fucking drivers!" Mort tossed his hands in his air and stormed past Jeff toward the holding room where over half of the last three days pickups were still being stored. "It doesn't matter," he called over his shoulder. "You and Luxor don't work here anymore. Clean your shit out of your locker and get the hell out of here."

"Wait a second," Jeff yelled as his boss flung open the swinging metal doors of the holding room. Jeff hurried down the hall after him. When he slipped into the holding room, Nevin was handing a clipboard to a new orderly. "I can prove I was here yesterday," Jeff said. "Ask Candy. He saw me and Phil leaving."

"Candy?" Nevin asked. "You mean Harry Kane?"

"Yeah," Jeff shot back. "Harry Kane. He'll tell you."

The orderly and Mort exchanged a quick glance before Mort turned back to Jeff. "Listen," he began, his voice low and measured. "I don't know what kind of sick game you're playing with me, French. But if you know what's good for you, you'll turn around and get the fuck out of here."

"No. I can't afford to lose this job, and I'm not going to because there's some mistake on my punch card. Now I was here yesterday, and Candy will verify that."

Mort stood still, his body clenched to the point of quivering. "He will, will he!" he shouted. "Let's just see about that." Without explanation, Mort pushed past the orderly and headed to the long wall of metal drawers that housed the stiffs. Plucking a set of keys out of his pocket, Mort went up to the drawer number 45.

As Mort inserted the key into the drawer, a cold understanding hit Jeff like an out of control ambulance. It slammed into his head, his shoulders and chest; his legs buckled and the hot taste of vomit filled his mouth.

"Candy was pickup number 4, two nights ago," Mort said, yanking the drawer open. Jeff looked at the drawer, but there was no body stretched out on the cold, metal table. What sat there was a long metal basin with a white sheet draped over its side. "Whatever killed Candy ripped him apart. Took his insides, his bones, everything. Shit," Mort said, his voice softening. "What we could find of him, we had to scrape up into in this bucket." Mort paused then shot Jeff a steely glance. "See for yourself."

Mort yanked the sheet off the basin revealing the hollowed out skin that was all that remained of Harry "Candy" Kane.

* * * * *

The pounding caused Phil to jerk himself out of a dreamless sleep. He waited, not sure if the sound was real or a mild hallucination brought on from exhaustion. He listened through the silence as his eyes adjusted to the darkness around him. The pounding came again. This time more forceful, more urgent.

Phil forced his tired body off the couch and headed for the front door.

"Alright, I'm coming," he yelled. He easily navigated the dark passageways from the living room to the front door. For the past three days he had been holed up in his studio, surviving on strong coffee and bong hits. As he came to the door he glanced at his watch. It was almost ten, but Phil wasn't certain if that was AM or PM.

Phil undid the three locks on his front door and yanked it open. "Jeff," Phil said casually. "I thought it might be you." Phil stepped to the side and motioned for Jeff to come in.

"What have you done?" Jeff said as he brushed past Phil into the apartment. "What the fuck have you done?"

Phil ignored Jeff's outburst and calmly closed and rebolted the door. "What are you talking about, Jeff? I haven't done anything."

As Phil turned, Jeff lunged forward and slammed his palms into Phil's chest, sending the artist into the wall. "Don't you lie to me!" Jeff grabbed a fistful of Phil's shirt then jammed his forearm beneath Phil's chin and started pushing. "You brought her back, didn't you? You and that fucking machine in the gallery!"

Phil struggled against the pressure of Jeff's forearm, but the former porn star was too strong and fueled by too much adrenalin for Phil to wiggle himself free. Staring into the wide, blood shot eyes of his former partner, Phil Luxor felt his throat about to be crushed and realized he was going to die.

Then the pressure disappeared and Phil fell to his knees.

Jeff took two steps back and collapsed ass first onto the floor. "You brought Kissy back, Phil. I killed her and you brought her back. And now she's killing again. Her and Metamorpho." Burying his face in his hands, Jeff began to weep.

Clutching his bruised neck, Phil swallowed a painful mouth of air as he shifted his weight from his knees onto his own rear end. "Calm down," Phil managed to choke out. "Just calm down."

His face still cupped in his hands, Jeff appeared not to have heard him.

Phil took three more deep breaths. Already the pain in his throat was subsiding. "How can she be back? You said you shot her head off."

Slowly. Jeff took his hands from his tear-stained face and glared at Phil. "It's not her body," Jeff said. "It's her spirit. Her soul. Whatever the fuck it is that she has. She's gotten inside of Metamorpho, and she's using it to kill."

Phil rolled his eyes and groaned. "Come on, Jeff. I know we're caught up in some pretty weird shit, but Metamorpho is not killing anybody."

"He is," Jeff said. "I saw him. He killed Stella. You know, the lady you stole the hairpin from. Metamorpho shoved his arms right through her back. Then he went over to Candy's place and ripped his skin off his body."

"Candy," Phil said. "Harry Kane from the morgue?"

Jeff nodded. "Yeah. Metamorpho killed him two days ago. I was there. Ripped him out of his bed and ate him. He didn't leave anything but his head and his skin."

Phil jumped to his feet and took a half-assed swing at Jeff that missed by over a foot. "Bullshit! Metamorpho is a fucking statue made out of chicken wire and metal pipe. He is not alive, and he is not possessed by the spirit of some succubus. That shit does not happen!"

"Yes it does," Jeff said softly. "It happened, and it's your fault." Slowly, Jeff pushed himself off the floor and started down the hall toward Phil's studio.

"Come into the living room," Phil pleaded as he followed Jeff through the hall maze. "You look like you could use a beer and something to eat."

Jeff shook his head and continued toward the studio.

"What are you going to do?" Phil asked when the pair

came upon the black door. Jeff's answer came without hesitation.

"Kill it." Stopping in front of the door, Jeff slipped his right hand into his leather jacket and removed the gun that had blown off Kissy Mantrap's head a year earlier. He half-turned and offered Phil a weak smile. "I've done it before."

Phil reached out to stop Jeff, but the younger man was too quick. Before Phil could get a hold of his coat, Jeff slammed shoulder first into the studio door and stumbled inside. The lights were off making it impossible for Jeff to see any more of his target than a large, shadowy outline. What was perfectly clear was the soft whir of Metamorpho's motor and the sound of a paintbrush scraping against the rough texture of the wall. The two sounds melted together perfectly into an inviting whisper.

Hello my pretty one.

A feeling of perfect calmness came upon Jeff as he aimed the gun at the base of the metal skeleton where he remembered the motor to be. He knew in all likelihood that his own death was just moments away; the spirit of Kissy Mantrap would awaken Metamorpho and send the statue to rip him apart. It would hurt like hell, too, but that was a small price to pay for finally being free of Kissy Mantrap.

"Eat this," Jeff said as he pulled the trigger.

In the small, square studio, the gunshot exploded with the sound of a barely muffled cannon. Phil screamed as a streak of hot light erupted from the barrel, illuminating Jeff's face for a split-second in a field of white electricity. Hidden beneath the sound of the gun's discharge was the high-pitched shriek of metal hitting metal.

Jeff took aim again, but before he could fire, Phil switched on the lights.

"Stop it!" he shouted, but Jeff didn't waver. With a clear shot now, he adjusted his aim and fired a second round into the motor at the base of Metamorpho's skeleton. This bullet struck true, blasting the mechanism into a dozen pieces. Metamorpho's skeleton hitched to the left then quickly dropped its right arm parallel with the floor splattering droplets of red paint against the canvas on the wall. The pattern reminded Jeff of the goop on the wall of Henry Wallace's kitchen.

"No!" Phil wailed, rushing to the now still statue. He glanced about at the ruined canvas then down at the twisted gizmos on the floor. "Damn you!" Phil wheeled around. "Goddamn it, Jeff. What the fuck are you doing?"

"Putting a stop to this," Jeff said blankly, the gun aimed at a spot directly behind Phil's head. "Now get out of the way. I have four bullets left."

"And then what?"

"Then Kissy will have nowhere to go and this will all be over. Now please, Phil. Get out of the way."

"It's already over," Phil said, moving to his left so he was no longer in the line of fire. "Look at Kissy's painting. I fixed it. She's no longer a succubus."

"You fixed it?" Jeff laughed slightly but did lower the gun. "How the hell did you fix it?"

Phil hurried to the tarp that covered the work-in-progress. "I found a copy of that movie you were in, *Hard Attack*. I saw the girl," Phil said, yanking the tarp free of the painting. "I saw what she looked like and painted her over the succubus."

The tarp was flung to the floor and the face of Kissy Mantrap in all her cold, sculpted beauty gazed down at Jeff from the canvas.

For a moment, the stunned expression on Jeff's face

bordered on the comical, but Phil didn't dare laugh. Especially since Jeff still had the Smith and Wesson. But then Jeff's entire body went rigid as if he had suddenly been hit in the head with a two by four. His eyes flew open wide and his arms shot out to his sides. The gun slipped out of his hand and smacked the wood floor with a loud thud, but Jeff didn't appear to notice. He took two staggering steps toward the canvas as Phil backed away from the painting. "It's her," Jeff said, half-whispering. "You really found her." He stared at the painting, shaking his head in disbelief.

Phil slid behind Jeff and picked up the gun. "Yeah," he said. "I found her."

With his back turned to Phil, Jeff continued shaking his head. "You found her pretty face," he whispered. "You found her pretty face."

Jeff turned around and Phil nearly shot him.

Jeff's piercing blue eyes, the eyes that melted the heart of Candy Kane, had turned jet black If Phil would have been closer, he would have seen a twin mirrors of his terrified face reflected back at him.

"You found her pretty face."

Shaking, Phil raised the gun and aimed it at Jeff's chest. "What are you?"

Phil told himself not to shoot; he forced himself to remain calm, even though his friend was staring at him with the black dead eyes of a succubus.

And he would have been able to remain calm if Metamorpho didn't rip itself free of the wire and pulley system that had controlled its movements.

Phil screamed, and though he was staring at the headless metal skeleton ripping itself free of the mechanism that housed it,

Phil fired three shots directly into Jeff's chest. Before he could fire a fourth time, Metamorpho freed himself and slapped the gun out of Phil's hand. Phil tried to turn and run, but the metal arms of his creation wrapped themselves around his chest in a bear hug and turned him so he faced the canvas.

Metamorpho clamped its sharp fingers over Phil's mouth, cutting off the scream that was exploding from his throat. Unable to free himself from the statue's grip, Phil watched in horror at what was happening to his ex-partner on the Bony Express.

Jeff stood with his back against the portrait of Kissy Mantrap after the force of the three bullets that struck his chest sent him staggering backward. He had his face upturned toward the ceiling and his arms outstretched as if he was being crucified. For a second, Phil thought he was going to call upon God to deliver him from evil, then Jeff's head slumped forward. His eyes were no longer black; they were crystal blue and glazed over with the look of a man with a bird's eye view of hell. Jeff's entire body quivered and started to fall forward.

But it never hit the floor.

Instead, it said fuck you to every known law of physics by snapping back as if tethered to an elastic band. Jeff hit the wall with enough force to dislodge the painting, but instead of falling, the portrait of Kissy Mantrap started to vibrate. Jeff's body flailed against the canvas as the image of Kissy Mantrap began to expand inside the painting. Her face and torso pressed against the canvas, her perfect nose and cheeks flattening as if she was smoshing her face against a window. In any other circumstance, the image would have been comical to Phil. But watching a figure from one of his portraits trying to escape the painting while another piece of his artistic handiwork trapped him in a bear hug was more than enough to send the former ambulance driver barreling down the road to insanity. After about half a minute's struggle, Kissy was able to push her arms free of the canvas and, dripping of warm, flesh-tone paint, wrap themselves around

Jeff's chest. She pulled the former porn star tight against the wall and squeezed.

And even with Metamorpho's fingers digging into the flesh around his mouth, Phil found a way to scream. It was the kind of excruciating scream that would have shattered a champagne glass if on would have been handy. But there wasn't any glass in Phil's studio, not even an old beer bottle lying around. So nothing shattered when Phil screamed.

Except for Jeff.

But he didn't really shatter; that would have been much cleaner with just a bunch of little pieces of Jeff strewn about the floor like a broken windowpane. Instead, Jeff exploded. One second he was standing there getting a hug from Kissy Mantrap, and the next second he was a cloud of human shrapnel flying through the air. Tiny shards of Jeff's bones slapped Phil's face, ripping dozens of razor sharp cuts into his flesh, his own blood mixing with the rust-colored mist that blanketed the studio. Phil's eyes and throat pinched shut, but his nostrils remained open allowing him to breath in the secret smell of Jeff French's internal organs. *Like burnt bratwurst,* Phil thought. *A hard roll and a side order of fries and we got ourselves a picnic.*

Phil wanted to laugh, needed to laugh, but he was choking on the taste of what he thought was Jeff's spleen and couldn't find a way to laugh. But that part of his brain that was heading down that highway to insanity had set the cruise control at ninety and found the whole thing hilarious. That part of his brain was busting a gut.

But the part of Phil's brain that appreciated the depth of the shit he was in stayed silent. It pushed away the taste of Jeff's innards and the urge to vomit and forced Phil to open his eyes. Through the blood-red haze, Phil watched as Kissy Mantrap stepped out of the painting and onto a puddle of guts and tissue. She glanced around the room, ignoring both Phil and what was left of Jeff. She sniffed in the air once, then forming a tight O with her mouth, she inhaled.

Immediately, the bits of flesh and blood that drifted like dust in the air were sucked into the cavity of her mouth.

This time Phil did laugh. To hell with sanity. Kissy Mantrap was inhaling the cloud of Jeff's blood the way Superman used to suck up the mustard gas that Lois Lane always found herself ankle deep in in that old T.V. show. But only Kissy wasn't doing the Hoover trick for truth, justice, and the American way. She was feeding and . . .

Phil's laughter melted into a sob.

Kissy was feeding and becoming . . .

Alive.

When the last of the blood cloud was sucked down her throat, Kissy closed her mouth and trained her black-eyed gaze on Phil. For a second, Phil could see his reflection in her eye, then Kissy blinked, and when her eyelids flipped back open, the eyes that stared back at Phil were a vibrant green. Kissy smiled, and Phil thought she was the most beautiful woman he'd ever seen.

"You found my pretty face," Kissy said. She glanced at the floor and gently pushed away some of Jeff's remains with the tip of her right foot. "I knew you would."

"You did?" Phil was surprised that he could speak.

Kissy nodded. "Certainly. You're a special man, Phil Luxor, but you're also arrogant." Kissy laughed and tossed her auburn hair back over her shoulders. "Did you really think the dead were contacting you? Begging you to help them metamorphosize?" Kissy stepped over what remained of Jeff's left arm and shoulder. Phil flinched when Kissy brought her arm out, but when her fingers caressed his cheek, Phil felt an undeniable stirring in his groin. "It's been me the whole time, Phil. I've been calling you. Telling you to steal those bits of soul for our metal friend there." Kissy's hand slipped from Phil's cheek.

Instinctively, Phil strained his head forward toward her hand. More than anything, he wanted to feel her fingers against his skin.

But Kissy denied him what would have been his last pleasure. She took two steps back, just beyond arm's reach.

"Jeff killed you," Phil managed to say.

Kissy didn't argue. "Some of me, yes. But not all of me," Kissy replied. "He didn't kill my eyes."

"Your eyes?"

Kissy nodded. "The eyes are the windows to the soul, Phil. As an artist, you should know that." Kissy took another step away from Phil which made the stirring in his groin even more pronounced. "When your friend told you about our encounter, he neglected to mention one thing. Before I died, I ripped his eyes from their sockets. Then I replaced them with mine."

"Why? I don't understand."

"So I could see. Isn't that obvious?" The blank look on Phil's face told Kissy that nothing was obvious. Kissy frowned. "Your friend took away my pretty face, Phil," Kissy said, running her thin fingers against her cheek and through her hair. "And I wanted it back. You see, I could have come back any time, but I needed something to come back through." Kissy turned to the blank canvas that hung limply from the wall. "That's why you were needed. Your arrogance and curiosity provided that for me." Kissy spun around to face Phil. "But before I could come through, I had to make sure that you painted the right face. The face I wanted. That's why I needed your friend. He carried my eyes. And you did all the rest."

"But the people," Phil began. "Jeff said you possessed Metamorpho and ate people. He said you ate Harry Kane."

"Jeff carried more than my eyes," Kissy said, moving toward Phil. "He carried my hunger. But enough talking. We have much to do." Phil screamed as Kissy's pretty face melted into the twisted mask of the succubus. "Time to become, artist."

* * * * *

Officer Lance Jacobs swallowed hard as he surveyed the bloody mess that was Phil Luxor's studio, and wondered how long he had to go until retirement. Thankfully, he didn't have to go in the room. That was a job for forensics.

"What do you think happened, Lance?"

Jacobs looked at his young partner, an ashen face rookie named Bill Steever. "Beats the hell out of me. I just know it was bad."

Steever nodded. "It looks like the guy got ripped apart."

"Two guys," Jacobs said blankly.

"Huh?"

Jacobs pointed to a mound of bones in the corner of the studio. "Look at the bones. I don't know a hip bone from the leg bone, but I sure as hell know what a hand looks like, and there's two hands in that pile."

Steever allowed himself a glance at the bones. "Yeah," he said. "So?"

"So look at that pile of shit beneath that painting."

"Oh man," Steever hissed as he recognized what his partner was pointing at. A left hand attached to the bottom half of a severed arm lay flattened on the floor.

"Yeah," Jacobs said. "Another hand. Another corpse."

Steever took his cap from his head and wiped the back of his hand across his forehead. He closed his eyes and took a deep breath. He was one bad smell away from blowing chunks, and he didn't want to do it in front of Jacobs. "What the hell happened here?" he asked, his eyes still screwed tight.

"Something bad," was Jacob's reply. "Something really fucking bad."

* * * * *

The cruise control of the Mustang convertible was set at seventy-five. With the top rolled down, the wind whipped her auburn hair in wild swirls about her face as she headed westward to the coast. Hidden behind a pair of mirrored sunglasses, her black eyes burned with hunger. She would need to feed soon.

"We're going to stop in the next town," she said, not taking her eyes from the road.

Phil Luxor's head lolled to the side.

"Do you understand what I said?"

Phil's lips parted. *It hurts.*

Kissy turned to face him. She smiled and brought her hand up to caress his cheek. The expression on Phil's face remained unchanged as she stroked it. It was the same expression he wore when she ripped his head from his shoulders, a fusion of terror and wonder. It was the expression the former artist would wear for eternity.

Or at least until the metal skeleton of Metamorpho could no longer support his head.

She looked over her handiwork, pleased at the way she was

able to stretch Phil's skin around Metamorpho's frame. It was a perfect fit, except for a portion of the lower torso where about twenty yards of Phil's intestines were twisted through chicken wire. That part of Phil's new body still needed some work.

But, after all, Phil was a work in progress.

It hurts.

Phil's head swivelled on the pipe that was pound through the top of his skull and soldered to Metamorpho chest cavity. Kissy noticed the looseness of the fit and made a mental note to insert a plate between the pipe and what was left of Phil's brain. But that could wait. For now she would feed.

"I'll fix you tomorrow," Kissy said.

A lone tear formed in Phil's eye. *It hurts.*

"Yes, Phil," Kissy said, turning her attention back to the road. "It's supposed to hurt. But think of it as suffering for your art."

Carrion Man

Joseph M. Nassise

Sheriff Tom Donaldson couldn't put off making the call any longer, not with the press and the town council breathing down his neck. Never mind the threats from the angry parents of the missing children. The time had come and that was that. There wasn't anything else he could do. He was out of options and down to his last straw.

If this didn't work out, they could have his job. *And good riddance, too*, he thought with a snort of disgust.

Picking up the receiver, he dialed Grayson Shaw's number from memory.

* * * * *

"I understand, Sheriff. The car will be here for me in half an hour. Yes. I'll see you then."

Grayson hung up the phone and sat back in his chair with a weary sigh. The call had finally come. He wasn't surprised, considering all that had gone on in the last several weeks, but he had hoped that this one could have been solved without his assistance. He'd been summoned for all manner of catastrophes in the past; earthquakes, floods, drownings, even the occasional murder investigation when the body had gone missing. But none like this. This one was different.

Children.

Fifteen of them.

Jesus!

He glanced heavenward, silently mouthing an apology, but damn if that wasn't how he felt about the whole mess. He had momentarily been tempted to tell Donaldson no. After all, the sheriff had sworn to the press that he wouldn't use any "hocus-pocus bullshit or psychic mumbo-jumbo" in solving this investigation. That public comment had been directed at him, and he had received the message loud and clear.

But that had been after victim number two.

With little James Newton now missing for over forty-eight hours, the official victim count was about to reach sixteen.

Considering the circumstances, Grayson had about as much a chance of saying no to Donaldson as he had of getting up and walking out of his wheelchair. It just wasn't going to happen. Not in this lifetime, at least. Which meant he was stuck with saying yes and getting involved in a case that he fervently wanted nothing to do with.

Forget the Lord, it's the American justice system that works in mysterious ways, Grayson thought ruefully as he wheeled himself down the hall toward his bedroom in order to get changed, since showing up for a meeting with the Sheriff in his bathrobe wasn't the best way for him to get back into the man's good graces.

* * * * *

Grayson was waiting at the bottom of the ramp that led to his front door when the police van arrived thirty-five minutes later. The driver got out, opened the rear doors, and helped Gray use the Tommy-Lift to get himself and his chair up inside the van. The Sheriff himself was inside waiting for him. Once the driver got back behind the wheel, they wasted no time getting underway.

"Do you know why you're here?" asked the Sheriff.

Gray nodded. "The children."

"Right. The children." A quick grimace of pain crossed the Sheriff's face at the thought, but he quickly suppressed it and got back to business. "The public is unaware of it, but for the last several weeks we've suspected that *this* man is the kidnapper and/or killer."

The Sheriff handed over a photograph of a middle-aged, heavyset man with long, greasy hair dressed in a tuxedo studded with rhinestones. Gray looked it over carefully, but he did not know the man. He told the Sheriff as much.

"No reason you should," answered the Sheriff. "His name is Jasper Michaels. He's the owner of the Great and Glorious Traveling Carnival and Circus, a roadshow that set up shop just outside of town about three weeks before the disappearances began. We've got a stack of circumstantial evidence a mile high that indicates this is our guy, but we don't have anything solid enough to charge him, never mind hold him. That's where you come in."

"I don't think I understand," said Gray.

"We've tried everything to catch this guy in the act, but he's good. He hasn't made a single mistake. Despite this, I've managed to talk Judge Stevens into giving us a search warrant for the carnival grounds. Because what we've got is so shaky, he's only given us a four-hour window though. If we don't find anything in that time, we're out of there." Donaldson shook his head ruefully. "It's crazy, but you're pretty much all I've got left. I need you to go in there, do that thing you do, and find the evidence we need to bust this guy. Understand?"

Gray nodded, "Yeah, I get it." He didn't mention the fact that his talent wasn't 100% reliable when it came this kind of thing or that Donaldson was grasping at straws in hoping Michaels was the culprit. He figured the Sheriff had enough to worry about without adding to the mix.

The ride took less than a half hour and they arrived to find several other squad cars parked alongside the carnival's front gates. The officers themselves were slowly evacuating the park, directing the crowds out the various exits. The driver parked the van behind the other cars and Donaldson got out to confer with his men.

It took over two hours to clear the grounds of the carnies and their guests. Gray sat in the back of the police van waiting it out at the Sheriff's request. The police department apparently did not want his involvement on the six o'clock news just yet, something with which he happened to agree.

Once the carnival was cleared, Gray used the Tommy-Lift at the rear of the van to lower his chair to the ground. Rolling off the lift, he turned in time to see Donaldson coming toward him from the passenger side of the vehicle.

"Remember, we've got the entire park to ourselves for the next four hours," Donaldson said. "That's all the time the warrant gives us. The only thing that can allow us to stay is if we uncover evidence that implicates Michaels. My men are tearing through the place as we speak, and if they find anything, they'll let us know asap. How do you want to handle your end?"

Gray had already considered his approach while waiting in the van. "Let's go down each of the main thoroughfares first, stopping at the most popular rides. From there, if we have time left, we can examine the booths and anything we think might deserve a second look."

"Fine with me. Let's get started," replied the Sheriff.

Before they could do anything, a large, hulking man dressed in an ill-fitting suit rushed out of the crowd, shaking his fists and yelling. Gray recognized him from the pictures the Sheriff had showed him on the drive over, Jasper Michaels.

"I'll have your badge for this, Sheriff! I'll sue you and the town for every single dime I lose over the next four hours. You can bet your ass on it!" Michaels hollered.

The Sheriff waved his hand and several officers moved onto an intercept course with Michaels. Prevented from reaching the Sheriff, the other man went on yelling. "You'll be on the street before morning, Sheriff! Mark my words! You and the damn Carrion Man both!"

Hearing the carnival owner shout his old nickname, Gray winced and ducked his head, doing his best to keep a low profile. He'd been the center of attention during a media blitz several years ago when he'd had been called in to help find several drowning victims after a flash flood. The papers had not been kind, particularly the supermarket tabloids. They'd called him a natural dowsing rod, one with a powerful talent. But unlike others with similar gifts, who could locate useful things like water or oil, Gray's affinity was for the dead. He was the human equivalent of a cadaver dog; he could locate a corpse from over fifty feet away, even if it was underwater or buried beneath the earth. The Weekly World Press, one of the worst offenders on the tabloid scene, began referring to him as Carrion Man, and the name quickly stuck.

He thought the public had forgotten about him, but he was clearly wrong. *At least the press never dug any deeper. If they ever learned the truth about what I can do, they probably would have burned me at the stake instead of just hanging me with a nickname.*

Michaels was led away, still yelling, by the officers who'd intercepted him. The Sheriff called for three of his other men to join them and the little group moved into the fairgrounds with Gray in the middle, surrounded by the officers. The men seemed slightly uncomfortable in his presence now that they knew who he was. They kept back several feet and repetitively cast furtive glances in his direction when they didn't think he was looking. Clearly agitated by Michaels' outburst, Donaldson wasn't talking any more than was necessary either, so the only noise that issued from the group as they moved onto the property was the sound of their footsteps against the hard packed earth and the electric whine of Gray's wheelchair.

Their first stop was the Ferris Wheel. It was an old ride, its paint cracked and peeling, its brightly colored lights dimmed from the dirt that had long accumulated over the bulbs. Its framework rose into the sky, reminding Gray of a mechanical skeleton looming high overhead, ready to drop and crush them beneath its bulk at a moment's notice.

Gray rolled up close to the machine, leaving the others behind. The smell of stale popcorn and machine oil invaded his nostrils. He reached out with one hand and touched the metal structure. He held his other hand over the dirt to the side of his chair, palm pointed at the earth. Closing his eyes, he cast outward with his power, looking for the remains of the missing children.

He was careful, extending his senses slowly, doing his best to detect even the slightest trace, but after several moments he put his hands back in his lap and opened his eyes.

"Anything?" asked the Sheriff from where he stood several feet off to the left.

Gray shook his head.

"All right, boys, let's keep moving. Time's a'wastin."

And so it went.

They stopped at the Tilt-A Whirl.

The Bumper Cars.

The Viking Longship.

Up and down the dirt thoroughfares, one ride after another, and each time it was the same.

Nothing.

For a moment he thought they had something at the carousel, but it was just the echo of an old death, a knife fight between two arguing carnies that had ended in tragedy. Gray shook his head and the group moved on again.

Ride after ride, with nothing to show for their efforts.

Until they came to the circus tent.

The minute Gray rolled inside he heard the dead calling out to him.

Begging.

Pleading.

Telling him all the awful things that had been done to them.

The barrage was momentarily overwhelming and Gray felt the world start to spin around him. He fought back against the din, using his power to block out the voices, building a mental wall to protect his sanity while he sorted it all out.

When at last he had regained control, he took a deep breath and slowly let the voices seep inside his mind once more. They were here; fifteen in all. Fifteen murdered children. He listened to them whisper in the back of his mind, felt their phantom touch scurry up and down the length of his spine, and learned all he needed to know about the events of the last three weeks. Of how they had been beaten, raped, and tortured. Of how they had been tricked into thinking they were going to be released, only to be forced to dig their own graves there in the center ring. Of how the dirt floor had grown stained with their blood, stark in the bright lights under the big top.

Gray was disgusted and shocked at the brutality that had been shown to those so young and innocent. It was a crime more heinous than any he had ever encountered and one that he knew in the marrow of his bones must go appropriately punished.

It was that thought that decided his next course of action.

Donaldson had noted his sudden hesitation and moved closer. "What is it, Shaw?" he asked. "Do you feel something?"

Gray put on his fake smile, the good one, one he used whenever he was forced to talk to the medicos about his disability. "Sorry, Sheriff. Just reacting to the smell of weeks of elephant shit and camel urine." He moved away from the group, out into the center of the ring, and went through the motions again for the benefit of those who were watching. As before, he shook his head in the negative and the group moved on.

Gray knew that if he told the Sheriff the truth, the bodies would be recovered from their graves and used as evidence. Michaels would be put on public trial, his fate to be decided by a system full of lawyers and loopholes.

A system that could just as easily let a vicious killer back out on the streets as it could send him to the electric chair.

A system Gray had absolutely no faith in.

So he kept his mouth shut. He went through the motions of using his ability for the rest of the hour that remained available to them. He even endured Donaldson's desperate disappointment and frustrated insinuations on the ride back to his home, just so he could be assured that Michaels would be dealt with in the just fashion he deserved.

One fact kept circling around inside his brain, a fact that kept him oddly reassured as he waiting for the coming of night and the cloaking darkness it would bring with it.

There had only been fifteen bodies buried beneath the big top, but there were sixteen missing children.

Which meant that there was a strong chance that Jimmy Newton was still alive.

But if he was alive, Gray didn't expect him to stay that way for long.

As soon as the sun went down Gray would be paying another visit to the Great and Glorious Traveling Carnival and Circus.

The Carrion Man had a date with the Ringmaster.

And, oh, what a show it will be, he thought to himself with a grim smile.

* * * * *

"Get in there, you little brat!" snarled Michaels, dragging the missing boy into the center ring and forcefully shoving him to the ground. He tossed a shovel at the boy's feet a moment later.

"Start diggin,'" Michaels ordered.

When the boy did not act quickly enough, the carnival owner drew back one booted foot and kicked him in the ribcage. "I said dig!"

Choking back tears and a howl of pain, the boy hauled himself up and reached down for the shovel.

Gray had seen enough.

"Leave it alone, James," Gray said softly from the shadows beneath the bleachers where he had been hiding for the last two hours. He activated the controls of his chair and rolled out into the light.

Both the boy and Michaels froze in shock and surprise at

the sound of his voice. Michaels knocked the boy back off his feet to the ground before whirling to face Gray. When he saw who it was, however, the anxious expression on his face turned to one of disdain.

"Look who's here, Jimmy. It's our resident freak, the Carrion Man himself." The carnival owner waved a hand dismissingly in Gray's direction. "You shouldn't be here, Cripple. You're going to end up hurt."

"I don't think so, Michaels. The only person who's going to get hurt around here right now is you," Gray replied calmly.

The other man laughed mockingly. "Yeah, right. You can't even get up out of that chair. How are you gonna stop me from killing you, never mind protect the boy?" To prove his point, he pulled back a foot and savagely kicked the youth again.

The sight caused Gray to grit his teeth in anger. "This time you've taken one too many, Michaels," he answered, his voice shaking with anger at the thought of all the children who had suffered at this pig's hands. "This time you will be stopped."

Michaels laughed again. "Oh, no!" he cried, in a high falsetto voice. "It's the Carrion Man! Run away!" He snorted in disgust. "Whatcha gonna do, freak? Use some psychic mumbo-jumbo on me? Wave your arms and turn me into a toad?"

"I don't intend to do anything," Gray replied. "They do." As he said the words, he took his hands off his lap and held them with his palms facing the bare earth on either side of his chair. He summoned up the true extent of his ability and pushed his power downward, felt it eagerly flow from his hands and into the earth around him. At first it flailed blindly, seeking, but then he felt it reach out and grab hold of the dead buried there beneath the big top floor, buried deep where the police cadaver dogs had been unable to find them the first time the carnival had been searched. His power reached out and gathered them all in, like a loving mother will her children, giving out new life to temporarily replace that which had been taken away.

Down beneath the earth, the dead began stirring.

Michaels hesitated for a moment, watching Gray's strange motions, but when nothing immediately happened his bravado reasserted itself and he began walking in Gray's direction. As he passed, he snatched up the boy's discarded shovel and slung it over one shoulder.

"What happened, freak? Your powers desert you?" Michaels laughed. "I warned ya, gave ya the chance to get outta here. Now I'm just gonna hafta bash your ugly little face in."

Gray ignored him, looking beyond to where James was slowly struggling to his hands and knees. The boy's dirt stained and tear-streaked face lifted toward him, the plea for help in his young eyes as blatant as if it had been spoken aloud. Gray smiled reassuringly. "You might want to look away, Jimmy. This isn't going to be nice."

The youth stared at him for a moment more and then nodded. He sat back down, burying his face in his hands so that he wouldn't have to see what was coming next.

Michaels ignored the exchange and took another step in Gray's direction.

Fifteen feet in front of Michaels, half the distance to where Gray sat calmly in his wheelchair on the edge of the ring, a child's hand suddenly broke through the surface of the dirt floor. The hand twisted and turned in the stark light, working its way free of the dirt around it. Grave mold grew across the back of the palm and, in some places on the fingers, the white gleam of bone shone through the graying skin.

Though he'd been dead for almost three weeks, life had returned to Tommy Williams' discarded body.

Life with a purpose.

Life with a grim, dark need.

Michaels stopped abruptly, staring at the hand jutting out of the earth before him. As if sensing his attention, it twisted in his direction, the fingers opening and closing rapidly, grasping out toward him.

The press had gotten it all wrong, those many years before, when they slung that oh-so-clever nickname on me, Gray thought with a smile. *Carrion Man indeed.* He was far more than just a human diving rod, attuned to the rotting remains of those who had passed on. Grayson Shaw was a necromancer, one from the old school, born to his art and trained in its use since birth. In his hands, he held the dark, forbidden power of life over death.

And he used it now.

He called out to them all, guiding them to the surface with the sound of his voice and the hum of his power as it coursed through the earth under Michaels' feet. He called for them to rise up, to do what he was afraid the halls of justice would not be able to do, to take revenge against the one who had so heinously torn their lives from them.

And they came.

Eagerly.

As little Tommy Williams freed his other arm and part of his head from the dark earth around him, Michaels screamed in terror and turned to run, only to find two of his earlier victims, Amy Smith and Rebecca Turner, had already managed to work themselves free of their earthly confinement and had cut off his retreat. Their eyes gleamed with an unholy light as they eagerly reached out toward him, their decaying lips curled into smiles of savage glee. A hand, missing almost all of its flesh and belonging to Michaels' first victim, Tad Stevens, burst through the ground

98

immediately beneath him and locked itself around his right ankle. As Michaels continued to scream, his other leg was trapped in the same fashion.

Unable to move, Michaels tried to use the shovel as a weapon, raising it over his shoulder and swinging it at his assailants. With supernatural quickness, the weapon was blocked by a skeletal forearm and then snatched out of the man's hands and tossed to the side.

Other shapes were moving in the surrounding darkness now, shambling into the light to join the fray. The smell of freshly turned earth and the cloying scent of rotting flesh wafted through the air. Gray inhaled deeply, pulling the aroma down into his lungs, a smile of satisfaction on his face as he watched the events playing out before him.

The coppery tang of blood joined the other scents filling the air inside the circus tent, and Gray laughed aloud as the predator became the prey. It didn't take long for Michaels to stop screaming, as the children tore him apart limb from limb.

When they were finished, when their victimizer was nothing more than a few vague scraps of raw flesh strewn about the center ring, Gray called the children to him. They came, like worshippers to a shrine, and he set their souls at ease as best he could before sending them back down into the earth to lie at rest.

In the end, only a few stains and a certain tartness to the air gave evidence to what had occurred. The ground in the center ring was once again smooth and unblemished. The remains of Jasper Michaels were nowhere to be seen.

Activating his controls, Gray rolled his chair over to where Jimmy was still crouched on the floor, his eyes shut tight and his hands over his ears to shield them from the screams. Gray reached down and gently shook the boy's shoulder to get his attention. "It's okay, Jimmy. You can look now," he said softly when the boy lifted his head and opened his eyes.

Jimmy lowered his arms and raised his head. He glanced swiftly around, looking for signs of his captor.

"It's over now, Jimmy. He's gone. He won't hurt you again."

The boy jumped up and hugged Gray, tears of relief falling from his eyes.

After a time, Gray gently forced the child back to his feet. Looking him in the eyes, he said, "I'm going to take you home now, Jimmy. Your parents and the police are going to ask you a lot of questions. I would appreciate it if you could leave me out of all this, if you'd just tell them that you escaped on your own when your kidnapper's back was turned. Can you do that? Can you do that for me?"

The boy nodded. "Yes sir. I can do that," he said.

"Good."

The two of them turned and slowly made their way back over to the entrance. Jimmy slipped out first. Before he followed, Gray turned back and faced the center ring once more. Letting a hand slip off his lap and face the ground, he sent a final, silent message.

"Sleep well, my children."

Deep beneath the ground, the dead smiled in their now restful sleep.

Selected Works

Down Among the Bosnian Dead

Joseph M. Nassise

They were being hunted.

After this morning's events, Sergeant Michael Raines, U.S. Special Forces, was convinced of it.

The only question he had left was who, or what, was doing the hunting.

It had begun innocently enough. The Fourth Cav had arrived by convoy over the swollen banks of the Drina River two months ago. Camp Walton, or Wasteland as if was unofficially known among the troops, had quickly been laid down on an area the size of three football fields laid side by side, smack dab in the middle of what the Dayton Accords had labeled the ZOS – the zone of separation that divided the Serbs, the Croats, and the Muslims. Concertina wire, claymores, and tank traps had quickly surrounded the camp, as if that muddy stretch of barren terrain had some inherent value that needed protecting from the broken remnants of the population that surrounded it. Barracks and command bunkers swiftly followed and the US military had hunkered down to do what they had come here to do.

Which, in Raines' view, was nothing.

The US Army was being used as a show of force, carrying out a political saber rattling exercise, with absolutely no intention of doing the citizens of this war-torn land the least bit of good. Like Mogadishu, Haiti, and a hundred other shitholes he had been in over the last few years, Raines knew that this place would go right back to the way it had been less than five minutes after they pulled out.

What a waste, he thought. He wasn't even certain if he meant the presence of the US military or the condition of the country around him.

Not long after the Camp had been established, the UN Peacekeeping forces sent in the forensic teams, tasked with investigating the reports of wartime atrocities that the press had begun to leak to the world at large. Walton had become a focal point for one such group, as it sat at the center of a stretch of ground that contained not one, not two, but four major burial sites where the Serbs had done their best to hide the evidence of their atrocities against their fellow countrymen.

The latest excavation had begun earlier in the week at a site designated on the map as Kilo Two-Zero. When he'd first heard the name, Raines had idly wondered if that meant this was the twentieth such site the forensic team had excavated and catalogued. After spending a day flying over the site in an Apache and estimating that there must be over eight hundred bodies concealed in that pit, Raines quickly came to the conclusion that he really did not want to know the answer to his question.

The prospect, if he was right, was too horrifying to contemplate.

He was better off not knowing.

The killings began shortly after the forensic teams had opened up K2Z.

In the last four nights, they had lost five men. After the first one, the Colonel had sent out a search party, assuming the missing private had simply strayed into town or had gone AWOL. The party itself came back one man short. The following night they lost the two men working the listening post just beyond the camp perimeter. Their relief found some equipment strewn about the ground, but no sign of the men remained. Convinced that the Serbs were up to no good, the Colonel ordered a full sweep of the town, but still no trace of the missing men could be found. Last night, a fifth man had disappeared on his way back from the latrine.

The fact that he had vanished inside the camp perimeter had thrown the troops into a frenzied panic.

The Colonel was on the phone all afternoon with his superiors, but Raines did not wait to hear what the outcome of those conversations had been. He'd been in the army too long to expect headquarters to be much help in this situation. Instead, he'd checked into things on his own, talking to the troops, walking the perimeter, even making a few forays into the surrounding area to talk to the locals.

Unfortunately, he hadn't learned a damn thing.

This morning, when the watch had changed, the partially eaten remains of the second man to go missing, Private Daniels, were discovered jammed in among the concertina wire on the west side of camp. The brass probably would have been able to make a case for the existence of a marauding pack of wolves with a taste for human flesh, if Daniels' head hadn't been discovered propped on a stake outside the east side of camp half an hour later.

The rest of the day had been sheer confusion, with the troops too afraid to leave the camp and the brass completely clueless as to what to do next. Fear and superstition ran amuck and everything from the Serbs to vampires was blamed for the attacks.

Now, about three hours after sundown, the camp felt deserted. Every building, tent, and bunker had been locked down for the night as best its inhabitants could manage and only those required to work sentry duty could be seen outside after dark. The rain was still falling steadily, obscuring vision and turning the camp into a sea of mud.

Snubbing out his cigarette, Raines turned away from his visual study of the camp perimeter and made his way through the maze of tents to one of the command bunkers. For a moment his form was silhouetted against the lights of the nearby tents and then he descended several steps between large mounds of sandbags and entered the scientific station in the bunker below.

"Talk to me, Simmons," he said as he walked inside.

The civilian technician seated at one of the computer consoles shivered at the sound of his voice. The memory of what Raines had threatened to do to him earlier in the day if he did not agree to use all that fancy equipment to figure out what was happening fresh in his mind. He knew it might be his head shoved onto a stake just outside the perimeter of the camp if Raines couldn't stop whatever it was that was out there. "Just a second, Sergeant. I'm bringing up the KH-10 images now."

KH-10 was one of the government Keyhole satellites, presently swinging past Eastern Europe on its nightly patrol. A moment later the set of monitors surged to life. A computer in the depths of the bunker overlaid the ghostly green images being fed from the satellite with known radar data and provided a ghostly map on the screens in front of the two men.

"Gotcha!" the tech said beneath his breath with satisfaction. In order to help Raines, he'd hacked into the KH data feeds, no easy feat. Once he was in, however, the system became much friendlier and in moments he had a variety of views laid out on the flickering screens. He pointed them out to the Sergeant.

"Okay, we've got UV over here. Gamma on that one. Spectro here. Infrared on the last screen to the left. The other three are real-time low light images."

It was these that Raines was interested in. He looked over the images, then pointed to a particular set of coordinates on the map. "Can you bring this in closer?"

Confident now, Simmons shrugged nonchalantly, "No sweat." He typed a series of commands into the keyboard. On screen, Raines watched the image jump closer in measured amounts, until it showed the area as if you were looking down on it from a height of about 5000 feet. The mass grave the scientists had uncovered earlier in the week showed up on the image as a large area filled with water. From this height, the bodies that Raines knew were piled more than ten deep in that pit were no more than dark, featureless shapes that occasionally broke the water's surface.

While Raines was studying the images, Simmons wandered over to another workstation. After a moment he swore beneath his breath and rushed back over to the console beside Raines. He frantically stabbed a series of commands into the keyboard and the screen to Raines' right suddenly blossomed with a cloud of pink light.

"What the hell is that?" Raines asked.

"Nitrogen," Simmons answered. "A big cloud of it. We planted spectrometers around the excavation site to try and understand just what we might be facing in there in regard to biological or chemical threats."

Raines pointed to the cloud on the monitor. "Is that normal?" he asked.

The tech continued to fiddle with the equipment, trying to further define the data as he answered. "The human body has a fair degree of nitrogen in it. When it starts to decay, some of that nitrogen releases into the air around the corpse. In this case, you've got several hundred bodies, maybe more, suddenly disturbed by us and by the rains. You'd expect to see some sign of that release on the graphs, but that cloud is way to big for it to be natural."

"Can we get in for a closer look at what might be causing it?" asked Raines.

"Not with the Keyholes. But I can probably have one of the spy boys' Predator drones overhead in about ten minutes."

"Shit! Why didn't you say so in the first place? Do it," Raines ordered.

In a short time the drone was sending back images from less than 5000 feet. At Raines' command, the tech ratcheted the image even closer until they were showing images in a ten-meter square from less than 1000 feet off the ground.

In the strange green light of the drones' night vision lens, Kilo Two-Zero looked even worse than it did during the day.

The incessant rains over the last four days had flooded the massive pit with several feet of water. The bodies that had filled the pit to near capacity now floated on the surface of the water or lay beached on its edges, like so much casually discarded waste. The steady downpour caused the image to shimmy and shift, as the camera lens did its best to filter out the interference. Every few moments the image would disappear altogether as lightning flashed across the sky, only to flicker and return seconds later as the equipment compensated for the light. The two men watched the screen for several long moments without seeing anything out of the ordinary.

"What's so special about this place?"

Raines shrugged. "Just a hunch, I guess." It was more than that, but he didn't have the energy to explain the connections.

Abruptly, on screen, a form surged up out of the water.

"Fuck!" Simmons cried, flinching away from the sight in surprise. Raines, having seen much worse during his time in the Army, barely flinched. His gaze stayed glued to the screens.

The man had probably once been a school teacher or a shop owner, though since he'd been dead for many months it would likely be difficult to tell conclusively at this point. What remained of his clothing showed he'd taken care with his appearance, dressing fashionably but inexpensively. Raines noted the bailing wire that was twisted savagely around the corpse's hands, as well as the entry wound just above his right eye, as if he had decided to face his fate and had looked up just as his executioner had pulled the trigger, and knew without a doubt that this man had never been a soldier.

The corpse bobbed upright for a moment in the water, face thrown back is if looking directly at the drone taking its picture overhead, and then twisted to the side and fell back into the water with a silent splash.

Raines looked over at his companion. "Are you gonna give me some natural explanation for that?"

The technician swallowed nervously and looked away, trying to regain his composure. "Expanding gases? A sudden shifting of the bodies? There are probably a dozen I could come up with."

Raines listened with only half of his attention. A sense of anticipation had swept over him the moment the corpse had popped into view. It was the same feeling he got when he was out on patrol or before he dropped into a firefight, that sixth sense veterans develop that says, "Here it comes." Something was about to happen, he was certain of it, and it didn't matter what type of explanation the technician came up with, not really.

A moment later another body surged up from down below, followed closely by a third.

Beside him, Raines heard the technician mutter, "*That's* not caused by expanding gases, I'll guarantee you that."

Raines' combat alarm was ringing full blast now and he had little doubt that his companion was right. He impatiently drummed his fingers against the tabletop. "Come on, come on, show yourself, you bastard," he whispered at the screen.

As if in response, something else suddenly emerged from that stagnant pool of water and death.

The rain and the lightning conspired to prevent them from seeing clearly, but it looked almost human. It was even dressed in the tattered remains of what had once been a business suit and had a few wisps of thin hair on its skull. That is where the similarity ended, however. Its fingers were longer than normal and even in the poor light Raines could see the claws that extended from their tips.

As they watched, the creature rose up out of the muddy water like an apparition from the depths of hell. It glanced cautiously left and then right, before rising to its feet and moving toward the corpses it had just rescued from the pit. It shook the water off itself like a dog and then grabbed one of the corpses by the arm, dragging it farther away from the water before squatting down beside it. Raising the dead flesh to its mouth, the creature tore off a chunk with its ragged teeth and began to eat.

"Jesus Christ!" Simmons exclaimed in disgust. "What the fuck IS that?"

Smiling grimly, Raines answered, "It's dead meat. It just doesn't know it yet." He moved to the other side of the console. "Can we get thermal and UV from the drone as well?"

Without a word Simmons activated two more screens.

Under the thermal imaging, the newcomer looked nearly identical to the corpses on the ground beside it, removing any doubt that what they were dealing with was even remotely human. If it had been human, it would have shown up under the infrared light. The ultraviolet light gave them no more information than had the infrared. Raines had Simmons go to the night vision lens, but that proved even less satisfactory than the other options they'd tried so far.

Frustrated, Raines went back to watching the creature under normal light conditions. It was enjoying its dinner and didn't appear inclined to move soon, which was something the sergeant was pleased to see. The creature also seemed oblivious to the weather, squatting there in the mud while the thunder boomed and the lightning flashed overhead.

As Raines watched, a sudden flash of lightning lit the scene, revealing something metallic hanging about the creature's neck. Just to be certain it hadn't been a trick of the eye, Raines waited until the next flash before turning to Simmons.

"Can you get any closer with that camera?"

Simmons thought about it and then answered, "I can bring it all the way down on the deck if you want. Thing is, that baby's pretty damn big. Its wingspan is something like fifty feet. Too much lower and that thing out there will know we're watching."

"I thought I saw something around its neck. Bring it down another 100 feet to see if we can get a better look."

Simmons complied. The picture improved only slightly, but the two men decided it would be best not to bring the drone any closer to the ground and chance scaring the creature away. After watching the thing for a few more minutes, Raines suddenly pointed at the screen. "Can you freeze that?"

The technician did and then printed a hard copy image. The picture was taken from the creature's left and slightly over its shoulder. Its face was turned away and tucked down out of sight, but the image clearly showed what it was that Raines thought he had seen earlier.

"Son-of-a-bitch," both men said at the sight.

Hanging around the creatures' neck was a set of US

military dog tags.

They had found their killer.

Instantly, Raines began considering what it would take to get to the site. It was about two klicks to the excavation. Considering the weather and the condition of the countryside, it would take him some time, even if he took one of the unit's ATVs. That would mean he would need Simmons to keep the drone in place and keep the creature under surveillance until he could get out there.

"How long can you keep the drone in the air?"

"Another forty minutes or so," Simmons answered, after looking at the fuel readouts on the control panel.

"Good enough," Raines replied, turning away and heading for where his equipment was stacked beside the door.

"Hey, wait a minute!" cried Simmons. "You're not really going out there alone, are you?"

Raines snorted. "Do you see anyone else lining up to volunteer?" he replied sarcastically. He pulled on his cape and picked up his weapon. "I'll take one of the ATCs. That should allow me to get there in about twenty minutes, even with the weather. I need you to stay here and let me know over the radio if that thing starts to move. Without you, I've got no way of knowing what its up to until I get too close to do anything about it. Got it?"

Simmons nodded and caught the headset that Raines tossed to him.

"Don't leave me hanging out there, Simmons, " Raines warned as he went out the door.

The rain had picked up in the last hour and was now

coming down fairly hard. Raines hoped it wouldn't cause any difficulties for the drone. Wrapped in his poncho, he passed through the camp like a wraith in the night, nothing more than a dark shadow against an even darker background. He entered the hanger that had been erected to serve as a vehicle pool and signed himself out one of the ATCs. The private on duty didn't ask to see his orders, no doubt figuring that no one in their right mind would go out on their own initiative after all that had happened.

The same held true for the men stationed at the perimeter. After a perfunctory check of his ID they let him out the side gate without any trouble. With a quick turn of the throttle, Raines headed overland.

He'd considered taking the main road, which would have gotten him to the site faster, but he couldn't quite break the years of habit that told him to remain undercover and out of sight. His pace was slower off-road than he would have preferred due to the weather and the condition of the landscape, but he felt that was a fair trade for his peace of mind and the decreased chance of falling victim to a sniper's bullet.

Not that anyone but a maniac would be out on a night like this, he thought to himself, grinning wildly and enjoying every minute of it. The rain pelted down with savage ferocity, whipped into a frenzy by the wind and the motion of his ATC. It wormed its way past the protection of his poncho to run down across his clothing beneath, leaving him cold and wet soon after setting out. Overhead, the thunder boomed and the lightning flashed, robbing him of his night vision at regular intervals.

The ground here had been carved into a seemingly endless series of trenches that stretched for miles, evidence of how savagely contested this area had been prior to the arrival of the UN peacekeeping forces. Raines was repeatedly forced to backtrack to avoid the shell craters and other debris that littered the landscape. At one point, riding along the berm between two deep trenches, he almost lost control when the ATC's tires slid sideways in the mud and left one rear tire hanging suspended over thin air, but a quick burst from the throttle allowed him to recover control sufficiently to escape the danger.

Fifteen minutes into the journey, a figure suddenly loomed out of the darkness in front of Raines as he crested a small rise. Raines expertly slewed the vehicle sideways with one hand and brought his weapon to bear with the other, but stopped himself from firing at the last second when he realized the figure wasn't moving. A closer examination showed it to be a scarecrow dressed in a soldier's uniform, bound to a crude wooden cross to hold it upright. Dozens more were revealed on the plain before him in the next flash of lightning. He could feel the weight of their stares like a physical thing, heavy and menacing in the gloom. For one long moment, he considered turning back, rather than making his way through that grim, silent company, but then his sense of purpose reasserted itself. Raines remembered how the Allies had used the same technique to make their numbers seem higher in the trenches along the Marginot Line in World War One. He wasn't about to let a bunch of scarecrows turn him away from the job that needed to be done.

Even if some of them looked suspiciously like real bodies instead of stuffed dummies.

He slowly began to wind the ATC through the silent throng.. On more than one occasion, he could hear the crunch of bones beneath his tires, but he did not stop the destruction of the ones forgotten in the mud of this aging battlefield. These were not comrades of his, and deaths months old held no interest for him.

Not knowing how good the creature's senses were, and not wanting to give it advance notice of his arrival, Raines used the GPS mounted on the handlebars of the ATC and stopped the vehicle several hundred yards away from the excavation site.

"Simmons, this is Raines. Can you hear me, Simmons?"

Simmons voice came back to him immediately, the high quality communications gear making it seem as if the other man were whispering in his ear. "I'm here, Raines. The thing hasn't moved. It should be about 300 hundred yards ahead of you, on the other side of that small hill to your right."

Raines looked around until he had spotted the landmark. "Got it," he replied. "I'm heading in." Dismounting, he slid his Mark 23 combat pistol out of its shoulder holster, chambered a round, and headed out on foot toward the site.

The mud was thick and pulled at his feet, while the rain and steadily increasing wind conspired to push him backward. He'd been trained by the best the US military had to offer, however, and very quickly crossed the remaining distance to the foot of the hill.

Speaking in a voice no louder than a whisper, Raines asked, "Simmons?"

The other's voice came back to him once more. "Still there."

Raines clicked his mike in reply. He bent lower to the ground and slowly made his way up the side of the hill. Just below the top, he lay face down in the mud and inched the rest of the way. With all the skill his training had given him, he slowly raised his head and peered over the top of the hill.

The creature was right where Simmons had said it was, less than 150 feet away on the other side of the excavation. It was turned partially away from him and was consumed with its dinner.

Raines slowly brought his arms up over the edge and pointed his pistol at the target. He got himself into a comfortable firing position, and then waited for the next crash of thunder. As soon as it began, he thumbed the switch that activated the targeting laser. A thin red beam of light shot across the watery grave and came to rest on the creature's right cheek.

Raines didn't waste any time; with the ease of long practice he fired two swift shots.

Both bullets found their mark.

Without a sound, the thing toppled over facedown into the mud.

"Nice shooting!" Simmons' voice whispered in his ear.

"Thanks," Raines replied dryly.

It had been far easier than he'd thought.

"I'm just about out of fuel on the bird," Simmons said. "Unless you object, I'm gonna bring her back in."

"Go ahead. Nothing more to see out here anyway. I'm gonna grab the body and head back to camp. I'll meet you at the motor pool in about half an hour."

Raines heard the hiss of an empty radio channel and turned off his headset. The open pit of the excavation separated him from the corpse, so with his weapon held casually in one hand, he carefully made his way back down the hill in the direction he had come, and then walked around the perimeter until he stood next to the creature's corpse.

Squatting down on his heels, Raines reached out with one hand and turned the thing over.

This close, Raines did not need any high tech equipment to recognize what he was looking at it. His Polish grandmother would have crossed herself at the sight and flashed the sign to ward off the devil. She would have called it an *upior*, but Raines was happy enough calling it by its American name.

Ghoul.

The creature's skin was wrinkled and gray, as if it had spent a long time submerged underwater. Its nose was partially decayed, resembling a snout more than a pair of human nostrils. Its teeth were yellowed and roughly filed sharp to help it tear the meat of its prey. Atop its misshapen head, a few straggling wisps of thin blonde hair were plastered down by the rain against its skull. Its eyes were closed, as if it were sleeping.

The bullets from Raines' gun had entered just to the left of the creature's nose and had blown a fist-sized exit hole right through the back of the creature's skull.

"Well my friend," Raines said to the corpse. "Whatever you were, ghoul or not, now you're nothing more than one dead critter."

Raines down, intending to remove the dog tags hanging about the creature's neck, when his gaze fell upon the picture of a Joker tattooed into the creature's forearm.

No Bosnian tattoo artist had done that detailed a job.

With a jolt, Raines also noted that the creature seemed to be wearing the tattered remains of a US Army uniform.

Suddenly suspicious dawning, the Sergeant snatched at the dog tags, tearing them from about the creature's neck with a quick yank. He held them up, waiting for the next flash of lightning to read the name stamped into them.

Private Jack Mahoney, US Army, they read.

The image of a blonde haired private from Oklahoma danced in the back of Raines' mind.

Blonde hair.

Horrified, Raines stumbled away from the thing that had once been an American soldier, his mind trying desperately to ignore the startling conclusion it had just come to.

It was at that moment, when Raines was distracted and disoriented, that the second ghoul dashed out of the darkness. With lighting speed, the creature grabbed Raines about the throat with one clawed hand and with the other knocked his pistol out of his grasp.

He watched in shocked horror as his weapon sailed through the air and landed with a splash out in the middle of the mass grave, disappearing from sight forever.

Overhead, the lightning flashed, revealing that this creature also wore the tattered remains of a military uniform. Blood red pupils stared back at Raines out of strange yellow eyes. All the world's malevolence seemed to be bottled up inside them and for the first time in what seemed like years Raines found himself frightened.

The creature then leaned forward and savagely bit his right ear off.

Shocked out of his immobility by the pain of his wound, Raines didn't hesitate to counter. His left hand flashed out and struck the creature on the pressure point below the rib cage while his right quickly sought the combat knife strapped to his right calf.

It was a good thing he had the knife because the percussive strike with his left hand was an absolute failure.

Instead of immobilizing his opponent as it was designed to do, Raines found his hand buried wrist deep inside the creature's ribcage.

The ghoul ignored the attack, clamping its free hand

around his neck alongside the other and squeezing them both tight, trying to cut off his air. The thing's hot, fetid breath splashed across his face.

Raines jerked his knife free and shoved it into the ghoul's side.

It had no more effect than the strike with his hand.

It was at that point that Raines started to panic. The creature's hands were slowly squeezing the life out of him. He'd been unable to draw a clean breath for almost a minute and in his exhausted state his vision was starting to gray out around the edges from lack of oxygen to his brain. He had to do something quickly to break free!

Raines pulled both of his hands free and desperately struck upward at the creature's arms.

The ghoul snarled in response, the sound like tearing fabric, but refused to let go.

Desperate now, Raines did the only thing he could think of.

He twisted sideways and threw himself, and the ghoul holding onto him, into the water-filled pit behind them.

The surprise move did what his attacks had not been able to do. For just a second the ghoul's hands relaxed their grip as it tried to react to its new surroundings.

That was all the time Raines needed.

He pushed away from the thing, then ducked beneath the reach of its arms and struck out for the bottom in an attempt to get away from it. He had gone no more than a few feet, however, when he swam straight into the submerged pile of corpses the forensic team had been unable to catalogue and remove.

The pile slipped free with the impact of his body from whatever had been holding them beneath the surface. Raines suddenly found himself tangled in a confusing whirl of arms, legs, and torsos. He thrashed against them, trying to work his way free, only to feel a hand with needle sharp claws clamp itself around his left ankle.

The ghoul had found him.

As he was pulled away from the drifting corpses, the ghoul struck again, this time opening a deep gash in his rib cage. Raines could feel the blood rushing out from his body and knew he couldn't survive much longer.

He thrashed and flailed his arms, trying to work his way free, and quite by accident discovered that he was still holding on to his combat knife. With strength born of desperation and a sudden overwhelming desire to not die in the disease infested waters of a mass grave in a country he could care less about, Raines struck downward with the weapon.

This time, his aim was true.

The knife sunk to the hilt through the rotten tissue of the creature's skull and pierced what was left of its brain.

Instantly, it let him go.

Knowing he had only seconds left, Raines struck out for the surface and burst upward into the night air in unconscious imitation of the corpses the ghoul had harvested for food.

Gasping, Raines dragged himself over to the shoreline and several feet away from the water before collapsing into the mud.

Seconds later he passed out.

Down Among the Bosnian Dead

* * * * *

Raines regained consciousness in the camp infirmary, his chest and head swathed in bandages. A nurse stood by his bedside taking his blood pressure. When she realized he had come to, she told him to lay still and ran to get the doctor.

Laying there, Raines could see that he was in a small ward. Only three of the ten beds were occupied, including the one in which he lay. A man with a leg in traction was in the last bed in the row on the far side of the infirmary, absorbed in reading a book. The bed directly next to Raines' was also occupied, this one by a man who appeared comatose, his face covered with a breathing device. The whine and hiss of his mechanical breather accompanied the rise and fall of his chest.

Raines' attention was drawn away from the man by the sound of the infirmary door opening.

"Well now," said the physician as he entered the room, a wide smile on his face. "Nice to see you've rejoined the living."

Raines didn't appreciate the joke, but he was too weak to protest. His limbs felt strangely heavy and his throat was incredibly parched. He managed to croak out a request for water and the doctor sent the nurse to fetch a cup of ice chips for him. After a few sips he was able to speak more clearly.

"How long?" he asked, his voice like gravel.

"Two weeks," replied the doctor, cheerily. "The morning after you went AWOL a long range patrol found you alongside the excavation at site Kilo Two-Zero. Your wounds were already filled with a raging infection, particularly that deep gash in your ribs. Frankly, I'm amazed that you didn't succumb to sepsis or the plague, considering where they found you. Just what on earth were you doing out there?"

The doc's cheery nature and casual reference to his

having been AWOL set Raines' self-preservation mode into high gear. The only person who knew what he'd been up to had been Simmons; so far, it seemed that he hadn't talked. Which meant that if Raines kept his mouth shut now, he could probably find a way to get out of this without any major problems.

Raines mumbled something unintelligible, dropped his head back onto the pillows, and pretended to drop back off to sleep without answering the doctor's question.

The ruse seemed to work. The doctor stood for a moment and then softly ordered the nurse to come get him when Raines woke up again. He had only taken a few steps toward the door, however, when an alarm from the bed next to Raines started blaring.

Raines opened his eyes slightly and watched as the doctor and his nurse rushed over to the patient. It appeared to Raines that the man had gone into cardiac arrest and the arrival of the defibrillator moments later confirmed that suspicion. The fight to resuscitate the man went on for over twenty minutes, Raines surreptitiously watching all the while, but eventually the staff gave up their efforts and left the man's body, and Raines, alone.

In the quiet following their departure, Raines actually did fall asleep, his injured body not yet fully up to the task of keeping him awake. His sleep was full of uneasy dreams.

When he awoke, it was night. Except for a few small utility lights and the illuminated dials of various pieces of medical equipment here and there about the ward, the room was dark. Surprisingly, Raines could still see fairly well. The injured soldier down at the end of the ward was fast asleep, blissfully snoring away. The body in the bed next to Raines was still there, though now a sheet covered it entirely with the exception of one errant foot that had somehow slipped out from beneath it and hung limply over the side of the bed.

Raines lay awake for several long moments without

moving, trying to gauge how he felt.

The long wound in his side where the creature's claws had torn through his flesh was tender and sore, but did not hurt as much as he had expected it to. The skin around it itched horribly, however, and he wondered if he was having some adverse reaction to the anti-infectants they must have spread liberally around the wound. He resisted the urge to scratch but then gave in to the need with a deep, perverse pleasure. His fingers dug into the flesh around the wound and left several long scratches in his skin, but he barely noticed. He was too intent in finding some relief from the itching.

He noticed a small washroom in one corner of the ward and decided to see for himself just how bad things were. Using the bed's handrail, Raines pulled himself into a sitting position and then swung his legs out from under the sheet and over the edge of the bed. The floor was cool on his bare feet. He waited a moment, double-checking he was up to this so soon after awakening from what was obviously a coma-like sleep, and then carefully pulled himself to his feet.

When he didn't immediately collapse in a wave of dizziness, Raines headed across the room in a slow, shambling gait. He managed to reach the doorway of the room without too much trouble and stepped inside, closing the door behind him. Only then did he turn on the light.

Excruciating pain surged through his eyes and into his brain.

Instinctively, Raines squeezed his eyes shut smashed his fist through two of the three fluorescent bulbs that provided lighting inside the room.

In the dimmer light, the pain slowly faded.

When he felt he could stand it, Raines opened his eyes and looked at himself in the mirror.

Most of his head was covered with a wide set of bandages, no doubt protecting the open wound on the side of his head where his ear used to be. His eyes seemed to reflect some of the light from the remaining fluorescent lamp and had a yellow tinge to them that told Raines he'd lost a fair share of blood. What was most disconcerting to him, however, was the fact that his skin seemed to be jaundiced as well.

Could he have contracted some weird disease from that water as the doc had said, he wondered, staring at himself in the mirror. Is that why he felt so queasy? Or was he having some kind of anaphylactic reaction to the medications they been pumping him with while he'd been in the coma?

He didn't know.

A sharp sting of pain shot through his mouth and Raines was surprised to find he had bitten his tongue without realizing it. If he kept this up, he'd never recover.

It was time to get some rest.

He turned the light off and opened the door to the ward. With slow, careful steps, he made his way back over to his bed. As he was getting ready to climb back up on the mattress, he noticed the foot that had somehow escaped the sheet the staff had placed over the corpse in the bed beside him.

He froze where he stood for several long moments, staring at it

Then, with a quick jerk, he pulled the sheet down further so that it covered the foot as well.

Selected Works

Funky Chickens

Drew Williams

"There it is!" Gail shouted in my ear. "On the left!"

I had just enough time to see where she was pointing before we sailed past the homemade, plywood sign that read OSGOOD FARM - 3 MILES. I was tempted to just keep driving, but Gail slapped me on the shoulder. "Turn around. The turn-off was back there."

I started to protest, but from the tone in her voice and look in her eyes, I knew it would be pointless. Married only three days, and I was already whipped. "Why in God's name do you want to see a two-headed chicken?" I asked, doing a U-turn in the middle of Route 45.

Gail twisted in the seat as far as the seatbelt would let her to face me. Loose strands of her long, auburn hair hung across her forehead, and the faint smell of her perfume drifted off her body. God she was beautiful. At that moment, the last thing in the world I wanted to deal with was barnyard oddities; it was only by a supreme effort of will that I didn't stop short of the dirt road that led to the Osgood Farm (Home of The World's Oldest Two-Headed Chicken), and take Gail like the four times the day before, and the three times the previous night.

"Because I want to," she replied, brushing the tips of her fingers against my jawline. "And the man at the hotel said it was authentic."

I made the right onto the dirt road and laughed. "No, dear. The man at the hotel said it was 'sure-as-shit-real.' I don't believe he ever used the word authentic."

The fingers moved from my jaw to my lips. "You know what he meant," Gail laughed, pinching my lips together.

"Mmmmm."

The road that led to the Osgood Farm was little more than a twisting path of red clay and gravel, barely wide enough for my Ford Taurus. Within a half mile, it seemed as if the car was being swallowed by a roving cloud of orange dust. The sound of small rocks hitting the sides and undercarriage of the car grew louder the closer we got to the farm. I slowed the Taurus so there would be less of a chance that the gravel would ding up the side of the car, so it took almost fifteen minutes to travel the three miles to the farm.

"There it is," Gail said. She slipped out of her seatbelt and pressed her face against the windshield. "Over to the left. I see the top of the barn."

I pushed down on the break, and as the Taurus rolled to a stop, the dust cloud drifted back to the ground. "See it?" Gail asked, turning to me.

I nodded. Just a few yards ahead, the dirt road became somewhat wider and straighter as it followed the natural incline of the land. Just beyond the ridge of the hill, where the dirt road seemed to drop off, I could see the long, red-pitched barn roof. Beside it was the top of something that looked like a giant cigar standing on end. "What's that?" I asked, pointing to the cylinder. "Next to the barn?"

"Corn crib," Gail answered without looking at me. "It's where corn is stored."

I felt a flush of momentary embarrassment as I detected the slight tone of exasperation in her voice. Gail grew up on a farm and was dismayed at my total ignorance of farm life. "But I'm a city-boy," I once told her in a feeble attempt to defend myself after asking the difference between a cow and a steer. "You're a dufus," she told me.

"Well," I said, easing my foot off the brake. "The two-headed chicken awaits."

Gail gave me a warm smile, the kind that says 'I really love you', and giggled. It really was funny to see how excited she was. "I imagine you've seen lots of two-headed chickens on the farm," I said as the car made its way up the hill. "Don't deformities like that happen all the time?"

Gail shook her head sternly. "Not like that," she said, her eyes fixed on the barn roof ahead. "For a chicken to hatch with two heads, in itself, is amazing. The fact that it survived . . ." Gail stopped and let out a long, low whistle. "The odds are astronomical."

"Lucky chicken," I said.

As we crested the hill, I realized that there wasn't much to Osgood Farm. I don't know what I expected, maybe scarecrows dotting rolling fields of corn, or at least the assorted chicken and pig running around the barn yard - the typical city-boy image of a farm. But besides the red barn and the corn crib, Osgood Farm consisted of a large, two-story farm house, two small chicken coops and a hell of a lot of uncut grass. I turned toward Gail, hoping that she wasn't too disappointed, but if anything, the smile on her face grew even wider.

"Isn't it great," she squealed. "It's just like my grandparents' farm. And look over there." Gail pointed to the right of the corn crib. "They even have a well."

If Gail hadn't said that the round wall of stones was a well, I never would have known it. The well was about four feet high, and lacked the little roof on it that all the other wells I've ever seen had. How Gail could tell the mass of bricks was a well, I don't know, but as we drove nearer to the farmhouse, I caught a glimpse of a tall, skinny boy coming from its direction carrying a bucket. He didn't seem to notice us and disappeared around the side of the house. "All that's missing is Ma and Pa Walton," I joked as I parked the car in front of the farmhouse.

"You be nice," Gail said, trying to hold back the grin that played at the corners of her mouth. "How often do you get a chance to see a genuine freak of nature?"

"Well, actually . . ." I drawled, but Gail had already pushed herself half way out of the car. I turned off the ignition and opened my door. Immediately a blast of dry heat slapped me in the face. "Man," I said, stepping onto the dusty ground. "It's got to be a hundred degrees out here."

"More like eighty-five."

Both Gail and I spun around at the sound of the voice. An enormous mountain of a man in blue coveralls and an orange shirt came from the side of the farmhouse and headed for the car. On the top of his massive head sat a sweat-stained John Deere ballcap. He plucked off the cap and wiped his brow with his forearm. "Yeah, not quite ninety," he said. "But hot enough."

I glanced over at Gail whose smile didn't waver at the big man's approach. "Are you Mr. Osgood?" she asked, extending her right hand. "The owner of the World's Oldest Two-Headed Chicken?"

The farmer slapped his hat back onto his head and burst out laughing. "That's me," he said, swallowing Gail's outstretched hand with his own. "You must be the newlyweds. Glenn Hubbard at the Carlson Arms called a little bit ago and said you might be stopping by." Mr. Osgood released Gail's hand and looked at me. "Glenn's always telling folks about my chicken."

I had to bite my cheek not to laugh. "Uh, yeah," I said. "I'm Neil Lincoln. This is my wife, Gail. We're on our way to Nashville, but when Gail found out that you had a two-headed chicken on your farm, we just had to stop."

Mr. Osgood nodded once in my direction then turned his attention back to Gail. "You're a farm girl, ain't ya?"

Gail blushed slightly. "Yes. How did you know?"

Another round of farmer Osgood's laughter filled the air. "Heck child, what other kind of people would want to see a two-headed chicken?"

Gail joined in the laughing, and to be polite, I threw in my own, weak chuckle.

"Well, she's over here," Osgood said, motioning toward the smaller of the two chicken coops. "But it will cost you five dollars."

Gail shot me a quick glance which I took to be the sign to fork over five bucks. I took out my wallet, removed the bill, and handed it to Osgood. As the farmer put the money into one of the pockets in his coveralls, I winked at Gail. I could tell she was relieved that I hadn't made some smartass comment about five bucks being a steep price to look at poultry.

"You know, sometimes," Osgood said as he ushered us

toward the pen. "The tour buses from the A.A.R.P. stops by. Twenty, sometimes twenty-five people come by to see Henrietta."

"Is that her name?" Gail asked. "Henrietta?"

Osgood nodded. "Yup. Every time I get a two-headed chicken, I call it Henrietta."

Gail's steps slowed. "You mean you've had more than one?"

"Uh huh. We seem to get one just about every seventh or eighth generation. The Henrietta you're going to see is the fifth one."

A puzzled expression crossed Gail's face. "But how can that be? I was just telling my husband that the odds of a two-headed chicken are astronomical."

Osgood allowed himself a slight chuckle and shrugged his shoulders. "Well, I don't know about odds. But I think I get them because we haven't had any new breeding blood around here since I was a kid. You just seem to get these kinds of things when you have a mess of inbreeding."

A mess of inbreeding. The phrase struck me as ominous, but from the look on Gail's face, I could tell she was satisfied with the explanation. "That would do it," she said, turning to me. "Sort of like a two-headed chicken trait being passed down generation after generation."

"That's what I've always thought," Osgood said as we neared the coop. "But my father was of a different opinion. You see, during the second world war, right before I was born, the government had troops stationed all throughout these mountains. A lot of the land around here was used for training but my father always said that the government was really doing some kind of secret testing out here."

"Uh, testing what?" I asked, forcing myself not to grin. Gail, too, was doing a poor job of not laughing.

Osgood shrugged his massive shoulders again. "Don't know," he said. "Secret weapons probably. Maybe even stuff involving the atomic bomb. At least that's what my father thought. He always said that the government didn't give two shakes of a rat's ass about the folks who lived in these hills. I don't know about any of that, but I do know that right after the army pulled out of here, an entire herd of his cattle died. Not long after that we had our first Henrietta. That was just a month before I was born."

I wanted to ask Mr. Osgood what his father ever did about his dead cattle, but we had come to the coop, a sturdy, miniature barn with a bright coat of red paint. "I keep the Henrietta in here, so there's no messin' with the other chicks. Plus this gives folks more room to see." Osgood slid back one of the coop doors. "And there she is," he said, waving his arm like a model on a game show.

I guess part of me never really expected there to be an authentic two-headed chicken. Up until Osgood opened the door, I really thought the thing would be some kind of hoax; that this great freak of nature would turn out to be a normal chicken with a fake rubber head glued to its shoulder. Or at best, some poor chicken with a massive tumor growing out the side of its neck.

But what stood in the middle of that miniature barn, just scratching away at the straw-covered floor that stunk of chicken crap and mold, was a sure-as-shit-real two-headed chicken.

From the breast down, it looked like any ordinary chicken with dirty-white colored feathers and thin legs that looked like orange sticks. Its wings, which flapped in surprise when Osgood opened the door, were now calmly folded across its plump belly giving off the impression that the chicken was used to people staring at it.

"Son of a bitch," I whispered beneath my breath. I turned to Gail who stood with her mouth open wide.

"Yeah, that's about the usual reaction," Osgood laughed from behind us.

Gail and I remained silent, neither of us able to take our eyes off the twin chicken heads. They were perched on separate flabby chicken necks that joined together like a Y. Unimpressed with our presence, the head on the left stretched to the floor and pecked at some feed while the other head stared at Gail with its black, unblinking, chicken eyes. It was a bit unnerving.

After a few more seconds of open-mouthed gawking, Osgood slid the coop door shut again. Just before it closed, though, the right chicken-head twitched, then joined its mate at the floor.

"Well, that was Henrietta. Sorry I can't let you look at her any longer, but after about a minute she starts getting a bit antsy and tries to escape." Osgood winked at Gail. "You know, fly the coop."

"Uh, yeah," Gail said, casting a backward glance at the coop door. "She's the real thing," Gail said softly. "I can't believe it."

"Seeing's believing," Osgood replied. He turned back to the farmhouse and made a motion for us to follow him. When we were about half way to the car, the front door of the house swung open and a tiny woman in a flowered sundress stepped onto the porch. Smiling, she came toward us carrying a pitcher in one hand and several plastic cups in the other. When Osgood saw her, he waved enthusiastically.

"There's Mrs. Osgood," he said, turning to me. "She always likes to greet our guests."

We met Mrs. Osgood at the car, and after a quick round of introductions, she offered Gail and me a glass of ice tea. "Just made it," she said, pouring the tea into one of the plastic cups. She handed the first cup to Gail. "Perfect thing for such a hot day."

Gail took the cup and thanked her. "I know what you mean. On my grandparents' farm, we had ice tea all the time. Even in winter."

Mrs. Osgood smiled pleasantly as she poured a cup for me. "Your grandparents had a farm," she said. "How wonderful."

I barely had my cup in my hand when Mrs. Osgood refilled Gail's. "This is fantastic," Gail said.

Mrs. Osgood beamed at the compliment. "Thank you dear. Osgood here and the kids sure like it. Why, we go through two gallons a day."

Gail glanced quickly about the yard. "Children," she said. "I haven't seen any about. How many do you have?"

"Too many," Mrs. Osgood laughed. "I got lots of mouths to feed."

Mr. Osgood joined in his wife's laughter. I looked at Gail and rolled my eyes. Behind the plastic cup of tea, I could see she was smiling.

I finished off my glass and handed it back to Mrs. Osgood. "Well, thank you very much," I said. "But we really should be going. We got a long drive ahead of us."

Gail, too, thanked the Osgoods who told us to drop on by anytime we were in the vicinity. "We sure will," Gail said, slipping into the passenger side of the Taurus. I slid into the driver's seat and started the car as Gail offered the Osgoods one last wave. Pulling away from the farmhouse, I saw the old couple in the rearview mirror standing side by side. They watched us for a moment then turned and went into the house.

"Nice people," Gail said when we came to the red clay and gravel path.

"Yup," I said before the car was again swallowed by the orange cloud.

****

The screaming has stopped.

They've given Gail a sedative, and the doctor said she should be out for another three or four hours. Before the doctor left, she asked if I would like a shot of something. I could tell by the way she looked at me that she was not making a routine suggestion.

I forced my best smile and said that I would be all right.

The doctor took me at my word because she hurried out of the room. Away from me. Away from Gail.

I take her small hand and softly kiss her fingertips. "Sleep," I tell her. "Sleep while you can."

We've been married for five months now, and in that entire time, I don't think I've thought once about the Osgood Farm and the two-headed chicken. Until twenty minutes ago, it was just another one of the diversions that made up the bulk of our honeymoon. When we got back home we told our family and friends about the two-headed chicken, but the novelty wore off quickly, and it was soon forgotten.

But how often do you get a chance to see a living creature with two heads? That's supposed to be a once in a lifetime thing.

It's not supposed to happen twice.

The memory of our trip to Osgood Farm is now coming back to me with burning clarity. It is almost as if the smell of straw and chicken shit is surrounding me now. I can hear Mr. Osgood's deep voice prattling on about the inbreeding of chickens and the government doing some kind of testing near his farm during the war.

And I can see tiny Mrs. Osgood with her pitcher of ice tea.

"Perfect thing for such a hot day," she said.

And it was. The perfect thing for those ninety degrees. So cool and sweet that Gail had two glasses.

"Your father was right," I want to tell Mr. Osgood. The government did do something to your land. They did something that killed your cattle. And then, whatever that something was, it got into your water supply. And it's still there. Still in the well where the water for that cool, sweet tea was drawn. I know because Gail had two glasses of it.

I told myself I wouldn't look at it again, but like that two-headed chicken, it's almost impossible not to stare at the flimsy, little five by seven strip of photographic paper. It's the kind doctors use for ultrasounds. On it is a remarkably clear picture of the baby growing inside of Gail. There's an arm, and at the end, if you look close, you can see five little fingers waving in a sea of amniotic fluid. And there's the chest and the shoulders.

And jutting out of each shoulder is a perfectly formed neck and head.

And I can tell by the way both heads are held erect, by the

way the eyes are set and the corners of both tiny mouths are curled up as if laughing, they know they are alive.

They are aware of who and what they are.

I want to run to my car and drive half way across the country to Osgood's farm and tell that mountainous son of a bitch that there's something wrong with his well. That the government poisoned it back in the forties, but that poison does more than just turn a regular chicken into a circus freak every seventh generation. I want to tell him more. I want to tell him that whatever is in his well can turn a healthy fetus, a healthy baby, into an abomination. But I don't. Somehow, I think Osgood already knows what the water can do to a baby.

As I look at the faces of my son, I can hear Mrs. Osgood's response to Gail's question about how many children she had.

I got lots of mouths to feed.

Yes, I'm sure you do, Mrs. Osgood.

Selected Works

Headlines

Drew Williams

Jack Klinger sucked on a Marlboro while Garth Guzman babbled on about the devil. Jack wasn't paying any attention. He just sipped at his fourth Budweiser and wished he could be anywhere but where he was. Unfortunately, it had been a long time since Jack had anything resembling a job, and Guzman offered him a hundred bucks for a little favor. Totally legal, Guzman promised. Legal or not, Jack was too hard up for cash not to accept.

"Do you believe in the devil?" Guzman asked. The pair was sitting in a back booth at Ruby's Roadside Diner, home of the Two-Pound Onion Burger and, according to Guzman, the best egg salad sandwich in Pennsylvania. It was the kind of seedy, out of the way joint Jack knew that Guzman preferred. "Well?" Guzman's question was filtered through a mouthful of egg salad.

"Nope." Jack tapped an ash onto the floor and stared at a speck of food dangling off Guzman's lower lip. It just hung there, a creamy white chunk of gravity defying eggwhite. For a second Jack was tempted to reach out and flick it off, then with a quick swipe of his tongue, Guzman retrieved the bit into his mouth. Jack turned his attention back to peeling the label off his beer. "Not particularly."

"Good." Guzman dropped the sandwich onto his plate and began fiddling with his napkin. "That's exactly what I need. Someone level-headed like yourself. Someone who knows when he's being served up a plate of bull shit."

His eyes fixed on the creamy, white blob of bread on the plate across from him, Jack couldn't help but laugh. Those were strange words coming from Garth Guzman, ace reporter for *The Pittsburgh Tattler*. Guzman's specialties were stories about Hannibal Lecter knock-offs and two-headed choirboys who could sing harmony. Guzman also wrote a weekly psychic advice and prediction column under the bi-line Madam Lorraine. To Jack, Garth Guzman and *The Pittsburgh Tattler* were connoisseurs of bull shit.

"So what's the job, Garth?"

Guzman smiled and returned to devouring his mammoth sandwich. "I was just getting to that. This week has been a real pain, and I'm way behind on the column."

"Madam Lorraine's Psychic Sight." Jack said dryly. He thought the title was garbage.

"Yeah. Old Madam Pain-in-the-ass. I've been putting her off for a few weeks, and now I need a month's worth of columns done in two days. I was going to knock them off tomorrow, but my editor sprung something on me at the last minute. She wants me to meet with some kids tomorrow who say they've found a pathway to hell in an old church."

Jack polished off his beer and groaned. "Pathway to hell. Christ, Garth, you got to be joking."

"No joke. These kids say they were partying in this abandoned church about an hour north of here," Garth said between bites. Thick chunks of egg salad sloshed about his mouth as he chewed. "A little town called Hilton. They were passing around a doobie when, low and behold, Satan materializes out of thin air." Garth waved what was left of his sandwich in front of his face. "Poof, and there he is."

Jack motioned for the waitress to bring him another Budweiser. "Bull shit," he said humorlessly.

"My sentiments exactly, but it gets better. See, the kids get all scared and take off. But the next day they get brave again and go back to the church to see if the devil is still hanging out."

"Let me guess," Jack interrupted. "Satan's waiting for them with a six pack and a pizza."

Guzman slapped his meaty hands together and laughed. "Nothing so dramatic. No, they say that the whole front of the church has been turned into some kind of pathway to hell. Seems like Old Scratch has got himself a subway depot right there at the altar with flames and shit coming out of it."

"Flames and shit," Jack repeated. Despite the pleasant buzz that was creeping up on him, Jack felt his mood turning sour.

Guzman held up his hands in mock surrender. "That, my friend, is a direct quote from the eye witnesses. 'Flames and shit.' Plus a few reanimated corpses. You know, the usual path to hell stuff."

Jack shook his head. "Come on, Garth. Why are you wasting your time with this garbage?"

Garth shoved the last bit of his sandwich into his mouth and frowned. "Because it's the kind of garbage that sells papers." He was about to say more but stopped when the waitress arrived with another round of beers. Once she left, Guzman leaned over the table and addressed Jack in a voice barely above a whisper. "Hell, Jack, I'm not exactly proud of what I write about. I know *The Tattler* isn't the most respected rag in the world, and the psychic hotline stuff is a flippin' joke. But it's a job, man, and it pays damn well. So until I get another one, I have to go where they send me. And right now my editor wants a story about the devil. So are you going to help me get it or not?" Guzman pushed himself back into his seat and wrapped his large hand around his beer. "Besides, Jack, can't you just see the headlines: "Satan's Sanctuary Found", or "The Path to Lucifer's Lair." Aw man, the possibilities are endless."

Guzman did have a point, Jack thought. *The Tattler* was never shy about printing sensational headlines, especially ones that had some connection with the supernatural. And if the story did find its way on to the front page, then Guzman would owe him, big time. "Okay. So what do you want me to do?"

Guzman's smile widened as he clinked his bottle against Jack's. "That's the spirit. Actually, it's going to be easy. All you have to do is go to the church and hide out there tonight. I'm supposed to meet with these kids tomorrow around nine, and I got a hunch there might be a few demonic artifacts strewn about for me to find. Know what I mean?"

"Got you. You want me to make sure these kids don't do a little interior decorating before your meeting. Spruce up the altar with, you know, 'flames and shit.'"

"Exactly. I'll drive you up there tonight around ten, then we'll hook up tomorrow about an hour before the meeting and you can let me know if anyone was screwing around with the church."

"Sounds simple enough. What about payment? You did say a hundred bucks."

Guzman chuckled and reached into his pants pocket. He pulled out two twenties and a ten and held them out to Jack. "Fifty now and fifty tomorrow. Though I should subtract a few for all the beer you've been drinking."

"Incidentals, my friend. Incidentals," Jack said, snatching the bills out of Garth's hand. "But one thing. What if this isn't a pile of crap? What if there really is a path to hell and the devil does make an appearance?"

Guzman stroked his chin thoughtfully. "Then I guess you're going to have one hell of a story. Satan: An Exclusive Interview by Jack Klinger."

Both men laughed.

* * * * *

"Son of a bitch," Jack cursed under his breath as he stood in the middle of the church. He had climbed through a broken stained-glass window and cut his right hand. Though the cut wasn't anything that would require stitches, it did hurt like hell. "Damn, damn, damn," he muttered, cupping the wounded hand with his left. When the throbbing in his palm began to subside, Jack fished his lighter out of his pocket and flicked it on. With barely enough light to see two feet in front of him, Jack examined his hand. All he could see was a two-inch surface cut across his palm that barely broke the skin. Disappointed that the wound wasn't something serious enough to squeeze a few more dollars out of Guzman, Jack wiped his bloody palm against his jeans and set about examining the church.

It was a large, stone church with a thirty foot ceiling and long narrow aisles. Embedded in the side walls were six enormous stained glass windows, each depicting one of the stations of the cross. Jack had broken into the church through the first of the stations, knocking out a section of Jesus' upper body in the process. Filtering in through the holes in the windows were thin streams of moonlight which provided just enough visibility for Jack to see two rows of pews stretching from the back of the church to a few feet from the altar. Even in the sparse light, Jack could see that nearly half of the pews had been ripped from the floor and overturned.

Making his way up the middle aisle, Jack carefully waved the lighter from side to side, but all the light did was create a weaving pattern of shadows on the floor in front of him. Rather than waste the butane, Jack flicked off the lighter and cursed himself for not bringing along a flashlight, but that was something Guzman said he couldn't do. Too much of a chance of being spotted, Guzman had told him. But right now, Jack didn't care too much about someone seeing him in the church; inching his way forward in the musty darkness, he was afraid he might trip and break his leg.

As he headed toward the altar, the noise from Jack's boots

made a dull, hollow thump that echoed throughout the building. The sound, like a mallet striking wood, grew louder as he neared the front of the church. Passing the last of the pews, Jack bypassed what was once the communion rail and walked toward the center of the altar. Where the altar table should have been, he found a few ripped up floorboards and piles of discarded beer cans and whiskey bottles. Kicking a few of the cans out of his way, Jack thrust his lighter out in front of him, flicked it back on, and leaned forward for a closer look. He stopped when he saw a diagram burned into the floor.

"I'll be damned," Jack muttered. A thick pile of black ash nearly three feet in diameter sat in the middle of where the altar should have been. As he looked down at the ashes, a sudden chill fluttered up his spine. Not that Jack believed in the possibility of a pit to hell, but maybe there was something more to this story than Guzman was letting on. Maybe these kids were doing a little more than smoking dope; maybe they were involved in some kind of ritual sacrifice. And if that was the case, there just might be one hell of a story here.

But when Jack reached down and scooped up some of the ashes, his initial twinge of excitement evaporated. The ashes were cold and mostly gray. Definitely not from a recent fire. He raked his fingers across the floor, but instead of finding shards of bone like he hoped, all he came across was a melted, plastic pocket comb and a few Old Milwaukee bottle caps. What had looked like a pentagram in the flickering light of his cigarette lighter was nothing more than an old campfire.

Jack stood up, disappointed, but not surprised, that there wasn't anything more grisly to the supposed path to hell. If these kids were trying to pull a fast one on Garth Guzman, Jack thought, they were doing a pretty lousy job. From what he could see in the lighter's glow, the altar looked more like the site of a weeny roast than a hole to the underworld. But then again, he wondered, what exactly did a path to hell look like? In his mind's eye Jack conjured up an image of a twisting yellow-brick road riddled with potholes and trash. But instead of the Scarecrow and Toto to help you ease on down this particular path, you get Hitler and a three-headed dog hungry for your balls.

Jack chuckled at the thought.

Now that had the makings of a great story.

Convinced this was a complete waste of his time, Jack took a last look around the altar before making his way to the back of the church. Behind the last row off pews he discovered an alcove that had originally been used for baptisms. Though the baptismal font had been removed, the thick, stone pillar that held the font was still in place. It would be a tight fit, but Jack decided that behind the pillar would be the perfect place for him to watch over the church. He slipped into the alcove and took a seat on the cold, stone floor. If the pot heads were going to show up and redecorate the altar, he could observe them without being seen.

Once he maneuvered himself into as comfortable a position as he could, Jack slipped a fifth of Southern Comfort, a present from Guzman, from his jacket pocket and cracked open the cap. When the pair had arrived at the church, Garth plucked a brown paper bag out from under his seat and handed it to Jack. "Keep yourself warm," he said. "I believe it was your favorite."

Jack accepted the booze without comment, slipping the bottle into his jacket and tossing the crumpled bag onto the floor of Guzman's car. The motion earned a brief look of disapproval from Garth, but Jack didn't care. The buzz he got this afternoon was beginning to fade, and the first seeds of a headache were starting to sprout in the back of his head. Jack glanced at his watch. 10:15. "The church is up this road about a hundred yards, right?" Guzman nodded. "And we'll meet back here tomorrow around 7:30?"

Guzman scooped up the paper bag and nodded a second time. "That's the plan. Just make sure no one sees you breaking in. It's still private property."

Jack ignored Guzman's warning and headed for the

church. Now, crammed into the space behind the baptismal font, Jack took a long, burning swig from the bottle and wished he'd never gotten mixed up with Garth Guzman.

It wasn't that Jack had anything against Guzman. In fact, there was a time in college when the two had been fairly decent friends. Jack was the editor of the campus newspaper, *The Weekly Rock*, and Garth was one of his top reporters. Both fancied themselves as hard-nosed newspapermen, willing to do anything to get a story. And their energy and willingness to spend countless hours making sure the paper got out on time made them the pride of the journalism department. Everyone who met Jack and Garth could see that these eager, young reporters had bright futures ahead of them. But Jack's bright future never really panned out. After college he never seemed to find his niche and ended up going from one dead-end job to the next. It wasn't that Jack was a bad writer; in fact, he was a damn fine one. His problem was that he could never put his ego on hold long enough to accept starting out on the bottom of the totem pole. Jack was too used to being the star, the ace reporter who always received the best assignments. When asked to do obits and human-interest stories, Jack rebelled, saying that type of writing was beneath him. In the end, the arrogance and tenacity that earned him the editorship of his college newspaper got him canned by every newspaper he worked for.

Garth, on the other hand, graduated from college and quietly inched his way up the journalism ladder. He took every job that came his way; copy-editing, type-setting, even writing household tips for a community paper in Western Pennsylvania. He also bounced from paper to paper, taking with him a growing reputation as a hardworking newspaperman and a pretty fair writer. He got his big break two years ago when Lisa Ferrel, the managing editor of *The Pittsburgh Tattler*, read Garth's story about the unsolved murder of a wino whose headless body was found inside the dumpster of a four star restaurant. The story wasn't one of Garth's best, but its factual reporting fused with just a hint of salaciousness convinced Lisa that Garth might have a future with *The Tattler*. A month later, Garth was on the payroll, and not long after, Madam Lorraine was born.

Jack glanced at the bottle, surprised that it was half empty. He would have to slow down if the booze was going to last the night. He took a small sip, savoring the burn as the liquid flowed down his throat. Wrapping his arms around his chest for warmth, Jack huddled up to the stone pillar and waited.

It was probably inevitable, Jack thought, that he and Garth would hook up again. Jack just wished the circumstances were different. Jack had been back in town only a few days when the two bumped into each other at a Seven Eleven. Garth was paying for gas and Jack was smuggling Ho-ho's and soda past the pimply teenager at the counter. When Jack got caught, Garth slipped the kid an extra ten bucks to look the other way, and the two old friends spent the evening getting royally loaded at a corner bar. Jack even managed to work up the nerve to hit Garth up for twenty bucks, and to Jack's surprise, Garth gladly handed over the cash. Since then, Garth and Jack got together two or three times a week, mostly to bull shit about the old days and polish off a few beers. Then yesterday, Garth called Jack asking him if he wanted to make some money doing a little newspaper work.

Jack glanced at his watch. 12:34. His legs were beginning to cramp up and his leather jacket was not proving to be enough to keep him warm. Some newspaper work, he thought. Freezing his ass off waiting for a bunch of punks to vandalize a church. So this is what his career had come to. Jack gulped at the bottle and laughed. Maybe it would be better if the whole thing wasn't a hoax and Satan did make an appearance. At least that wouldn't be boring.

A sudden thought popped into Jack's head that made him sit up. It was so simple he couldn't believe that it took this long for him to think of it. He could write the story himself. It would take a couple of hours for him to hitch back to town, and then maybe two or three hours at the computer. But if he moved his ass, he could have a story for Guzman's editor just about the time Garth was supposed to pick him up. It would be easy to crank out a real, honest-to-goodness eyewitness account of the Lord of Darkness and his pathway to hell. Shit, he virtually had a sacrificial fire on the altar. So what if nothing had been sacrificed? That was a minor detail he could iron out later. All the ingredients for a story were here; a moonlit night, a desecrated church . . . *That's the angle to take,* Jack told himself. *Desecration always sells.* Plus the story would feature the big boy, Satan himself.

That old excited feeling started welling up in Jacks's gut. Since Guzman's editor had the teenagers as witnesses, there wouldn't be any reason for her not to run the story. And if this Lisa Ferrel was as smart as Guzman led on, she'd recognize a great story and a top-notch reporter when she saw one. Sure, he would be scooping his old friend, Jack thought. But screw him. Garth had enough breaks; it was high time Jack got one.

Jack started to laugh. To hell with this sitting in the dark waiting for Beelzebub to show up. His chance to get back into the game was staring him right in the face. All he had to do was get to work. A bit unsteady from the booze, Jack pushed himself off the floor. He shot back the last few drops of Southern Comfort, then let the bottle slip from his hands onto the floor. "Screw you, Satan," Jack yelled. "I got a story to write."

"Screw you too," a voice answered from out of the darkness.

Jack spun around just in time to see the dark outline of a machete as it came at his neck.

* * * * *

Garth Guzman looked up from his desk as his editor walked unannounced into his office. Smiling, she waved a white piece of legal-sized paper above her head. "I don't know how you do it, but you got another one."

"Oh. Got another one what?"

"Another dead ringer from Madam Lorraine. Your

prediction last week that the Hilton Headhunter would strike again. Well, some slob got his head separated from his shoulders last night." Lisa handed Garth the sheet of paper, a fax copy of an incident report from the Pennsylvania State Police. "Three decapitations in eight months. I love it," she squealed. "Three. That qualifies as a serial killer. Can you believe it? A freakin' serial killer right in our own backyard. This is fantastic."

Guzman took the police report and began reading. "Decapitation. An abandoned church just outside of Hilton." He held the paper out to his boss. "Any ideas on who the guy is?"

Lisa took back the report and said no. "Nothing. Guy didn't have any I.D. No driver's license, no wallet. Nothing. The cops think he was some drunk sleeping off a hangover in the wrong place at the wrong time. They found an empty fifth of Southern Comfort near the body, and there was some evidence that he broke into the church."

"How about that?" Garth started to rise from his desk. "I better get up there and check things out. This will be a great piece to go along with Madam Lorraine's column this week."

Lisa nodded. "My thoughts exactly. That's why I got a car and a photographer waiting for you. So you better get a move on"

Garth arched his eyebrows at his boss, a small grin played at the corners of his mouth. "A car, for me. Now that's a first. Could this be some kind of a promotion?"

"It could be," Lisa said, starting for the door. "It could just be." Before she was out of the office she stopped and turned back to Garth. "One thing though," she said. "How did you pull that one out of your hat? It is kind of creepy."

Garth shrugged his shoulders. "Not really. Madam Lorraine's been making some pretty general predictions about Hilton for the past three months. You know, a violent act, nighttime, the usual kind of vague details. I worded the predictions so she could take credit for predicting just about anything with a little bloodshed."

Lisa snorted and slapped her palms against her thighs. "A little bloodshed. That's rich. Christ, Garth, the police report says they haven't found the head yet."

"I don't know what to tell you. I just got lucky, I guess. Or," Guzman said, squinting his eyes and lowering his voice dramatically. "I'm turning psychic."

"My ass." Lisa laughed and headed out the door. "Now just get up to Hilton and bring me back a story."

Guzman watched his editor disappear down the hall. Lisa was a good editor, and she had been a good friend. There was only one small problem. She had a job the ace reporter wanted. And like everything else in life he wanted, Garth would figure out a way to get it. All he had to do was be patient. The right moment always came along.

"Anything you say, boss. I'm already on it."

In the Eye of the Beholder

Joseph M. Nassise

Steven Jessup stood in the midst of the gallery and gazed in amazement at the painting on the wall before him. It was good, which was expected, since the world-renowned artist Kensington Wales had painted it. That was not what had brought Jessup up short and forced him to stare in stupefied wonder at the canvas. It was the haunting familiarity to the scene that did it, the way the artist had captured the precise moment in which the sun had dropped below the water out past the boardwalk at the edge of town, the rays glinting off the brass fittings of the sailboat that was just at that moment slipping past the marker buoy out in the center of the channel. Ignoring the obviously high degree of talent the artist possessed, this scene was like a thousand other seascapes that were hanging in hundreds of other galleries along the boardwalk outside.

Except it wasn't, for Jessup had witnessed this exact scene yesterday from his seat on the pier, had watched that very boat slip its mooring and head on out to sea, the reflected sunlight forcing him to raise a hand to shield his eyes from the intensity of the glare.

Even that wasn't all that unusual. Artists worked from reality all the time and Jessup wouldn't have been surprised if he had been in any of those other galleries up and down the boardwalk and seen this painting with its carefully recreated scene hanging there.

But he was here.

In Kensington Wales' gallery.

Which should have been impossible, for besides being a complete and utter recluse, Kensington Wales was as blind today as the day when he had lost his eyes to the accidental splash of loose chemicals in a paint factory fifteen years before.

The itch that had earned Jessup two Pulitzers went off in the back of his head.

There was a story here; he was certain of it.

The gallery was full of people, but, as usual, the artist himself wasn't anywhere to be seen. His manager, Geoff Crenshaw, was in full form, however, moving about the crowd extolling his client's virtues to anyone with a checkbook and the slightest inclination to buy.

At the moment Crenshaw was deep in discussion with a waifish blonde in a strapless black dress. Jessup had also run into her earlier in the evening, and while he did not find such women interesting, he did remember her because of the fact that she had the most unusual colored eyes he'd ever seen, a strange mix of amber and green.

Ignoring the girl, Jessup kept his attention on Crenshaw.

Jessup knew that if anyone had access to Wales, it would be Crenshaw.

That was where he would begin.

＊ ＊ ＊ ＊ ＊

Jessup was behind the wheel of his rental car, parked several yards down from where Crenshaw stood waiting for a cab outside his Beverly Hills apartment. He had been following Crenshaw for the past seventy-two hours and had not left the car in all that time. The backseat was littered with discarded fast food wrappers and the smell of food past its prime. What seemed like his forty-seventh cup of coffee rested on the edge of the front seat between his legs.

When the doorman finally managed to hail a cab for his tenant, Jessup pulled out into traffic and followed.

As he drove, he reviewed what little he had managed to learn about the famed artist and his faithful employee. Wales had burst onto the scene some three years ago, with an initial showing in New York that had sold out in less than forty-eight hours. Successes such as that were few and far between, so much so that within days everyone who was anyone in the art world wanted a piece of Kensington Wales.

This was not to be, however.

Unlike most newcomers, Wales chose to stay aloof, to avoid the media interest that would have made him a household name overnight. Which, in turn, created a media frenzy the likes of which had not been seen in the art world since Mapplethorpe offended everyone back in the early nineties. Wales refused any and all interviews. He rebuffed local reporters, national news media, and every major print magazine that came calling. He even turned down a chance to come out and meet his adoring public on the Tonight Show. As far as he was concerned, he simply wanted to be left alone to paint.

Crenshaw had been there from the start, handling the initial showing in Soho and then very quickly moving his client to the higher-class galleries on Rodeo Drive in Beverly Hills. He'd helped Wales relocate to the west coast, acting as both his business manager, and near as Jessup could tell, his only contact with the outside world.

For the last three days that Jessup had been following him, Crenshaw left his apartment every day at about this time, traveled into the canyons to the mansion where Wales had ensconced himself, met with his client for anywhere from twenty minutes to five hours, then went about his normal day's work of meeting with the media, visiting each gallery that featured Wales' work, and other assorted managerial activities. It had been mind-numbingly boring for Jessup; all he'd managed to discover was that Crenshaw had a penchant for cheap French cigarettes and liked to flaunt his access to the artist in front of the media.

Jessup knew today was going to be different as soon as the taxi headed south instead of north. He followed at a discreet distance as it moved down the coast for some thirty miles, before pulling into the parking lot of a small family-owned restaurant that sat on the edge of a public beach and boardwalk.

After paying the driver, Crenshaw went inside and sat by himself at a table for four. Jessup waited a few moments and then wandered in with a cultivated look of casual indifference, taking a seat off to the side with a clear view of both Crenshaw and the front door. Five minutes later he was rewarded for his patience over the last three days.

Two men came in, looked around, and immediately joined Crenshaw at his table under the windows. They were dressed in nicely tailored suits, but to Jessup's trained eye it was clear they were another class of citizen than Crenshaw's usual companions; nothing more than street hoods in fancy clothes. Crenshaw's distaste for the men was obvious, though it was equally evident that he had been expecting the two of them.

Jessup watched as the three men conversed briefly. A thick wad of money changed hands, and with that, the meeting was over. The two men stood and had the waitress reseat them at another table, leaving Crenshaw seated alone.

It seemed the meeting was over just in time, for several moments later Crenshaw was joined by another guest.

This time, it was the waifish blonde from the party.

Jessup was amazed to see Crenshaw suddenly transform into a gracious and charming host. He and the woman enjoyed lunch together. If Jessup hadn't known better, he might have actually believed Crenshaw was as charming as the blonde obviously considered him to be.

After lunch, Jessup followed the two of them as they took a leisurely stroll down the boardwalk. The boardwalk was mostly deserted, due to the chill in the air and the warning of rain later in the afternoon, so Jessup had to remain at a respectable distance. He did not miss the fact that he wasn't the only one following the duo, however. The hoods from the restaurant were doing the same thing.

Now we're getting somewhere. Jessup's pulse quickened.

The couple stopped at one of the boardwalk's observation points, directly opposite the entrance to a beachside hotel. Crenshaw came up with a couple of quarters and the two of them playfully began to use the telescopes the city had mounted there. Jessup hung back, taking a seat on a nearby bench and watching them at a distance. The two hoods were not so circumspect. They walked over to the same observation platform, but ignored the other two.

Out of nowhere, a homeless man appeared at Jessup's side. "Spare some change?"

"No. Go away." Jessup replied, without looking away from the others.

"Hey man. I'm talkin' to ya," said the man, moving to stand in Jessup's line of sight.

"I said go away!" Jessup said forcefully in a low voice. He did not want to make a scene and call attention to himself, but at the same time he needed to get rid of this guy.

It was not to be, however. The man would not go away, continuing to badger Jessup for money. In exasperation, Jessup finally hauled out his wallet and gave the man a twenty.

Money in hand, the man disappeared down the boardwalk as quickly as he had appeared.

But the damage was done.

When Jessup focused his attention back on the observation point, he was dismayed to find the two hoods standing there alone.

Crenshaw and the blond were nowhere in sight.

Where the hell did they go?

Jessup got up and walked down the boardwalk in the direction of the two men. As he drew closer, he could see that one of the men was carefully watching a balcony on the second floor of the hotel behind them. A casual glance in that direction allowed Jessup to catch the face of the blonde as she turned away from the window, her interest suddenly captured by something in the room behind her.

One of the hoods chuckled as his partner said something crude in response.

It was suddenly obvious to Jessup just where it was Crenshaw and the blonde had disappeared to, causing the reporter a brief moment of embarrassment. Yet that swiftly passed when he considered the situation. If Crenshaw and his companion wanted to disappear for an afternoon quickie, they certainly could do so without the oversight of a couple of street toughs.

There was more here than met the eye, the reported thought to himself.

He passed the two men and continued walking for several more yards until he came to another observation platform. He settled into one of the benches that overlooked the water and casually kept watch on the other two men.

He did not have long to wait.

Less then fifteen minutes after Crenshaw had disappeared inside the hotel, one of the hoods followed him in. He was not gone more than ten minutes before Crenshaw came out the front door, still rebuttoning his shirt, and went to lean over the railing overlooking the ocean once more.

Jessup cursed. He got up, intending on moving closer, when the hood suddenly re-emerged from the front entrance of the hotel. In his right hand he now carried what looked to be a small Rubbermaid cooler.

Rejoining his companions, the three men had a brief conversation before the hood handed the cooler to Crenshaw. The two hoods then walked off, back in the direction they had come.

"*What the hell?*" Jessup thought to himself. His journalistic instinct told him he'd just witnessed a vital piece of the puzzle surrounding Kensington Wales, but he'd be damned if he could figure out just what it all meant.

He had to get a look at what that cooler contained.

Crenshaw, however, was not about to give him a chance. He walked back down the boardwalk past Jessup, cooler in hand, and returned to his car. Less than five minutes after the exchange, Crenshaw was back on the highway headed north toward Hollywood in the direction that he had come.

Jessup followed closely behind.

They retraced their route back into town and it was soon obvious that Crenshaw was headed for a meeting with Wales. Jessup decided that this was one meeting he didn't intend to miss. He passed Crenshaw and went on ahead. He'd spent the last few days studying aerial maps of the canyons and knew that he could get access to Wales' place through the adjoining property. A few well-placed phone calls had also revealed that the owners of that property were away on vacation, which would make the transit that much easier.

The sun was just setting when he pulled off the main thoroughfare and parked in the driveway of the target property.

He quickly walked around the house and crossed the back lawn to where the property was set off from the next one by a high stone wall. With some help from the branches of a nearby tree, he scaled the wall and pulled himself up.

From his position atop the wall, Jessup could see that the rear yard was shrouded in darkness. A wide porch surrounded the back of the house and led down to the pool area. Both were presently unlighted. Light from inside the house spilled out onto the porch, revealing the room just beyond the sliding glass doors to be the mansion's main living area, a room that had the appearance of both comfort and regular use.

Betting that this was where Wales would receive his guest, Jessup clambered down off the wall and crossed the darkened yard in a half crouch. Reaching the porch steps, he quickly climbed to the top, crossed the porch, and settled in behind a brick barbecue close to the sliding glass doors that led inside. This close, he noted one of the sliding doors to be partially open and he hoped he had not made too much noise in getting in place.

After a few moments of relative quiet, he breathed a sigh of relief.

He had apparently not been seen nor heard.

He found a comfortable position and settled in to wait.

It did not take long.

Fifteen minutes passed before he saw Crenshaw, cooler in hand, led into the room by the butler, who in turn disappeared up a staircase off to the left that Jessup had not noticed before. A few moments passed, during which Crenshaw helped himself to a drink from the liquor cabinet and paced about the room, then Wales appeared at the top of the staircase.

From his vantage point, Jessup watched the artist move

down the stairs and into the living room where he greeted his guest. Crenshaw helped the older man over to a chair close to the sliding glass doors, offering Jessup an almost unobstructed view of the old man's face.

What Jessup saw there made him gasp in surprise.

He had known Wales was blind. What he hadn't known was that the man wore no cosmetic replacements for his eyes. His damaged eye sockets were empty; raw angry looking holes in his weathered face that seemed to pulse with a strange life of their own as the blood that once served his eyes coursed there beneath his skin's ravaged surface.

Because of the open door, Jessup was easily able to listen in on their conversation.

"You've brought the next set?" Wales asked, his voice dripping with need, like a heroin junky on the edge of withdrawal.

Crenshaw took a seat next to Wales and placed what he carried between his feet. "Yes, of course, Wales. I've got them here, as usual," Crenshaw replied, absently patting the cooler with his left hand. "You'll have them very shortly, as soon as we've discussed a few things."

Wales waved his hands in impatience. "Yes, yes, Crenshaw. By God, don't be such a bloodthirsty leech. Take whatever damn cut you please. You know I don't care as long as the house is maintained and my painting can continue. Just give me the next set and get on with it. This darkness is driving me crazy."

Jessup watched a smile of satisfaction cross Crenshaw's face and understood immediately that the artist was being blackmailed by his manager, and apparently not for the first time. What he did not understand, however, were Wales' comments about the darkness. *Wasn't that all a blind man ever saw?* he thought. *Darkness?*

"Of course, Kensington, " said Crenshaw, the smile still on his face. "Silly of me to even bring it up. You are a reasonable man and always agree to my equally reasonable requests."

Wales snorted in exasperation. "For Christ's sake, where are they?"

Crenshaw reached down and picked up the cooler, placing it on the coffee table in front of the two of them. "Relax, Kensington" he said. "I've got them right here, as promised. And I must say that the boys did an excellent job this time around. I know you'll be quite pleased."

Jessup watched as Crenshaw drew on a pair of rubber gloves, then carefully opened the cooler.

A thin fog swirled out of the open container.

Dry ice? What is so important that they have to keep it preserved with dry ice? Jessup thought to himself.

Crenshaw reached into the cooler and withdrew a small, frost covered container. Jessup could see two smaller objects, roughly the size of walnuts, nestled inside the container, but Wales leaned forward in eager anticipation just as Crenshaw was opening the case, obstructing Jessup's view. For several long moments all he could see were the backs of the two men on the couch before him; Crenshaw gently handing something, presumably the contents of the container, to his client and the older man just as carefully raising whatever it was to his face.

Jessup's curiosity got the better of his patience. He shifted position, hoping to see better.

In doing so, his left shoulder brushed up against the set of cooking utensils precariously balanced on the edge of the barbecue, knocking them with a clatter onto the porch.

Both Wales and Crenshaw whirled around in Jessup's direction.

Jessup gasped in surprise.

A pair of amber eyes with green flecks stared back at him from a face that only moments before had contained nothing but raw, empty eye sockets.

Outrage warred with horror in Jessup's soul as he realized that he had seen those very eyes in someone else's face earlier in the week.

Jessup's gaze locked on Wales' new eyes, but the man's next statement made it immediately clear that the artist was not seeing the intruder at all, but something far more personal, something that should have belonged to no one but the true owner of those most unusual eyes.

"Excellent!" exclaimed Wales. "Crenshaw you've outdone yourself this time. Quick, bring me my canvasses! I must get to work immediately!"

Understanding dawned in Jessup's mind and he knew beyond a shadow of a doubt just how it was the Wales had been able to paint a scene with such detail and clarity that he himself could not have witnessed.

Jessup began backing away from the glass doors, Wales' continued exclamations of delight and calls for his paints ringing in his ears.

He made it off the porch and was halfway across the lawn before he noticed the large, muscular shapes closing in on him from all sides out of the darkness.

* * * * *

One month later.

The media presence was almost, but not quite, better than Crenshaw could have hoped. A representative from almost every major news station and print magazine for five hundred miles was on the premises and milling about the gallery. The only topic on their lips was Kensington Wales. For the first time in the man's fifteen-year career, he had produced two different series of paintings, two totally different themes in his work. It was an unprecedented event and Crenshaw had made certain that it was receiving the attention that it deserved.

He watched as Michael Patterson, Art Critic for the Los Angeles Times, approached out of the crowd.

"Quite a change for Kensington, isn't it Crenshaw?"

"Whatever do you mean, Michael?"

"Oh, come on! You know as well as I do that this is completely unlike the Kensington Wales that has been dazzling the art scene for the last decade. No grassy green meadows, no pretty-as-a-picture sunsets. Instead, we get this," Patterson said, casting a hand outward at the canvasses so artfully arrayed on the walls before them, scenes of partly-revealed passion, arms and legs entwined in diverging angles while light and shadow danced in their interplay. "You've got half a gallery of soft porn, for heaven's sake, while the other half no more than B-grade horror with monstrous shapes and half glimpsed figures looming out of the shadows! What were the two of you thinking?"

Crenshaw looked over at the critic, a mocking half smile on his face. "Just because you don't care for it, Michael, doesn't mean the public won't."

Crenshaw's smile grew even wider.

"After all, beauty is in the eye of the beholder, isn't it?"

Selected Works

Riding The Dragon

Drew Williams

This siren is different.

It's not the dull, long note in g-minor we've all grown accustomed to over the past few weeks. It's not the same sound that has been sending us to the shelters, testing to see how quickly an entire city can force itself into a few square blocks of brick and mortar cellars.

This siren is beeping, a high-pitched staccato strangely reminiscent of a machine gun. When this siren goes off, we all turn toward the large glass exit doors, each of us straining our necks for a better view of what is coming, but all we see is the blue sky and the reflection of the sun off the cars lined up in the parking lot. It only takes a moment for our eyes to comprehend the absolute normalcy of the moment before we turn to each other, our faces mirroring each other's fear.

The girl behind the cash register gasps and drops the quart of milk she was ringing up. It hits the floor sideways and splits open. She pauses, only for a second, to look down at the low fat milk that is slapping against her shoes like tiny waves. Then she starts to run.

She heads for the glass doors, which open automatically. She doesn't look back, she just runs out into the parking lot and the warm sun of this perfect day. Then she turns to the left and sprints toward the shelter that is nine blocks away.

For a moment, we all stand still, listening to the ripping sound of the siren and watching as the counter girl disappears amidst the minivans and SUV's. When she is no longer visible we react. Pushing aside shopping carts and display cases of potato chips and batteries, we push as one toward the door. No one shouts, no one says a word. We just move.

For the past few weeks we have been told that there was a chance that they might have the ability to deliver a nuclear attack. The chance was slim, almost nonexistent, but the air raid sirens that had lain dormant for fifty years were brought back into service. As were the shelters, antiquated recesses in the basements of buildings designed to withstand the bombs and missiles of an enemy that had long ago graduated to much more powerful and lethal weapons.

We were assured that the drills were only precautionary; that events would never come to this. So we jogged and walked to the nearest shelter each time we heard the siren's long, low blare. We went laughing, smiling and waving to each other, enjoying the camaraderieofsecurity. But this siren is different.

I'm almost to the open door when my son's hand slips from mine. At first I don't realize that he is no longer beside me, and I take another three steps to the door. Then I feel his absence from my side and I turn.

My son is two, a miniature replica of me but only with his mother's eyes. He's grinning and pointing to a spot hidden behind a newspaper rack. I take a step toward him intent on scooping him into my arms and dashing the mile to the nearest shelter. But I've seen that grin before; and I know what is concealed behind the wall of newspapers.

It's a six-foot green dragon wearing blue sneakers and a lopsided red baseball cap, an oversized model of the supermarket chain's mascot. My son runs up to the dragon and strokes its smooth, metal sides. He turns to me and holds out his hand. It's our game, our supermarket ritual that we have played out ever since his first steps.

He giggles and points to the coin slot, oblivious to the burping siren, unaware of what is heading our way.

What just a few minutes ago was a slim to nothing chance.

All he knows is that this is the point in our game where I

hoist him onto the dragon's saddle and slip a quarter into the slot. It is the prelude to the sixty seconds of gentle shaking that make up the ride.

I still want to run, overwhelmed with a hopeless but instinctive drive for self-preservation. I still want to do some kind of gesture, no matter how primal, that I can take with me that will attest to the fact that I tried to protect my son.

But I also have quarters in my pockets.

I always do when we go to the supermarket, and my son knows that. It's part of the game.

So I lift him onto the saddle and slip a quarter into the slot and watch as he rides the dragon. He laughs and I can't help but smile even though I know the last precious moments of his childhood are being counted down by the wagging tail of a metal dinosaur.

When the ride stops I estimate it has been three minutes since the siren went off. How much more time, I wonder. Six? Seven minutes?

Probably less than five.

That's it. Five minutes and then everything changes.

My son swivels atop the dragon's back and takes my hand.

"Again," he says.

Could I run a mile in five minutes while holding him?

Would it matter?

"Again."

There are three quarters in my pocket, and I start to panic. Then I remember where I am. I take a quick glance over my shoulder at the open cash register pregnant with quarters.

Sure, I tell him, and slip another coin into the slot.

And as long as the quarters hold out, my son and I, his hand cradled in mine, will be one and ride the dragon together.

.

Soft, Sweet Music

Drew Williams

I was eleven when I found the finger in the abandoned lot behind my parents' house. I had spent the better part of that morning looking for field mice, and just as I had given up and was about to head home, I saw it there in the dirt next to a pile of leaves and a broken beer bottle. At first I thought it was a big, brown worm, so I took out one of the finishing nails I had in my pocket and bent over to find the meatiest part of the thing. I intended on impaling the creature to the ground, but when I crouched down and jabbed it with the tip of the nail, some of the loose dirt on top of it fell off, and I saw the unmistakable circle pattern of a knuckle. Four small lines within a circle about the size of a penny. But before I could examine it further, I heard my mother call out to tell me it was time for lunch. I glanced in the direction of my house then back at the finger. Without hesitation, I scooped it up and deposited it into my pocket along with the nails and ball of string before running home to my mother and the bowl of chicken with stars soup that I knew would be waiting for me on the table.

After lunch, I locked myself in my bedroom and dumped the contents of my pocket onto my bed. On top of my white, woolen blanket, the finger looked like a crooked, brown turd. I poked at it with my much smaller and lighter index finger, rolling it back and forth across the bed. I half expected it to leave a brown stain on my blanket, but when it didn't sully my clean bed spread, I gently stroked the length of the finger as if I was petting a mouse. The finger was pleasantly smooth, but there was a hard layer of blood and mud crusted around the end where the flesh should have joined with the third knuckle. I picked a few flakes off and brought them to my lips.

They tasted of salt.

What took me by surprise was the fingernail. It was perfectly trimmed without a trace of dirt in it. It looked a lot like my mother's nails did after she got a manicure.

I examined the finger a few more minutes then went into my parents' bathroom and got a bottle of rubbing alcohol. I went back to my room and scrounged around my closet until I found a mason jar. I popped the lid, dumped out the rocks and teeth I had collected over the years, then filled the jar half way with alcohol and dropped the finger in. It sunk turd-like, twisting twice before resting at the bottom of the jar. Bits and pieces of dried mud broke free of the finger and discolored the alcohol. I scolded myself for not thinking of washing the finger off before tightening the seal on the jar and stashing it beneath a pile of old comic books in the back of the closet.

Perhaps I should have told someone about what I had found; that would have been the appropriate thing to do. But from the moment I saw the finger on my bed, its brown darkness set against my clean, white blanket, I knew that I was in possession of something dangerous, something wonderfully more mysterious than just a discarded piece of flesh and bone. I felt as if I had been let in on a great, wicked secret. A secret apart from my parents, apart from classmates, a secret that, for the first time in my life, was wholly and truly mine. I never wondered where the finger came from, or how it ended up in the lot behind my house. Its history didn't interest me. All that mattered was that it was mine now, and I was going to keep it.

That night I had the dream for the fist time.

The dream is always the same. I'm sitting naked on the floor of my mother's kitchen. I'm on the floor because all the furniture has been removed. The floor is cold, and I can feel my legs and butt growing numb, but I don't move. I can hear the sound of a piano playing softly in some far distant room. I don't recognize the melody, but it is soothing.

I ignore the cold and pain that is creeping into my legs and concentrate on the music. I am just on the verge of identifying the piece when a shadowy outline wavers in the darkness in front of me.

I know that it is a man, but there is no body, no substance for my eyes to fix on. It is just a gray cloud, slightly lighter than the blackness that surrounds me moving in harmony with the sweet, distant, music. As I stare into the shadow, a long, brown finger with a finely polished pink nail emerges from its depths. It is my finger, the one in the mason jar, only now it wears a diamond ring. The finger hovers inches from my face, pointing at the spot between my eyes. I don't speak, I don't move; I simply stare at the ring and know that I have been chosen.

I didn't look at the finger everyday. I didn't have to. Just knowing that it was tucked beneath my comic books was enough to send me into dizzying fits of ecstasy. I possessed something that no one else had; an extra finger. A finger that wore a bright, diamond ring in my dreams and whispered secrets to me while I slept. And I never revealed the secret of my finger to anyone. In fact, very rarely did I remove the finger from its hiding place, though sometimes at night after a day of enduring the monotony of my parents' company or the abuse of my school mates, I would put it on the end table next to my bed and stare at it. I imagined that it wiggled at me and I would wiggle my finger back. We'd play that game for hours until sleep would finally overtake me, and I would have the dream.

For six years, every night, the same dream.

Then I found the hand that had lost my finger.

Not long after my eighteenth birthday my parents died, and I came into possession of their not unsubstantial estate. I no longer saw the necessity of an education, so to the dismay of my classmates who delighted in torturing me, I dropped out of school. And since my parents' home was now entirely mine, I no longer saw the need to hide my finger, so I removed it from its corner of my closet and stationed it on the mantle in my father's den where once rested a rather bland family portrait taken in the summer of my thirteenth year. I threw that portrait, and the rest of the family photographs into the garbage.

175

I was perfectly content in my solitude with my finger for company, but occasionally I would feel the need to surround myself with strangers, to walk unseen amongst them. I began to take the subway into the heart of the city where I would pick a random exit and wander the streets. Sometimes I would spend a few hours in one of the dive-bars that littered nearly every corner. I would drink Tequila and sit in a corner smoking cigarettes and breathing in the hot air that reeked of body odor. I would grow drunk from the stale smell of sweat. Often, I would bypass the bars and just walk the streets and alleys, watching the people - the nameless, faceless people who side-stepped me on the street. I liked to watch them as they hurried by, wondering where their hands and feet had been.

One night when I was overcome with the urge to mingle, I took the subway to the West Fipse Street exit. I was heading west into the heart of the city when I heard the sound of a guitar. At first, I could barely recognize the sound as music, but as it grew louder, the delicate strains of the guitar became more familiar. With a cold dread, I came to recognize the song as one I had heard countless times in my dreams played on an unseen piano. I hurried down Fipse Street, drawn forward by the music, but then a man's voice stopped me cold. In a raspy, bass he sang:

> *I got them four finger blues*
> *Yeah, the four finger blues,*
> *Ain't ya heard the news*
> *I gots them four finger blues*

I rounded the corner of Fipse and there he was, an ancient black man strumming a weathered Gibson guitar. Though he was sitting cross-legged on the sidewalk, it was obvious that he was tall and painfully thin. Draped in a tattered brown raincoat, his head swayed to and fro in time with his music while his left hand easily slid up and down the neck of the guitar in a seamless flow of G - C - D chords. All the while his right thumb stroked hard against the steel strings.

> *Oh yeah, you know it's true*
> *Them old four finger blues*

And where his index finger should have poked out from his hand was a shriveled stump of flesh.

I couldn't speak, I couldn't move. I just stared at the gnarled stub of knuckle. Its weathered pink flesh glistened in the pale light like a diamond.

As I stood there, the old man looked at me and smiled. "You got a dollar friend?" he asked, his voice softening just a trace. "I sure could use one." He cocked his head toward a worn fedora in front of him. I glanced at its contents - four singles and a handful of change. When I looked back at him, the smile had grown larger, almost menacing. "Yup, sure could use a dollar."

He knew.

I don't know how, but he knew that his missing finger was in a mason jar in my home. And he wanted it back. I could see it in his wide, green eyes. They fixed upon me like a pin stabbing at my throat, boiling with hatred and envy.

give me what's mine - give me what's mine - give me what's mine

I grabbed the handful of bills in my pocket - tens, twenties, I don't know, and threw them into his hat. The music stopped and for a moment, his eyes darted away from me toward the wad of cash in front of him. Released from their grip, I spun around and ran back toward the subway. But the further away I ran, the louder and stronger I could hear his song in my mind:

Gonna get my finger back
You just better believe it, Jack
Man can't mess with fate or fact
Yeah, I'm gonna get my finger back

That night, for the first time, I was afraid of the dream.

Nothing about it had changed, every feature, every sensation was as it had always been. But sitting on the cold floor of my parents' kitchen, I trembled in fear. My finger pointed at the spot between my eyes, and I sensed its rage because our secret had been discovered.

Failed me - failed me - failed me

When I woke up the next morning my forehead burned as if it had been branded with a coat hanger. My finger had spoken to me in the dream, seared its command directly into my brain. The pain of that command was horrible, but welcome; I had been given a chance to redeem myself.

That night I took the subway back to West Fipse and headed once again to where the blues man sat the night before. From nearly three blocks away, I could hear his song:

Gonna sleep well tonight
Gonna sleep fine tonight
Ain't got no bed
But that's ALLLLL RIGGHHHHTTTTT

Each note was like a nail being pounded into my skull. And each nail reminded me that this was my only chance at redemption.

A back alley spills out onto West Fipse Street about a dozen feet from where the ancient musician sat playing his guitar. A small crowd of people were gathered around the man, so I was able to slip unseen by him into the narrow alley. Slithering into the tight space behind a dumpster that sat about twenty feet from the entrance to the alley, I waited.

I didn't have long to wait, three maybe four hours at the most, before the music stopped. The sun had long since set, and the old man needed to take a piss. Oblivious to my presence, he shuffled past me into the dark alley, then slipped into the doorway of an abandoned building.

I held my breath, waiting for the telltale sound of urine splashing against brick. When it came, I sprung. In four quick steps I was on top of him, ready to plunge the butcher knife I had hidden in my jacket into his neck. Before he could react, I buried the blade up to its hilt in the soft spot at the base of the man's skull. He stumbled forward and managed to turn around before he fell dead into a pool of his own urine. From his wide-eyed stare I could tell he recognized me; he knew why I had to kill him.

I had to tug the knife with both hands to get it out of his head, but after a few moments I was able to work it free. I slipped the knife into a plastic freezer bag and put it in my inside jacket pocket. Out of my side pocket, I removed the garden shears that I had been sharpening all day and another freezer bag.

A minute later I was out of the alley, heading back to the subway and home.

* * * * *

Spread across my white bed sheet the fingers look like smooth, round piano keys.

Piano Keys.

Yes, that's what they look like. And when I place my old fingers in between my new ones, I can see the resemblance clearly. But I am dreadfully short of keys. I'm not sure how many keys are on a piano, but I know that I'll need more to hear the soft, sweet music of my dream.

Many more.

Soon on Video

Drew Williams

It was a difficult decision; gang rape and revenge or sadism and mutilation, but after ten minutes of deliberation, Jay Nixon chose rape and revenge.

The choice was especially hard since the video boxes were equally titillating. In his left hand Jay held *I Spit on Your Grave* with its picture of a mud-splattered woman in a pair of cutoff shorts that ran up her ass as she waded knee deep in the swamp. Beneath her firm, muddy, left butt cheek the tag line read: "No jury in the land would convict her." In his right hand Jay held the case for the equally low-budgeted flick, *Blood Suckers,* featuring a midget in a Bill Clinton mask holding a dismembered head. Stamped below the title was the warning: BANNED IN 24 COUNTRIES! "But not here," Jay mused before tossing *Blood Suckers* back onto the rack.

Eyeing Jay as he made his way to the checkout-counter, was a bald man with basketball-sized sweat stains beneath his armpits. Jay thought the guy looked out of place. Most of the counter jockeys at the Video Plaza were kids in their late teens, skinny geeks with bad hair and nose rings who thought working at a video store made them part of the movie industry. But this guy was different, much different. He was easily in his mid-forties, a thick, squat man with an absurdly round face and an upturned nose that made him look faintly bovine. Three greasy strands of hair were parted over his forehead just inches above his dark and deep-set eyes. When Jay reached the counter and held out the case for *I Spit on Your Grave*, the bald guy broke out into a grin. "Find what you're looking for?"

Jay ignored the question and tossed the case onto the counter along with his driver's license and a five-dollar bill. The man scooped up the license and video with quick, pig-like fingers. "*I Spit on Your Grave*, excellent choice." The pudgy counterman stole a quick glance at Jay's license. "I mean if you're into this kind of stuff. Right . . ." Another quick look at the license. "Mr. Nixon?"

Jay grunted and tapped his fingers against the counter. "Yeah, I guess."

The counterman ran a bar scanner over the video and typed Jay's license number into his computer. "Okay, Mr. Nixon. That will be two dollars." Jay nodded toward the bill. "Of course." The fat fingers flew across the counter a second time. "You'll have to excuse me, I'm new here. Actually, I just bought the place." He jerked his thumb over his shoulder toward a sign taped to the window. On both sides read, UNDER NEW MANAGEMENT. "I'm Bob," he said, pushing Jay's rental toward him. Atop the video case sat three crisp one-dollar bills.

Jay glanced toward the sign, surprised he hadn't noticed it on his way in. "Uh huh."

"I'm glad you like the slasher flicks," Bob said. "I've ordered a lot more titles. A lot of the old classics."

Without a word, Jay made his way to the exit.

* * * * *

It was a stroke of good luck for Jay that the Video Plaza was under new management, especially if the porky new owner came through on his promise and got some new Horror movies. There weren't many films in the section that he hadn't seen, and though he often rented action movies and the occasional erotic thriller, Jay always found himself drawn back to Horror, back to the monsters.

Hopefully this Bob character won't be full of shit, Jay thought when he got back to his apartment. He lived alone in an upscale complex full of hotshot young bankers and assorted professionals who cheated on their taxes and drove thirty-thousand-dollar sports cars. Jay was probably the only unemployed person in the building, but ever since his trust fund kicked in after his old man's death, he had a guaranteed sixty thousand a year for life. Jay didn't worry about money or a job, and he certainly didn't give a rat's ass about the yuppies who lived around him.

Jay grabbed a Sam Adams out of his well-stocked refrigerator before slipping *I Spit on Your Grave* into the VCR. Stretching his six-foot-three-inch frame out on the couch, he hit the play button. As the opening credits rolled, Jay wondered if the gay stockbroker in the next apartment would ever rent a movie like *I Spit on Your Grave*. Probably not, Jay thought. Probably too good for such entertainment. Jay took a long swig at his beer and settled in for the evening, the remote control resting snugly in his palm.

* * * * *

"So, how was it?" Bob asked the next afternoon when Jay returned the tape. The counterman had changed his shirt but new sweat balls were starting to peek through. For a second the acidic smell of body odor wafted unpleasantly up Jay's nostrils. Jay crinkled up his nose and tossed the tape onto the counter.

"It sucked."

Bob looked surprised. "Really? Even the gang rape scene? That's my favorite part." Bob's bushy eyebrows arched as if he expected a response.

Jay shrugged slightly. "Well, that part was okay. The rest stunk."

His eyes still fixed on Jay, Bob snatched up the tape and casually deposited it in the return bin. "They should have killed her, you know."

"Huh?"

"The guys in the movie, they should have killed that girl. It's pretty stupid to gang rape a woman and then let her live. What were these guys thinking? That she wouldn't come after them?" Again came the raised eyebrow.

Jay nodded in agreement. He had been thinking that very thing the night before. "But if they would have killed her there wouldn't have been a movie."

Bob laughed out loud and slapped his stumpy fist against the counter. "Can't argue with that. No sirreee." He was about to add something else when the front door swung open and an elderly woman shuffled inside. "Excuse me," Bob said when he saw the new customer. He slipped out from behind the counter and met the woman near the Drama section. Jay turned and headed straight for Horror. As he scanned the titles, some of them new, he heard Bob tell the woman, "I have that, but it's in the back room. I'll just run and get it."

As Bob shuffled off to the back room, Jay looked over the new Horror videos. Most were of films he had never heard of, many of them foreign. One tape that caught his eye was for a movie called *Night Terrors*. The box showed a long, wooden bridge, a thin noose hanging from its side a few feet above a reddish black river. Beneath the river, scrawled in blood-red letters, was written *"Suicide Was Only the Beginning."* Jay flipped the box over, saw that the film ran for an hour and forty minutes, and took it up to the counter.

As he waited for Bob to return, Jay spied *I Spit on Your Grave* atop the return bin. It was odd how his and Bob's reaction to the film were the same. The only part of the movie that was decent, that actually got Jay excited, was the ten minutes when the four rednecks raped the chick. The whole revenge plot after that was all garbage.

Jay stared at the tape and began drumming his fingers against the counter top. Four fingers tapping on the Formica, one finger for each time he rewound the rape scene.

"So did you find something?"

184

Startled at the sound of Bob's voice, Jay snapped his hand off the counter and into his pocket. "Yeah, I think so," Jay said, handing over the case for *Night Terrors*. Bob looked at the title and gave it an enthusiastic thumbs-up.

"Good flick. You ought to read the book."

Jay mumbled yeah under his breath as Bob pulled up his account on the computer. "Whoa," he said when the record appeared. "You've been renting four, sometimes five videos a week." Bob put his finger against the screen. "And they've all been Horror or Action." When Bob pulled his finger back, it left a smooth, greasy smudge on the monitor. "You must like the blood and guts stuff, huh?"

Jay didn't answer, he simply pushed a five-dollar bill across the counter. Bob, however, wasn't going to let the subject drop. "You must have a lot of time on your hands to watch so many movies," Bob said, taking the bill from Jay and slowly dragging it toward himself. Jay watched the movement, fascinated by how much Bob's fingers resembled slugs. Thick, pink slugs. "You must not like going out and socializing much."

"I don't have friends." Jay was surprised how quickly and automatically the words tumbled out of his mouth. He immediately regretted them. "I just like movies," he added. "Most other stuff bores me."

Bob tilted his head and let out an understanding "Ahh." "Boredom, of course. I completely understand. Ennui."

Jay took his tape and his change, but didn't turn to leave. "On what?" he asked.

"Ennui. It's a French word. It means boredom of the soul. Actually, a kind of emotional and spiritual emptiness. To suffer from ennui is to suffer from a hollow soul." Bob stopped abruptly. "Oh hey, I'm sorry. It's kind of a hobby of mine. You know, philosophy." A sheepish grin spread across the counterman's round face. "Sometimes I get carried away."

"Yeah," Jay replied. He pocketed his change and was turning to leave when Bob's hand shot out and clamped itself around his wrist. The strength behind Bob's pudgy fingers surprised Jay.

"Oh, I almost forgot. I was wondering if you could do me a favor." Bob released Jay and ducked beneath the counter.

"What's that?" Jay asked the top of Bob's shiny head.

Bob popped back up holding a black videocassette. "I just got this new series of Horror flicks this morning, and I haven't had a chance to preview them yet. Since you seem to be a connoisseur of the genre, I was wondering if you would take a look at this and tell me what you think." Bob held the tape out for Jay to examine the title. *The Birth of Evil: Vol. 1.* "No charge," Bob added.

Jay shrugged his shoulders and accepted the film. "Sure, no sweat."

"Great," Bob said, slapping his meaty palms together. "You'll be doing me a big favor."

Jay nodded and headed for the exit with a video stuffed in each of the side pockets of his jacket. As he stepped out onto the street he heard Bob call out:

"Have a nice day."

* * * * *

The digital clock blinked 2:15 in bright, red numbers. Besides the flickering gray static on the television, it was the only light in the room. For over an hour Jay pointed the remote control at the television, but he couldn't find the strength to press down his thumb. He was tired, drained almost to the point of passing out. But rippling beneath his exhaustion was an undercurrent of nervous energy, a thrilling cocktail of adrenalin and fear.

After leaving the video store, Jay grabbed a quick dinner at a sub place and downed a few beers at a bar next to his apartment complex. After a wasted hour of trying to talk a brunette into coming back to his place, Jay said to hell with it and went home to watch his movies.

Night Terrors was first, and Jay had to admit that it wasn't bad. Lots of death, including a pretty gruesome decapitation. And on a stomach full of beer, it was well worth the money.

Then came *The Birth of Evil*. It was near eleven when *Night Terrors* ended, and Jay wasn't sure he could stay up for the second movie. His early evening buzz was starting to wear off, and he was having trouble keeping his eyes open. But then he thought of the woman at the bar. Kelly was her name. She designed web pages and made it quite clear that she wasn't interested in anything Jay had to say. A sudden burst of anger snapped Jay out of his lethargy as he remembered the condescending smile that spread across her pretty face when she told him that she didn't think it would be a good idea if she gave him her phone number. At the time Jay laughed off the rejection, but what he really wanted to do was call Kelly a teasing bitch and toss a beer in her face.

"To hell with it," Jay muttered. He picked himself off the couch, grabbed a fresh beer from the refrigerator and flicked on *The Birth of Evil*.

When the tape began, Jay did not have high hopes that it would be any good. With its hand-printed label pasted to the cassette, *The Birth of Evil* had all the looks of a quickie piece of indy. trash. Shot in black and white with a jerky handheld camera, the movie's first scene appeared to be nothing more than silent home movie of a fat guy cooking sausage.

Barely a minute into the film, Jay pronounced it crap and was about to shut it off when the scene switched. The fat guy was no longer in the kitchen; now he was in a small backyard surrounded by a dozen or so laughing children. The same shaky camera filmed the fat guy twisting balloons into animal shapes before passing them out to the kids. Jay leaned closer to the television for a closer look.

And recognized the costume and the smiling grease-painted face of John Wayne Gacy.

Absently, Jay set the remote on the side of the couch and watched as Gacy silently led the children in some song before overseeing a skinny blond woman in slicing up a birthday cake.

Then the scene shifted again and Gacy was back in his house. The clown suit had been discarded, replaced by a baggy pair of boxer shorts. In one hand Gacy held a meat cleaver, in the other, a can of Old Milwaukee. Gacy was talking to a young man whose back was to the camera. Tied to a chair, the man frantically tried to free himself as Gacy strolled to his side, winked once at the camera, then plunged the cleaver into the man's neck.

Jay slipped back on his couch, mesmerized as Gacy hacked away at his victim. When there was nothing substantial left to chop up, a blood-splattered Gacy picked up what was left of the young man and carried him to a trapdoor in the kitchen that led to the crawlspace under the house. As he was depositing the body in the crawl space, the film went black. A moment later, a smiling, fully dressed Gacy was ushering a handsome, red-haired boy into his living room.

An hour and a half later, after watching Gacy torture and mutilate over two dozen young men, Jay watched the final scene: John Wayne Gacy being taken away in a squad car. Then the screen went black. No THE END, no credits, just static.

"Fuck me," Jay whispered when the movie ended, the highest compliment he could pay a film.

* * * * *

"Well? How was it?" Bob asked when Jay returned *The Birth of Evil*. "Is this something I should put on the shelf, or should I send it back to the distributor?"

Jay told him to keep the tape. "It was good. I wasn't so sure what it was supposed to be. It wasn't like a regular movie. But it was creepy. And the guy playing Gacy, he looked just like him."

Bob brought his chunky hand to his face and stroked his chin. "Yeah, the distributor told me the actor playing Gacy was a dead ringer for the real one." Bob accepted the tape and tossed it into the return bin. "Glad you liked it," he said. "Get you anything today? I got a few new straight-to-video flicks and the new *Witchcraft* movie. I think it's number 12."

Jay shook his head and asked Bob if he had any more of *The Birth of Evil* tapes.

Bob looked a bit surprised. "Well, they're not in my system yet, but I'll tell you what. If you rent a movie at full price, I'll let you preview the next one like last time. Sort of a two for one thing." Bob plucked the second volume from under the counter and held it out to Jay. "Got a deal?"

"Sure." Jay eyed the black case in Bob's hand. "That's cool." He turned from the counter and grabbed the first movie off the nearest shelf. "I'll take this one," Jay said, handing the tape to Bob.

Bob eyed the tape, amused at Jay's choice. "Hmm, *Farewell My Concubine*. Interesting choice." Bob slid the tape across the bar scanner. "Two fifty," he said.

Jay handed him the money and took the tapes without comment, though he had no idea what *Farewell My Concubine* was about.

189

* * * * *

Volume two of *The Birth of Evil* was just like the first one, no sound, black and white, and shot with a handheld camera. Only, this film was about Ted Bundy.

And just as in the case with the guy playing Gacy, the actor playing Bundy was another dead ringer. Same steely-eyed good looks, the same arrogant swagger.

When the film began, Bundy was sitting in a library next to an attractive, dark-haired woman. After a few silent minutes of small talk and giggling, Bundy motioned with his head to a place somewhere off to the left. The girl looked in that direction and closed the book in front of her. Always the gentleman, Bundy stood and took the girl's hand.

Jay held his breath as he watched the scene's inevitable progress. Bundy escorted the girl to a secluded spot on the third floor of the library. There he wrapped his hands around the surprised girl's throat and squeezed it shut. As Bundy dug his fingers deeper into the girl's neck, Jay felt his own fingers coiling into the smooth fabric of his sofa, his heart thumping madly inside his chest as if a live wire had been attached to the organ. Oddly similar to the expression of Bundy's victim, Jay's mouth flew open and a wave of air flowed down his throat expanding his lungs until they were on the verge of bursting. Every muscle in Jay's body was flexed, every nerve and fiber of his being was on fire.

The exquisite flow of electricity pulsing through his body lasted another ninety minutes, intensifying with each of Bundy's kills. When the tape finally ended and the screen faded to black, the energy that had gripped Jay switched off like a light, leaving him in darkness.

* * * * *

Bob asked him a question but Jay wasn't paying attention.

"*Farewell My Concubine*," Bob repeated. He folded his thick arms across his chest, watching as Jay shifted his weight from foot to foot. "I can't let you take out *Vol. 3* until you return *Farewell My Concubine*."

Jay muttered a feeble apology, but Bob dismissed it with a wave of his hand. "No problem. I just have a policy about renting tapes to someone who has unreturned movies. That's all." Bob plucked a video case from beneath the counter. "But I got all the tapes in the computer system last night," he said. "And look, I was even able to put on new labels." Bob thrust his hand out so Jay could read the one-word label taped to the case.

DAHMER

Jay sprinted the eight blocks to his apartment to fetch *Farewell My Concubine*.

* * * * *

By the time Jay returned to his apartment with the third volume of *The Birth of Evil*, he was exhausted and feeling more than just a little stupid. He couldn't explain the urge that had gripped him when he woke up that morning. Perhaps it was left over adrenalin, the residue of the heart-pounding excitement he felt while watching the Bundy tape.

Or it could have been the dream. Jay could only remember hazy bits of it, a foggy night and the smell of smoke. And there was the sensation that his hands were on fire. Even in his sleep, Jay could feel his fists opening and closing and the agony of white-hot metal being seared into the flesh of his palms. When Jay woke, the details of his dream slunk back into the bowels of his subconscious, but his fingers burned as if they had just been plucked out of a pot of boiling water. All over his body, his flesh tingled and only one thought filled his waking mind; he needed to get his hands on the next volume of *The Birth of Evil*.

But by the time he returned to the store with *Farewell My*

Concubine, the compulsion that seized him earlier was gone. He rented the Dahmer tape, but the overpowering need to do so had left him like the memory of his dream. Still, he paid Bob his three dollars, slipped the tape into his jacket and walked sullenly back to his apartment.

That gave Jay enough time to realize that the compulsion had left him about the same time Bob starting talking about cul-de-sacs. The conversation began with Bob asking Jay how he liked *Farewell My Concubine*. Still gripped with the urgency to get his hands on the third tape, Jay told Bob that he hadn't watched it. Bob smiled knowingly. "Didn't watch it, huh," Bob said. "I figured as much. You're the kind of guy who only goes in for the bloody stuff, right? Murder, rape, gore. You know, all that good stuff that gets the old heart pounding." Bob tucked his meaty paws into his pants pockets and rocked up on the balls of his feet. "Why do you think that is, Jay?"

The question took Jay off guard. "Don't know," he said, his panting breath slowing to normal. "I just do."

"Uh, huh," Bob said flatly, making no move to retrieve the tape Jay wanted. "No particular reason, huh. You were just born that way, right?" Bob rolled his eyes and shook his head. "You don't think you might have some kind of power issue, do you, Jay? You know what I'm saying. You feel like you don't have control over things, maybe like you don't really belong, so you find an outlet in the Horror flicks. Watching people get diced up by an unstoppable monster provides a pretty thrilling vicarious experience, don't you think?"

Fully recovered from his run, Jay straightened up to his full height. Easily half a foot taller than Bob, he glared down at the portly counter man. "What the hell are you talking about?"

A crooked smile played around the corners of Bob's mouth. "Hey," Bob said apologetically. "I'm not trying to bust your chops or anything. It's just another of these hobbies of mine. Junior psychologist, you might say." Bob chuckled to himself. "Hell, I'm into the chicks-behind-bars movies." The laughter grew stronger. "Guess a shrink would have a field day with me."

Jay's expression remained unchanged.

Bob stifled his laughter and pulled out volume three of *The Birth of Evil*. But before he handed it to Jay, Bob asked if Jay knew what a cul-de-sac was.

"Yeah. It's a dead-end street."

Bob scrunched up his piglike nose and frowned. "Not exactly. It's a turn-around really. A circle that is both an ending and a beginning. If you enter a cul-de-sac, you don't really come to an end. You just get turned around and sent back down the road you've come up." Bob slid the tape across the counter. "Do you know what I mean?"

Jay wasn't certain if Bob expected an answer or not, but he was tired of small talk. He just wanted his movie and to get the hell out of there. Jay tossed three singles onto the counter and snatched up the film. As he neared the exit, he heard Bob add:

"Oh, Jay. Be kind and rewind."

* * * * *

The third volume of *The Birth of Evil* sat unwatched atop the television. For nearly an hour Jay stared at the thin, black cassette, his mind wrestling with what Bob had said. Critical self-evaluation was never something Jay allowed for himself, but Bob's off-hand remark about power issues started a chain reaction in Jay's mind that was dangerously close to spinning out of control. The shards of truth in what Bob had said were too sharp to ignore. The counterman was right, Jay had never felt as if he belonged; not at home, not at school. All his life, Jay never permitted himself to become a part of any group; he preferred to remain on the fringes of society, satisfied to watch life from a distance.

Nor was he exaggerating when he told Bob that he didn't have any friends. Even as a child, Jay didn't have friends; he didn't want them. Nor did he ever desire companionship, especially from his neighbors and classmates. Early on Jay accepted that he was an outsider, a loner who craved isolation. As he matured, he had become involved with a few girls, but nothing serious ever came of it. To Jay they were simply short-lived sexual flings. But sex was never more than a diversion for Jay, and in the past year, that diversion was becoming increasingly unfulfilling. Like that bitch from Carters the other night. At the time, Jay was certain he wanted to get her into bed, but now he wasn't so sure. Now he realized that a part of him wanted the woman to reject him, to humiliate him just so he would have an excuse to become angry with her. A disturbing epiphany pushed its way to the front of Jay's mind; he liked that all-too-brief moment of pure, unadulterated rage he felt when the woman spurned his advances. He liked the way it made him feel dangerous, as if he could do anything.

Jay's eyes darted back and forth between the tape and the television. And what about the Horror movies? As far back as he could remember, they were the only kind of movies he truly enjoyed. The bloodier the better. Was that the kind of power issue Bob was talking about? Was his fascination with them someway of . . .

"Oh, this is bull shit!" Jay shouted, springing up from the couch. So what if he liked Horror flicks, he told himself. That didn't mean he was some kind of sicko or had power issues. "Screw Bob," Jay said out loud. That fat bastard didn't know anything about him. So what if blood excited him; so what if he masturbated during the rape scene of *I Spit on Your Grave*.

"Doesn't mean I have issues," Jay convinced himself.

He slapped the cassette marked DAHMER into the VCR and hit the play button.

* * * * *

A thin veil of mist clouded the starless night. It wrapped itself around Jay, shrouding him in the scent of rain and oil. It was a foreign smell, but one Jay found oddly familiar.

Jay was standing at the corner of Pirl and Helms, a half mile from his apartment complex breathing in the delicious aroma of the night, tasting its subtle blend of copper and sulphur at the back of his throat. He had no idea how he got there or where he was heading. All he knew was that he had to walk. To go west.

For a few moments he stared at the mist above him before resuming his march westward. As he walked, the cold wind buffeted his face and chest. Instinctively his body began to shiver, but Jay's mind didn't register the cold. All he could feel was the burning sensation deep within his lungs. He felt on fire, a living, breathing wall of flame.

And the taste that filled his mouth. It too burned, singeing his tongue and throat with the succulent flavor of boiled flesh. Jay wheeled about, pirouetting in the middle of the sidewalk. He was drowning in the sweet aroma of the night, his brain overloading on the tastes and smells that assaulted him from every side. He looked down at the sidewalk and saw a crimson trail snaking its way down the street. It flowed across the rough concrete, spilling over the curb and splattering rivulets of amber against the pavement. Jay opened his mouth as wide as he could and gulped in the night air. It tasted hot and alive. Jay tossed his head back and screamed in pleasure.

Then he began to run, following the bloody path flowing down the sidewalk.

And when he stopped he was in front of Bob's video store.

Jay pressed his face against the glass front door and peered in. Back lit by a dull, yellow streetlight, Jay could barely see the video racks in the store's center. Toward the back of the store the darkness swallowed the last few rows of videos. Jay concentrated on the darkness, forcing his eyes to see deeper into its inky blackness. After a few seconds he thought he saw a tiny red dot, only a pinprick of light, glowing in the back of the store.

Someone was smoking.

Jay put his palms against the door and pushed it open.

"We're closed for the night, Jay," Bob said from out of the darkness. The red ash rose about two feet and flared up. As Bob inhaled, Jay could see the man's face briefly illuminated by the red glow of the cigarette. Even in the dark Jay recognized Bob's bovine features and the loose strands of greasy hair dangling against his forehead. Jay could also see that the counterman's deep-set eyes glowed the same sharp red as the tip of his cigarette. Then Bob lowered the smoke and was once again invisible.

Jay stepped through the door, letting it bang shut behind him.

"I told you that we're closed, Jay." Another puff, another peek. "Or do you have something to tell me?"

Jay fixed his eyes on the red glow and moved toward it. "They're real, aren't they? Gacy, Bundy, Dahmer. Those weren't actors in those movies, were they?"

Jay heard Bob chortling softly in the darkness. It was a deep, throaty sound, almost a growl. "Of course they are actors, Jay. I don't know what else you could call them but actors." The cigarette went back up to Bob's mouth. As Jay drew nearer, the red flame grew more intense. Jay could tell that Bob was smiling, his eyes now narrowed to razor-thin slits. "But if you are asking me if what you witnessed was the real Gacy and Dahmer, the answer is yes. They were the real deal, giving the performances of their lives. In the end, Jay, all those murders were scripted. Performed beautifully by actors with very specific parts to play."

Jay stopped just arm's length from where Bob stood. "I watched Dahmer," Jay said slowly. "When he ate those people, I could taste them."

"And you didn't turn off the tape, did you, Jay? You just went on watching and feasting. And you loved it, Jay. Every delicious morsel of it."

Jay nodded in the darkness. "How?" he asked.

"Trade secrets," Bob replied quickly. He took another puff on the cigarette. "But '*how*' doesn't seem to be important, does it? *Why* seems to be much more of an appropriate question."

"Why?" Jay asked. "Why show it to me?"

Bob dropped the cigarette to the floor and ground it out with his heel; however, the red glow still hovered about his face. "Tell me something, Jay. Have you ever seriously considered just how twisted humanity has become? How it revels in evil, glorifies violence, pain, rape. Think of the movies I hawk right here. How many rapes and murders do you think are in this room alone? How many times have you watched someone tortured, perhaps impaled on a spike, and called it entertainment?"

Jay shook his head. "But they're not real. They're only movies."

Bob thought that was funny. "Who's to say what reality is and isn't, Jay? When you watched the girl being gang-raped in *I Spit on Your Grave*, wasn't your erection real? Wasn't your orgasm real? Real or not, the movies I peddle convey a very simple message: Human life doesn't mean shit."

Bob paused and grinned. "Aren't you amazed just how much humans relish pain and degradation? How much they love to wallow in the filth of their own excesses? Come on, Jay, we both know this world is sick, but have you ever wondered how much sicker things will get? How much worse it can become?"

"I never thought about it," Jay whispered.

"Of course you haven't," Bob said. "Nobody does. It's as if humanity just takes it for granted that the world has always been so demented. Well, let me clue you wise. It hasn't, Jay. Not by a long shot." Bob stuck out a pudgy finger and winked. "I'll let you in on a little secret. This world can't get any sicker. It has embraced every possible perversity, and it still can't get enough. It's always hungry for more; more filth, more decadence. And do you know what the best part is, Jay? You've become so used to being surrounded by filth and perversity that it's no longer shocking. Every kind of deviant behavior has been analyzed and rationalized and ultimately excused. You see, Jay, it's not fashionable to believe in evil and the devil anymore. Oh no, the existence of the devil is much too simplistic for such a modern world. And as for sin, it simply no longer exists. Your academics and psychologists have taken care of that. Sin is just another construct, something to work through in therapy."

Bob chuckled softly. "You see, Jay, what was called evil in the past is nothing but entertainment today. Something to watch on the Springer show or the nightly news." A satisfied grin spread across Bob's fat face. "You're living at the nadir of human civilization, Jay. This moment, right now, is humanity's lowest point."

Bob reached behind him and placed his palm on a door that had been hidden in the darkness. "Look in here," Bob said, flinging the door open. Jay was immediately blinded by a searing blast of white light.

Jay felt Bob's meaty hands hook into his arm and usher him into the room. "Open your eyes," Bob said softly. "It will be alright."

Jay opened his eyes to find himself standing in an enormous storeroom of videotapes. Thousands of simple black boxes with plain white tape down their sides, lined countless feet of shelving.

"I lied to you," Bob said, releasing Jay's arm. "*This* is the complete collection of *The Birth of Evil*. Over eleven thousand tapes and growing."

Jay stepped past Bob to examine the tapes, his hands reaching out toward the smooth plastic boxes. "Elizabeth Batory. Baron Giles DeRais. Joseph Stalin." As Jay read the litany of names, the same burst of electricity that gripped him when he watched the Bundy video surged throughout his body. Jay's heart began to pound faster and his skin grew unbearably sensitive. He could feel the air around him. It flowed over and through his pores, invigorating him with a thousand burning pinpricks. His vision, too, had become unnaturally acute. Jay took the video labeled 'Mao Tse Tung' and held it to his face. Its lines and contours snaked in a crisscross pattern, weaving to and fro until a sharp silhouette of the Chinese dictator emerged. When Jay saw the face, the black box gently shuddered in his hand as if it was breathing.

But it was his hearing that was most affected. At first, when his fingers found the boxes, Jay heard a low humming noise like the whir of a refrigerator motor. But as the currents of electricity flowed within him, the low hum evolved into a frenzy of voices. The voices of thousands of murderers spoke as one, all whispering their tales into Jay's ear. And Jay heard each one, each lurid description of strangulations - and rapes - and beheadings. He listened to the tales of betrayal, of poisonings and revenge. Tales of blood and flesh. And with each story, the power coursed stronger through Jay's body.

"Take them all," Bob said soothingly. "Hear what they have to tell you."

And Jay did, furiously grabbing the videos from the shelves. As he clutched them, they pulsed with life within his hungry fingers. Jay didn't know how long he was in the storeroom, maybe six minutes, maybe six years. For Jay, time seemed to stop. It was only after he heard the whisper of the last murderer that Jay came back to his senses.

199

He turned to Bob, his body about to explode from the energy that pulsed beneath his skin. "Is this it?" he asked. "Is this the end?"

Bob shook his head slowly. "The end? Oh no. Quite the opposite, in fact. You see, son, just like the title says . . ." Bob spread his arms out wide and spun about the room. " This is the birthplace of evil, the place where it breeds and grows until it can no longer be contained." Bob stopped spinning and looked Jay squarely in the eyes. "This is where a man like you discovers his destiny."

"Destiny?" Jay repeated.

"Certainly, my boy." Bob gestured to the racks of videos in front of him. "Just like you, all the actors in these passion plays were equally as lost. Loners who could find no useful place in society. And like you, they were bored. Empty vessels with no direction or purpose. They found their way here and I cured their ennui. I filled their emptiness with the power of evil and sent them out to fulfill their destiny."

Bob stepped forward and placed his hands on Jay's shoulders. "Remember what I told you about cul-de-sacs. How they aren't dead-ends, but turn-arounds? Well, Jay, like I said, this moment in time is the cul-de-sac of humanity. It is the lowest point of human existence. And since your kind cannot go any lower, all the depravity and evil born today must be turned around and sent back out."

"Where?" Jay asked. His fingers twitched, greedy to return to the long row of smooth, black cases.

"Not where, Jay. When. You see, the evil in all these boxes is born right here, right now. But this world is saturated with evil; you're drowning in it. So in order for it to thrive, evil must be turned around in time and sent back. Sometimes to the far past, sometimes, like the videos you watched, to more recent times. But to be sent back, it needs a vessel. Someone to carry it, to make it come alive. Do you understand what I am saying, Jay?"

Jay nodded mutely.

Bob smiled and patted Jay on the shoulder. He reached behind his back and produced a black videocassette. "Take this," he said, handing the box to Jay. "This will explain everything."

As soon as Jay's fingers touched the video, a surge of electricity exploded up his arm and engulfed his body. His fingers burned, twitching with an unquenchable desire to wrap themselves around smooth flesh. And in his mouth, Jay began to salivate at the taste of burnt skin. He looked down at the tape and read the name.

Bob gave Jay another pat and ushered him to the back door. "Have a good time." Jay said nothing as Bob maneuvered him to the rear of the storeroom. The plump shopkeeper threw open the exit and motioned for Jay to step outside. His fingers wound tightly around the video, Jay stepped back into the night. "Enjoy," he heard Bob say.

Jay turned to say something to Bob, but when he did, he found himself facing a soot-covered wall. Unfazed by the disappearance of the door to the video shop, Jay examined the rough brick wall for a few moments before turning toward the street. Around him the fog had become a dirty yellow, heavy with the smell of rain and oil. A series of tall gas lamps lined the street, casting a feeble light onto the men and women who hurriedly brushed past him. From out of the fog, the sound of horses' hooves echoed down the cobblestone street. Jay smiled, knowing for the first time in his life who he was and what he was to become. His life of isolation, his anger and boredom had led him to this wonderful, inescapable destiny.

As if possessing a consciousness of their own, Jay's fingers began to drum against the plastic video case. Only now, in this place and time, it was no longer a video case. In Jay's hand was a smooth, weathered, leather bag. A doctor's satchel, to be exact.

And inside, Jay knew, would be a scalpel and a chisel. And a firm iron mallet.

Jay hugged the bag to his chest, and the taste of flesh grew stronger in his mouth.

"Ello darlin."

Jay casually turned his head to the side in order to get a good look at the whore. She was a short, round woman. No longer young and attractive. She smiled a gap-toothed smile at Jay and said in a thick, Cockney accent, "Buy a lady a drink?"

Jay smiled pleasantly at the woman and patted the bag that held the tools of his profession. The bag that, in his life at the cul-de-sac of humanity, had been a case for a videotape. A videotape with a strip of white tape down its side where was written a single name:
Jack the Ripper.

Jay extended his hand to the woman, who eagerly accepted it. "Lead on, my dear," he said, ushering her in the direction of a darkened alley.

"To our destiny."

That Cleansing Fire

Joseph M. Nassise

The Lear jet banked suddenly, the abrupt action jolting Cade Williams from his uneasy sleep. Glancing out his window, he could see the lights of the city far off to the left and knew that the pilot must be starting his preparations for landing. That meant Cade had another twenty minutes or so before he and his team would be on the ground and in the thick of things.

Like most of the Order's equipment, the interior of the aircraft was spartan. Gone were the leather seats and the recessed mini bars, the inflight entertainment centers and the four star meals. Only that which was functional and necessary had been left in place, though they had left the privacy curtain that separated the rear compartment where Cade was sitting from the main cabin just ahead.

Looking past the curtain, he could see Matt Billings seated about halfway up center aisle in the main cabin. As Cade watched, his teammate stripped his weapon and began cleaning it with deft movements and the ease of long familiarity. At the sight, the voice of O'Malley, Cade's first drill instructor at the academy, echoed in his mind, "If you have no other assignment, see to your weapons." It was advice he heeded during his fifteen-year career with the Special Tactics and Operations team of the Boston Police Department and brought with him to the Order when he had been recruited. He had enforced that unwritten rule on his squad from the very first day and now, five years later, it was as habitual to them as breathing. Cade knew without looking that his other team member, Gavin Jones, would be in the seat opposite Billings, doing the same thing to his standard issue handgun.

Having a perfectly operational weapon might just make the difference between life and death for his men, particularly on this run, Cade thought to himself with some resignation. They had been asked to take the assignment by the Preceptor himself, something that didn't happen too often, and therefore couldn't turn it down, despite the fact that Cade felt uneasy about it from the beginning. The situation was not one to inspire confidence. Two months ago, the local Catholic diocese had requested help through the Vatican in dealing with a particularly violent blood cult. The parish pastor had catalogued a number of problems ranging from intimidation of his parishioners to a sudden lack of street people appearing at the soup kitchen. He was convinced that there was evil afoot and believed the local authorities had neither the desire nor the manpower to be able to handle the situation. His request had gone through the channels and had been passed to the Order for investigation.

Contrary to what most people believed, the Holy Order of the Poor Knights of Christ of the Temple of Solomon, or the Knight Templars as they are popularly known, were not destroyed at the hand of the King of France when he burned Grand Master Jacques De Molay at the stake in 1314 for heresy. Following Molay's death, the Order had gone underground, protected through a secret pact with the Vatican, only to emerge centuries later as a hidden military arm of that organization. Its primary purpose was to defend mankind against the evils that walked in the world, unnoticed in a society that was preoccupied with science and that scoffed at superstitions, regardless of the truths they might contain.

The Order agreed that the situation merited a closer look. A team was sent in, led by a veteran Knight Captain, and instructed to look into the situation and assist the parish in whatever manner they found necessary.

Three weeks after their arrival, the team abruptly disappeared.

Using equipment that was left behind, the parish pastor communicated directly with the Preceptor and had requested further assistance.

206

Since Cade's team was closest to the site, and presently unoccupied, they drew the short stick and were asked to take the assignment.

That was two weeks ago.

As was standard procedure, Cade sent his fourth team member, Bishop, in ahead of the rest of the team, with instructions to set up a secure location unknown to the locals and then rendezvous with the parish pastor. Bishop carried out both tasks without a hitch, relaying the address of the safe house during his regularly scheduled communication a few days ago. He checked in the next night as well, leaving a brief message that he believed he had some information about the fate of the first squad and that he would see the rest of the team in a few days.

The night after that he missed his call.

Cade wasn't too concerned at that point. His team was trained to use secondary and even tertiary communication schedules just in case any activities they were engaged in prevented them from making the primary one. When Bishop missed the second check-in, however, Cade grew more concerned.

By the time he missed the third, Cade had the rest of the team and the necessary gear loaded onto one of the Order's jets ready to get underway the moment the Preceptor had given them the word.

Now, as the pilot made the announcement that they would be landing soon, Cade reached over and picked up the long, thin case resting on the seat next to him. Balancing it on his knees, he opened the case's three clasps and raised its lid.

Inside, on a smooth bed of white silk, lay the sword that had been given to him during his investiture, the night that he had pledged himself and his life to the Order.

The weapon itself was an unadorned English long sword. Its hilt had been specifically molded to match the grip of Cade's right hand. Along the length of the blade that was facing upright in the case, the word *Defensor* had been inscribed in silver.

Translated, the Latin word meant Defender.

Cade carefully withdrew the sword from the case and held it up in the aisle, turning it slightly to and fro so that the dim lighting of the cabin made the script sparkle and shine. According to the Code, a knight in the Order was allowed personal ownership of only a few, specific items. The sword given to them during their investiture ceremony is one of them, a symbol of their fidelity to the Order and their unrelenting dedication to its ideals. The weapons are supposed to remain undecorated, chaste if you will, just as the knight who carries them pledges to do the same. Enhancing the weapon in any way after it is awarded is cause for a variety of punishments, for doing so is considered a sin of pride.

Cade ignored this rule, just as he ignored more than a handful of others over the last several years when the success of his missions required it. On the day after the ceremony, he secretly commissioned a silversmith to help him add a second word to the same exact location on the opposite side of the blade.

Now, as he turned the weapon over, he smiled grimly at what he had written there.

Ulciscor.

Vengeance.

It was the driving reason behind Cade's daily existence and the true reason for his membership in the Templars.

He gently replaced the sword back in its case, this time with the opposite side facing up. Tugging the thin, cotton glove off his right hand, he traced the Latin word with the tip of his right index finger. He could barely feel the inscription through his skin, but his Talent sent the raw emotion locked in it back to him with the force of a thunderbolt. For several long moments, he reveled in the flow as all that rage, determination, and utter hatred for the Adversary washed over him like the torrent of a raging river. Just as he had on the day he awakened in the hospital five years before, he vowed to find the Adversary and make it pay for the loss of his wife and for the changes it had wrought in him.

His encounter with that supernatural entity left him with a scarred face, hands, and soul. It also left him with several unique abilities, something he was certain the Adversary never intended. The first, what he liked to call his Talent, was more properly known as psychometry. When a person handles an inanimate object they leave traces of their passing on it, a psychic residue so to speak, as the emotions and thoughts passing through the individual's mind are left on the surface of the object. With just a simple touch, Cade could read those impressions and know something about those who handled the object before him. The ability had a dark side too, however, for it denied him even the most casual physical contact with another person. Touching someone was far worse than touching an object, for an object held only a few, brief glimpses into the individual who last handled it while touching a person had all the pain and emotion locked inside them. Even a casual brush against another person overwhelmed Cade with a sudden influx of foreign thoughts and emotions. He suspected continual contact could even result in a loss of his own identity, as his psyche was overwhelmed by another's, though he had never tested his theory. Because of the danger of such contact, Cade was forced to wear thin cotton gloves at all times when he was out of the safety of his own home, preventing his Talent from activating.

His other ability, less troublesome from a practical sense but more disturbing emotionally, he called his Sight. Where the Adversary had touched Cade's face, nothing but scar tissue now remained. His eye was destroyed on contact; the skin around it melted and cauterized in seconds, leaving so much scar tissue that removing the damaged orb and fitting a prosthetic would have been impossible without extensive surgery, something he had no intention of undergoing.

In spite of the damage, or perhaps because of it, Cade could now see into the realm of the dead. He could see all manner of ghosts and supernatural beings. Not just when *they* wanted to be seen, which contrary to popular belief isn't very often, but any time *he* wanted to see them. Cade had learned that there was another layer of reality superimposed upon our own, a place he had come to simply call the Beyond. It was within this realm that the dead normally resided, cut off from humanity by the smallest of margins. The Beyond is almost a mirror image of this world, but fashioned out of emotion instead of material substance. The stronger the emotions, the better. It is emotion that allows a shade to exist, to hang around some aspect of their former lives that were particularly important to them. To haunt those places, if you will. Just as an accident victim will wander that lonely stretch of highway where they lost control of their vehicle, so will a murder victim revisit the scene of the crime. The shade of an adult might even return to the home they knew as a child, if such a place held a strong emotional attachment for them. When a person sees a ghost firsthand, it is nothing more than a fleeting glimpse into this aspect of reality.

Cade had also learned that having the ability to see into the Beyond had its share of dangers, though. Ghosts and other supernatural beings hunger for the attention of the living the way a heroin junkie hungers for a fix. They quickly take notice when we suddenly drop into their world. Cade had been hounded by all manner of phantoms when he'd spent too long across the barrier.

Being on the other side isn't easy, either. The real world constantly calls out to you, so your concentration is often split between this side and that. A momentary lack of caution can get you killed in our world. In the Beyond, the old saying that there are fates worse than death is more than just a saying, it's a reality to live and die by.

A mechanical sound vibrated through the aircraft's frame, announcing the lowering of the landing gear, and bringing Cade's attention back to the situation at hand. He replaced his sword in its case and sealed it up before replacing the case on the seat beside him. Unbuckling his seatbelt, he moved forward into the main cabin.

His men looked up expectantly when he entered.

"Ten minutes to go," Cade told them. "Get those weapons secured and sealed away. Once we're on the ground, Billings and I will unload the gear while Jonesy goes for the rental car. I want us loaded and on our way to the safe house in less than thirty minutes. If we get lucky, maybe we'll pick up Bishop's trail from there. Any questions?"

Both men shook their heads.

"Good. If everything goes smoothly, we'll be back at the commanderie by this time tomorrow."

Leaving his men to their tasks, Cade went forward to talk with the pilot and see what arrangements had been made for their landing.

* * *

Cade waited with Billings at the foot of the aircraft stairs while Jones went to get the rental car. While they waited, they helped the pilot unload the four larges cases of equipment from the cargo area of the plane. Each case was locked tightly and was sealed with the emblem of the Holy See, making them the sovereign territory of the Vatican itself, off limits to all but their intended recipients. It was the same type of diplomatic protection afforded to the staff members of a foreign nation's embassy and it allowed the Order to move cargo of all types, including firearms, explosives, and supernatural artifacts, about the country with no resistance from the authorities. If the authorities couldn't see what was in the box, they certainly couldn't prevent it from arriving at its destination.

Jones pulled up next to the aircraft behind the wheel of a black Ford Explorer. Cade and Billings quickly loaded the gear into the rear of the vehicle before climbing inside. A few moments later the three of them were speeding out of the airport gate.

Not knowing what happened to Bishop, Cade had no choice but to assume the safe house was compromised. Instead of going there as was originally planned, Cade had Jones drive around for a while until they found a run-down Holiday Inn on the outskirts of town. Cade went inside and got them three adjacent rooms on the ground floor in the back of the hotel, where their comings and goings would be mainly unobserved. Jones parked the truck in front of the door to the center room and they made short work of unloading the equipment.

Ten minutes later they met in Cade's room. After a brief discussion, it was decided that they would go to the safe house first, in the hopes that Bishop might simply be injured and unable to make contact. If he was not there, they would do a thorough search of the premises in case he had left a message or some other clue as to his whereabouts. If, after that, they still came up empty handed, they would then try to make contact with the church pastor who had first requested assistance. All three of them agreed that the pastor himself might be compromised, or worse, in on the problem from the beginning, so that any trip to the church would be treated as a journey into hostile territory. They would secure the premises first and ask their questions later.

Just after sunset, the three of them suited up. Each team member pulled on a set of white ceramic body armor that had been blessed by the Holy Father himself and displayed the red cross of the Templars prominently across the chest. Jumpsuits of black flame retardant material went over these. In a shoulder holster, each man carried a standard issue HK Mark 23 .45 caliber handgun, complete with a 12 round magazine, a flash suppressor, and laser-targeting device. A combat knife was either affixed to their belts or in a calf sheath on the outside of their boots. Two spare magazines were affixed with Velcro to their left wrists. Their swords, held in tear-resistant nylon sheaths, were slung across their backs, the hilt of the weapon extending just beyond the right shoulder for easy access in the heat of combat. Lightweight Kevlar tactical helmets with built in communications gear was worn on their heads.

In addition to the pistol, each man carried his choice of personal weapons. For Billings, it was a Mossberg 590 12 gauge combat shotgun. He was the team demolitions expert, so he also carried an assortment of plastic explosives and detonators in the chest webbing he wore over his armor. Jones carried an HK MP5 compact submachine gun, though on occasion he would swap that for a Barrett Light .50 caliber sniper rifle if the situation demanded it. Bishop had been an expert with all kinds of throwing knives. Cade was the only one who didn't carry anything in addition to his standard pistol.

His other, more esoteric abilities were all that he needed.

When they were ready, they left the hotel behind and climbed into their vehicle.

* * *

The safe house was located in a quiet, residential neighborhood on the south side of town. A thick stretch of woods occupied the right side of the street, while several older homes occupied the left. Cade had Jones drive down the street slowly, occasionally using his high beams to illuminate the house numbers painted on the sides of the mailboxes before moving on. To the casual observer, it would look as if the men in the car were looking for a particular address. In reality, Cade and Billings were using the time to study the target property, noting entry and egress routes and watching for motion behind the darkened windows that faced out onto the street.

After passing the house once and not finding anything obviously amiss, Cade had Jones drive around the block and pull over to the side of the road in the shadows beneath a stretch of trees, where Cade and Billings slipped out of the vehicle.

The night was dark, the sky above covered with a thick curtain of heavy storm clouds and with the rise of the moon still a half hour away, helping them in their effort to remain concealed. Keeping to the shadows, the two men made their way back down the block until they were hidden in the woods directly opposite the front door of the safe house. Cade clicked his mike twice, giving the signal that they were in position. A moment later Jones came back down the street in the Explorer and parked along the curb in front of the house. He flipped on the interior light and pretended to study a map.

His companions watched the house carefully, looking for any reaction to Jones' presence, but none came.

So far, so good.

Cade clicked his mike again.

Upon receiving the signal, Jones turned off the interior light and exited the vehicle, the map held in his left hand, leaving his right hand, his weapon hand, free. Jones walked up the front walk and rang the doorbell. The plan called for him to ask for directions to the airport if someone answered the door, while Cade and Billings covered him from the street. If no one answered, Jones would signal to the others and they would advance on the house themselves, at which point they would enter the home with the key Bishop had previously sent to them.

Cade watched tensely as Jones headed up the walk. This was the dangerous part of the plan; if Jones was attacked and dragged inside the house before the others could get to him, he would be on his own with his companions locked outside, unable to help.

Jones waited a moment after ringing the bell and then, after receiving no answer, rang it again. When it went unanswered the second time, he stepped off the front steps, checked the street one time to be certain no one was watching, and then walked around the side of the house, headed for the rear.

Cade and Billings crossed the street and found him waiting at the back door of the house, key in hand. The two men moved into position and Cade signaled for Jones to go ahead and open the door.

Inside, the house was dark. Using hand signals again, Cade indicated they were to do a search. The three of them fanned out and swept through the small dwelling with the aid of their flashlights, but didn't find Bishop. The refrigerator and shelves were stocked with food and several city maps were on the coffee table in the living room next to the briefcase containing Bishop's communications equipment, evidence that he had been here, but that was all.

There were no clues as to what had happened to him.

Or where he was now.

They were going to have to check out the church.

* * *

The St. Margaret Catholic Church occupied a small, half-forgotten lot sandwiched between two abandoned tenements. It was made of brick that had long lost its newness, coated as it was by the dust and grime of the city. A small, squat rectory was attached to it by a short covered walkway. A broken-down chain link fence surrounded the property. Here and there small piles of wind-blown trash could be seen trapped up against the fence in the light of the now risen

215

moon.

Cade parked the Explorer along the curb in front of the grounds and the three of them got out. The streets were quiet, hushed even, as if the buildings around them were holding their breath, waiting to see what these intruders would do in their domain. Cade could feel the electrical tension that comes from being watched, but couldn't identify were the feeling was coming from.

They pushed open the gate and made their way over to the church entrance. Once they drew close, they were able to see that the heavy, oak doors of the sanctuary were left partially open. Considering the neighborhood, it was a clear sign that all was not right here.

They entered the church like it was hostile territory.

Billings shoved open the door and let his companions slip inside before taking up a position behind them. Stretching out before them was a large central aisle that extended to the altar fifty feet ahead and divided two sets of pews into equal parts, with aisles stretching down the outside of each section against the walls. On either side of the altar, two small wings formed the horizontal axis of the cross and stretched out of sight. The building was shaped like a cross and the team had entered at its base. The interior was semi-dark, lit only by the soft breath of moonlight that were streaming in through the four windows that were evenly spaced along the wall. The red beams of their laser sights danced about in the semi-darkness like the lights at a rock concert before swiftly coming to rest on the body that had been left laying across the altar at the front of the church.

Making certain that the building was clear was the first priority, however, and so the body would have to wait. Without a word, Billings moved to the left-hand aisle and Jonesy moved to the right. Cade waited until they were in position and then gave the hand signal for them to advance simultaneously toward the altar. This would allow them to provide fire support to each other while at the same time make use of the wooden pews as cover should it prove necessary.

They made it to the foot of the altar without incident. Billings and Jonesy circled the outer wings without finding anything out of the ordinary before rejoining Cade at the apex of the central aisle. Only at that point, once they were satisfied that they were alone, did the three of them advance on the body laying on the altar.

The man was dressed in the black casual clothing and white clerical collar of a Catholic priest. One leg was draped over the front of the altar, the other hung over the side, bent at the knee. The priest's hands were arranged on his chest with an antique wooden crucifix clasped upright between them.

If it hadn't been for the condition of his skin and face, you might have almost been able to believe he was sleeping, Cade thought idly. Of course there was no way you'd ever make that mistake once you'd gotten a close look at what had been done to him.

Had the man spent the last two hundred years baking in the Arizona deserts, he couldn't have looked any more drained of substance than he did now. The skin of his face was stretched tightly over his skull, as if the flesh beneath had been sucked away, leaving just the thinnest barrier between the air and bone. A quick glance down at the man's hands let Cade know the condition extended there as well and from that Cade guessed that it extended across his entire body. The man's eyes were gone, the empty sockets staring at the ceiling far above. From the position of the man's jaw, it looked like his mouth was frozen open in a silent scream, but the several strips of grey duct tape that were wrapped around his lower face made it difficult to tell for certain.

Jonesy was the first to speak.

"Vamps!" he cried, using the common name for

something that was in truth far more vicious than the blood-sucking monsters immortalized by Bram Stoker's Dracula. "Why the hell did it have to be vamps? I hate vamps!"

"Ch'iang shih," Cade corrected softly, using the proper name for the Chinese creatures, but he agreed with the general sentiment. If the blood cult they had supposedly been called in to investigate actually turned out to be a pack of Ch'iang Shih, he and his team were in for a nasty fight in the not so distant future.

While his team had never had to face this particular supernatural menace, he had been thoroughly briefed in the past. He did his best now to recall what he had been told.

Also known as the Gui Ren, or Demon People, they were some of the fiercest supernatural creatures ever encountered by the Templars. They had their origins in China and were routinely seen throughout Central and Southeast Asia, but they had rarely been encountered here in the States. According to Asian tradition, they are formed when an individual has an outstanding karmic debt that must be paid, a debt so enormous that it prevents the soul from moving onward through the Great Cycle and forces the body to rise again from death. More often than not, the higher, rational aspect of the soul, the Hun, becomes dormant, leaving the P'o, or the lower, bestial aspect of the soul, in control of the resurrected creature. Neither truly living nor dead, the Ch'iang shih are creatures without Chi, the essence of life, and therefore must constantly steal it from the living in order to sustain their existence while they seek to redeem their debt and rejoin the Great Cycle.

The drained, lifeless husk that is left behind after such a theft had become the Ch'iang shih's signature the world over. No other creature left such evidence of its passing in their wake, making them easily identifiable for hunters like Cade's team.

Identifying them was the easy part, however.

Finding and defeating them was another matter entirely.

Leaving Jones on guard, Billings and Cade did a more thorough search of the church, looking for anything that might indicate what had happened to the missing advance team, Bishop, or the church staff.

After an hour of searching, they came up empty-handed.

Which left the body itself and the need for more drastic measures.

With Billings and Jonesy on guard around him, Cade bent over and examined the corpse on the altar before him. The priest had clearly been middle-aged; his thinning gray hair and liver spotted skin gave evidence to that. A close look at the shrunken flesh of the right side of his face revealed a large bruise. The black cloth of his shirt and pants was ripped and tattered, mainly about the arms and lower legs.

Cade removed his gloves and placed them in his pocket. He checked to be certain his men had control of the situation, receiving a nod of confirmation from each of them, and then turned back to face the altar.

It was time to go to work.

There was no way Cade was going to use his Talent on the body itself. The priest had no doubt suffered greatly at the hands of the Ch'iang shih and Cade had no desire to relive any of that experience. Instead, he was going to take a reading from the surface of the altar itself, in the hopes that it would filter enough of the horror out of the encounter to allow him to understand just what had happened here.

Cade took a deep breath, mentally preparing himself for the task ahead. Using his Talent was never easy. It physically drained him of energy at an alarming rate, leaving him weak and disoriented for several long minutes afterward. The need to constantly guard against being overwhelmed by another's thoughts and emotions made it mentally demanding as well. Staying immersed too long in the flow made it difficult for him to regain his own identity, and though he had never tested the theory for obvious reasons, Cade believed that his physical form could be affected by what he was seeing through his Gift as well.

When he was ready, he reached out and laid his palms flat on the altar's surface.

Hands.

Hands carrying him, perversely caressing him, while others seize hold of his arms and legs and haul him bodily into the air.

Our Father, who art in heaven…

Movement, the whisper of bodies parting to get out of the way, a low murmuring of anticipation filling the air.

He's dropped onto a hard surface (the altar?) and his limbs are pulled out and away from his body, his captors' claws clicking against each other as they expose the skin of his wrists and legs.

Hail Mary full of grace, the Lord is with thee…

The cloying scent of rancid meat hangs in the air.

More hands seize his face, forcing his jaws open, the taste of something metallic as an object is shoved into his mouth while gnarled fingers snatch at his tongue.

Pain, terrible pain, as his blood flows freely, filling his mouth…

With a sudden cry Cade snatched his hands away from the altar top, the coppery taste of phantom blood sharp in his mouth. He turned his head and spat on the carpet to clear it.

When he looked up, Billings and Jones were looking at him expectantly.

"Vamps, all right," he told them, as he pulled his gloves back on. "A lot of them. And they left us a calling card." Cade reached out, held the corpse across the forehead with one hand and, with the other, yanked the pieces of duct tape off the corpse's mouth. The man's mouth remained locked open, so Cade peered inside and then reached in with two fingers to draw something out.

Cade held the object out for the other men to see.

It was a gold signet ring set with a ruby stone in the shape of a cross. It was identical to the ring that each team member wore, the same rings they were given on the night of their initiation into the Order. On the reverse side, directly beneath the stone, were the initials JKB.

"Bishop's ring," Cade said.

Billings swore.

Cade handed the ring to him, removed the glove on his right hand and then extended that hand back toward his teammate again.

"You sure you want to do that, boss?" Billings asked.

Cade nodded. "We don't have any other choice. They obviously want us to know that they have Bishop. The ring might be able to tell us if he is still alive, and if he is, where they might be keeping him."

Shaking his head in resignation, Billings gently dropped the ring into his teammate's open palm.

This time, Cade's Talent was a bit more generous.

Pain.

A deep, throbbing pain that pulsed in his left side, right where the vamps had slashed him with his own weapon. He knew he was still bleeding; the wet trickle that marched down his ribcage and under the waistband of his pants clearly told that story. His right wrist hurt as well, where two of the vamps had locked their vile mouths on his flesh before their leader had stopped them from draining him dry.

He was bone-weary, evidence that the two junior vamps had taken a fair amount of life force from him before the stronger one had intervened. Still, he was alive, and as long as he was had no doubt that his team would make an effort to rescue him.

Which meant he had to stay that way until they could get to him.

He knew he was in the warehouse district; he'd seen as much when they'd grabbed him at the church. While he'd been unable to determine the exact location of the building to which they had brought him, he had been able to catch a glimpse of the sign out front. "Markhams Slaugh..." was all he'd been able to see before they'd dragged him inside.

A quick search of a phone book was all they needed after that.

Markhams Slaughterhouse was located on South 52nd Avenue, near the intersection with Grand. Billings went out to the car and returned with his computer equipment. Using coordinates from a GPS device and some mapping software, he quickly pinpointed the exact location of the warehouse in relation to their current position. It was less than fifteen minutes away.

Neither Jones nor Billings were surprised when Cade suggested they head directly for the warehouse. The fact that Cade had "read" anything at all off of Bishop's ring meant that he had been wearing it sometime in the last forty-eight hours, for this was how long any given object could retain the psychic impressions imprinted on it. While forty-eight hours was a long time to be trapped in the hands of the Ch'iang shih, the possibility remained that their teammate was still alive.

They couldn't take the chance and leave him to the vamps mercy.

They had to try to get him out, as he had known they would.

Cade had no intention of going into a nest of vamps without someone knowing what had happened to them, however. Using Bishop's computer equipment, he sent a coded email directly to the Preceptor, informing him of everything that had occurred so far and letting him know what they planned to do next. If they did not return, at least the Order would have the information amassed to date and could plan an appropriate response to the situation.

Cade had every intention of surviving, but it never hurt to be prepared.

* * *

The warehouse seemed to be deserted.

Cade and his fellow knights stood just inside the entrance, their weapons held ready for use. The cavernous interior of the warehouse stretched away before them, illuminated by a series of old arc lights strung across the ceiling. A few piles of discarded crates and equipment lay in the far corners of the room.

One of the lights shone down directly on the bruised and bloody face of a man whose slumped body was tied to a support pole halfway across the room.

Bishop.

Cade looked carefully around the interior of the warehouse, searching for any sign of movement either in the shadows that lined the walls or among the rafters and catwalks that stretched high overhead.

Nothing moved.

With Jones and Billings ready to provide covering fire, the three men cautiously made their way across to their fallen companion. While the others stood guard, Cade knelt down beside the pole and gently touched Bishop's face. The man's skin was icy cold.

They had arrived too late.

Keeping one arm around his teammate's body, Cade leaned around the back of the pole and cut through the cords that bound the body to it. With its support suddenly released, Bishop's corpse slumped against him. Cade gently eased Bishop to the floor.

Just to be certain, Cade leaned in close and listened for a heartbeat.

Only silence was returned.

Cade raised his head and looked down at his teammates' dead face, burning it into his memory, another victim he would now have to avenge.

Bishop's eyes suddenly popped open.

His gaze met Cade's confused one and a wicked grin scurried across his lips.

"Sorry, boss," he said, without a touch of remorse, and his hand whipped around toward his former leader, a razor sharp set of talons extending from his fingertips and seeking Cade's face.

At that exact moment, most likely the result of some

undisclosed prearranged signal, the rafters suddenly vomited a scurrying, seething horde of ravenous creatures that descended the walls with spider-like grace and came rushing across the warehouse floor toward Jones and Billings.

"It's a trap!" Cade yelled, throwing himself away from Bishop and out of reach of those deadly claws.

His warning was unnecessary, for Jones had already caught sight of the swarming horde. Without hesitation the Templar opened fire with his MP 5, pouring 800 rounds per minute into his foes. Billings followed suit, his combat Mossberg booming in the echoing confines of the warehouse in sharp contrast to the buzz of Jones' weapon.

Cade rolled away from his opponent and came up in a crouch, his pistol held securely in his right hand. He could see that Bishop had already risen to his feet and was snarling in rage at having missed his target.

As his enemy came charging toward him, Cade triggered his Sight.

In the Beyond, the warehouse was a darker, more ominous place, full of the shadows of pain and suffering caused by the slave-driving mentality of the owners that had driven its workers for so long. Here, the true nature of the team's attackers also revealed themselves, as their thirst for the team's life force was an almost physical presence pulsing out from them in waves of need and desire.

There was no mistaking the fact that the warehouse was full of very hungry Ch'iang shih.

Nor was there any doubt as to what had happened to Bishop.

Cade calmly noted his former teammates altered condition - his savage hunger, his unholy rage, and his dual existence in both the real world and in the Beyond – and then he was out of time. As his former teammate rushed in to savage him, Cade fired point blank into the man's face.

Bishop went down, hard, with a bullet hole just beneath his right eye.

In the fifteen seconds it had taken Cade to dispense with Bishop, Jones and Billings had cut down the first wave of charging vamps with their blistering firepower. The staccato stutter of Jones' weapon was interspersed with the booming tones of Billings', but still more of the creatures swarmed off the rafters high above and charged toward them. Worse yet, many of those that had gone down were now starting to get back up.

While Bram Stokers' fictitious creations had access to regenerative powers, the Ch'iang shih did not. Such powers were not really necessary, for their bodies were really nothing more than animated corpses given new life by the hunger and desire of their souls. As such, bullets, even high powered ones from a weapon like Jones' MP5, did little to actually stop them. Those Ch'iang shih who had gone down under the Templars' onslaught did so more from the sheer velocity of the striking ammunition than from any physical harm the bullet might have caused them. A bullet hole to the chest was of little concern for an undead creature and was nothing more than a few moments worth of inconvenience as they were knocked off their feet.

Cade quickly took in the situation. "Go for their legs, " he yelled to the others. When it appeared they did not hear him, he stepped up between them and directed his own fire at his chosen targets. It only took a moment before his companions caught on to what he was doing and followed suit.

The warehouse was filled with a cacophony of sound; the bark of Cade's handgun, the booming sound of Billing's shotgun, the shrieks and wails of the Ch'iang shih as they were cut down in mid-step by the precision shots of the knights. Conversation between Cade and his men was next to hopeless. It was only the steady training and discipline that Cade enforced on his team that allowed them to operate as a cohesive unit even in the face of such an overwhelming assault. As one man's weapon would run dry, the others would step up their volume of firepower, allowing him to reload and rejoin the fray.

Eventually their supply of ammunition began to dwindle and then disappeared altogether.

As one, the knights dropped their weapons and drew their swords, turning to stand back to back in one of the oldest defensive positions known to man. The vamps closed in, anticipating an easier time of things now, only to discover that the knights' still had plenty of bite left.

Soon the floor around the knights' feet was littered knee high with vamp bodies.

In the face of the savagery of the knights' defense, the vamps retreated to the darkness among the machinery in the far corner of the warehouse. Those wounded that could still walk followed suit, while still others, their shattered legs and kneecaps now useless, used their arms to drag themselves along the floor in pursuit.

The three knights took a moment to catch their breath.

"Bishop's gone," Jones said matter-of-factly as he kicked a still twitching forearm away from his boots.

Having already written off his former teammate, Cade glanced over to his right where he had left Bishop's body before joining the fray. That section of floor space was empty. Jones was right; Bishop was gone. But had he gotten up of his own accord or been dragged away by his comrades?

Before Cade could ponder the question further, the vamps attacked again.

This time they came drifting in and out of the Beyond, so that Jones and Billings were mostly unable to see them coming. Nothing more than an occasional whisper of movement could be seen as the vamps streaked in toward them at inhuman speed, flickers of motion they caught out of the corner of their eyes and desperately tried to counter.

The vamps had not counted on the changes the Adversary had wrought in Cade, however.

Cade's Sight showed the vamps clearly, even when they stepped fully across the barrier into the Beyond where they believed they were safe. As the vamps closed in, Cade kept up a constant stream of information, calling out commands to his men, telling them where and when to strike. He danced in and out of the battle like a whirling dervish, his sword flashing in the light, striking his foes with savage grace.

But his fierceness was not enough. By the time the vamps retreated for a second time, all three of the knights were bleeding from multiple wounds and their energy was getting dangerously low. They would not be able to hold the vamps off for much longer.

Across the floor the knights could see the vamps gathering together again, preparing for another assault. They must have abandoned their previous tactic, for they were clearly visible to all three of the Templars.

Grimly, the knights waited for the onslaught.

Much to their surprise, it did not come.

At least, not yet.

The milling group of Ch'iang shih suddenly parted ranks and an Oriental woman of extreme beauty stepped to the front of the group. She was dressed in a traditional Chinese gown of flowing green silk that matched the emerald hue of her eyes. Her midnight black hair flowed loosely across her shoulders and down her back where it hung almost to the floor behind her. One hand held a Chinese war fan across her upper face and even from across the warehouse Cade could see the gold lacquer that covered nails several inches in length.

Behind her, like a faithful servant, came Bishop.

His face bore the evidence of Cade's marksmanship; a large swatch of flesh and bone had been torn away just below his right eye. It did nothing to dim the unholy light in his eyes, however, and only served to increase the hatred in his heart for the living knights standing before him.

The woman spoke up in a voice like a softly lilting breeze. "Why have you come here?" she asked.

Cade ignored the question and gave the standard Templar response when encountering a supernatural being. "Your kind is not welcome in this place and is an insult to the Lord. Renounce your evil ways and let the Order send you to the rest you deserve."

In a voice pitched so low that only his fellow knights could hear him, Jones said, "You get better at that line all the time, boss."

Billings laughed. "You sure have a way with women," the knight joked.

Cade ignored them, though their quiet humor in the face of almost certain death made him proud. He had trained them well. He did not expect the Ch'iang shih princess to accept his offer, but the demands of the Code required that he offer such succor to any supernatural creature he encountered. It was a throwback to the days before the Inquisition, when the Order would offer surrender to all their foes before resorting to force. Personally, he thought it to be complete foolishness, but he had taken a vow to follow the Code and where it did not conflict with his own personal mission of vengeance he strove to do so.

At this point it served to gain him a few more precious seconds to try and figure a way out of their current predicament.

Cade had no doubt that many a foolish young man had fallen for the woman's innocent façade but the sudden guttural bark of laughter that escaped from her near perfect lips revealed the animal hidden beneath that glamorous form. Her razor sharp teeth flashed into a smile.

"You are as arrogant as the commander of the last team that invaded my territory." Indicating Bishop with a disdainful wave of her hand, she said, "Like this one here, I will make you into my personal lap dog for your audacity."

Cade smiled and all the hatred he'd harbored for years against the agents of the darkness spilled forth from his gaze. Raising his weapon in front of him, he said, "I think you'll find me more difficult prey than my lieutenant. But feel free to give it your best shot. At the very least, it should make for an exciting end to a fun evening."

The Ch'iang shih leader snarled, spittle dropping from her lips. With a wave of her war fan she gave the signal for her troops to attack.

Cade and his men braced themselves for the onslaught, knowing that they had very little chance of surviving.

The Ch'iang shih dashed forward, their shrieks of rage filling the confines of the warehouse.

Before they had crossed even a quarter of the distance to their prey, however, the warehouse was suddenly filled with the booming thunder of several dozen firearms and the front ranks of the ravenous creatures were cut apart like confetti.

Cade glanced behind him, the direction from which the firepower was still continuing.

High above, on one of the catwalks that crisscrossed the building, stood a large group of local law enforcement officers, including what appeared to be members of the city's rapid response team. They lay down a blistering wave of covering fire over the heads of Cade's group as other members of their team began flinging hand grenades into the seething mass of oncoming vamps.

Pure chaos ensued.

Under such overwhelming firepower the Ch'iang shih stood very little chance of surviving. From his position on the opposite side of the warehouse, Cade watched the vamp leader scornfully turn her back on her followers and disappear back into the darkness.

With a last angry glance at his former leader, Bishop followed suit.

The knights and their unexpected allies made short work of the remaining vamps after that.

When it was over, the rescue squad commander, Special Agent Miles Covington of the FBI, walked over to where Cade knelt on the floor tending to an angry looking but otherwise shallow wound on Jones' back.

"Agent Williams?"

Cade turned, taking in the government hair cut and JC Penney suit the other man wore, as well as the manner in which he had been addressed and the grim, angry expression on the man's face. "Yes?" he answered cautiously, not quite knowing what to expect.

"Your boss got in touch with us about an hour ago. The next time the Customs Service intends to stage a hostile raid on a Triad smuggling ring in my city, I'd sure like to be notified beforehand, not in the midst of the raid. It's a good thing I decided to make sure you hadn't stumbled into something over your head or we'd be picking your bodies up off the floor instead of theirs. Are we clear, mister?"

Cade was too relieved to give the government agent any grief. He made the appropriate apologies and acted quite thankful for the assistance his team had received, which wasn't too difficult considering that was exactly how he honestly felt. Mollified, the FBI agent turned away to take command of the clean-up operation, leaving Cade to tend to his wounded teammates.

"She got away, boss," Billings said, through a wince of pain as Cade bandaged his broken ribs.

"Bishop, too," Jones added.

Cade nodded. "I know. We'll deal with them both at another time. For now, let's just get you two out of here and back to the commanderie. We'll debrief there."

Gathering their gear, the three men limped over to the warehouse entrance, now standing wide open to admit the many ambulances lined up outside ready to transport the bodily remains of the Ch'iang shih to the morgue, and left the warehouse behind. They slipped through the ever-increasing number of patrol cars and emergency vehicles that were rapidly filling the warehouse parking lot and crossed the street to where they had left their own vehicle in an adjacent lot.

After he'd gotten his men seated in the vehicle, Cade turned and gave the warehouse one last look.

He knew that it would not be the last time they would be hearing from the charismatic vamp leader or from the former Templar who now walked at her side. The Order had encountered another enemy today, one to add to the every-growing list of evils that would have to be dealt with before long.

But that could wait for another day.

For now, it was time to take his team home.

Twilight at The Cairo

Drew Williams

Ignoring the 12 MPH sign posted at The Cairo's entrance, Morgan Liddle sped up the gravel driveway past the blank marquee and into the drive-in movie theater's enormous parking lot. Spraying a cloud of dust and rock into the air, Morgan turned his rented Lexus off the driveway just as he passed the three-story movie screen that towered over the eastern end of the theater. For a moment, Morgan paused to look at the enormous blank screen softly lit in the pale moonlight, noticing that it looked like a giant sheet suspended in the black night. But his attention was directed elsewhere. At the opposite end of the parking lot was the projection booth, a squat, brick building just large enough to hold two men, a 70 millimeter projector, and a cooler of beer. A thin sliver of light spilled out of the small hole in the front of the blockhouse. Morgan looked away from the light, fixing his eyes on the ancient Ford pickup truck parked alongside the building's entrance. *Damn it*, Morgan cursed as he steered toward the rusty vehicle. *Damn you, Harry Stetz.*

Harry Stetz had been a pain in Morgan's ass since Morgan first started the process of buying The Cairo for Harley Kane of Kanemart. Harry Stetz had been managing The Cairo for forty of his sixty-three years, and he wasn't going to give up his debt-ridden drive-in without a fight. Harry swore that he would stop the sale of The Cairo, even threatening to shoot Morgan's ass full of buckshot if he stepped foot on the property. But after four weeks of hammering out details with The Cairo's creditors, Morgan had the deed to the drive-in, and Harley Kane had a clear path to build Kanemart number 76. But now Harry Stetz had returned to the property, and though Morgan didn't think the old man was serious about his threat to shoot him, Harry's presence made the lawyer nervous.

The Lexus came to rest just inches from the bumper of Harry Stetz's truck. "Stetz," Morgan shouted, angling his large frame out of the car. "Are you in there?" A few seconds passed before Harry Stetz appeared in the doorway. Stetz was a short man, razor thin with a slight stoop in his back. He wore a green ballcap that nearly swallowed his head, but his eyes, wide and intent, hinted at the fire still left in the old man's body. They were fixed on the burly attorney.

"Yes, Mr. Liddle. It's me."

Morgan shook his head when he saw The Cairo's ancient projectionist. "Damn it, Harry. You know you're not supposed to be here."

"I'm just getting some tools and things I left behind," Harry said. "I ain't gonna steal nothing, if that's what you're worried about." Turning sharply, Harry slipped back into the blockhouse.

Morgan hurried after him, but when he stepped into the blockhouse, the lawyer wasn't prepared for the stench that greeted him. Four decades worth of cigarette smoke and Harry's beer-farts had been burned into the fiber of the brick building. Morgan jammed his fist to his mouth and fought back the urge to gag. When the initial shock of the blockhouse funk dissipated, Morgan thrust his finger at the ring of keys suspended from a belt loop on Harry's stained trousers. "You were supposed to turn in all your keys last week at the closing, Harry. If I wanted to, I would be perfectly within my rights to call the police and have you arrested for trespassing."

Harry kept his back to Morgan. "Yeah, I guess you would," he said slowly, making no motion to remove the key ring from his belt loop. "You know all about what's legal and what isn't. That's how you were able to steal this place."

Morgan shook his head. "I didn't steal anything, Harry. I bought The Cairo."

"Not from me," Harry shot back.

"You didn't own it," Morgan replied. "The bank did."

236

Turning to face the lawyer, Harry wretched up a thick wad of phlegm from his chest. "The bank," he said, spitting the massive lugie at Morgan's feet. "That's what I think of your bank."

"It wasn't my bank," Morgan said, eyeing the round ball of snot. It splattered against the concrete floor at least six inches from Morgan's shoes, but that didn't stop the lawyer from taking a wary step backward. He was certain that Harry wasn't capable of acting on his threat of filling his ass up with buckshot, but Morgan wasn't so sure that the next of Harry's snot rockets wouldn't find its mark. "It was your bank, and you were about to default on the loan. Another two months and the bank would have foreclosed. So, by buying the loan now, Kanemart saved you a lot of grief and heartache. Besides, Kanemart Enterprises is going to bring a lot of jobs to the area. And that's going to give this town a fresh infusion of capital. Capital that this antiquated drive-in theater is not producing."

Harry eyed Morgan for a moment before plucking a bent cigarette out of the breast pocket of his filthy tee shirt. With a crooked smile, Harry lit the cigarette and tossed the match over his shoulder. "Cripes, Liddle. Can't you turn off the lawyer bullshit for a minute? I heard it all before." Harry sucked sharply on the cigarette, holding the smoke deep within his lungs. When he finally exhaled, he shot the stream of smoke in Morgan's direction. "And what do you mean by antiquated? The Cairo has kept up with the times."

Morgan shrugged. "Face it, Harry. With videos and thirty screen multiplexes, the drive-in theater is a dinosaur that just takes up valuable commercial real estate. It's a thing of the past, and you just have to accept that."

Harry shook his head from side to side. "You don't know what you're talking about, Liddle. You have no idea what kind of place The Cairo is, or what it means to the folks in this town."

For this first time since he entered the blockhouse, Morgan relaxed his stiff posture. "That's not really true. I do know what The Cairo means to the people around here. My parents were from town, but they moved to Atlanta before I was born. When I was growing up, they used to tell me stories about The Cairo all the time."

Harry gave Morgan a puzzled look. "Your parents used to come to The Cairo?"

Morgan nodded. "Uh, huh. Thirty years ago. They told me that this was their favorite place to go when they were dating. In fact, if it wasn't for their stories, I would never have known that this property existed."

The irony of Morgan's last statement was not lost on the old projectionist. "Don't that beat all," he said. "Your folks tell you what a great place The Cairo is and you have to come up here and rip it down." Harry leaned his crooked back against the wall of the blockhouse and closed his eyes. For the past four months he had fought Kanemart's takeover of The Cairo with every ounce of energy he possessed, but now the fight was over, and he had lost. He sniffed loudly, and for a second, Morgan thought Harry was going to send another lugie his way. Instead, the older man took another slow drag on his cigarette and opened his eyes. "So what did your parents say about the place?"

Morgan allowed himself a small laugh. "Oh, that they came here with all their friends just about every Friday night. Lots of times they would drive up after high school dances and park in the back rows and drink beer. They especially liked it when you showed the old horror movies from the fifties."

Harry chuckled. "Yeah, the kids always liked those. Sometimes I'd dress up as a vampire or the mummy and go around scaring the shit out them. You know, banging on their car windows and whooping around." Harry brushed his hand across his forehead as he remembered the days when he could still run around the parking lot. "That was a lot of fun."

"My mother said her favorite was *I Was a Teenage Werewolf.*"

Harry's eyes widened. "Oh yeah. I used to show that every summer in the 70's. That was always one of my favorites too. Michael Landon chasing them teeny boppers through the gym. Whenever I showed that, I would borrow some kid's varsity jacket and put on this old werewolf mask and jump on people's cars." Harry slapped at his thigh and started to laugh. "Boy, that used to scare the shit out of the kids back then." After a few seconds the laughter trailed off, and Harry wiped at his brow again. This time the weathered hand lingering a long few seconds at the corner of his eye.

"Ah hell, Mr. Liddle. I got nothing against you doing your job. The Cairo's been on shaky ground for a while now, and you're a smart businessman. Heaven knows I ain't. And I guess I should be grateful. I ain't going to end up bankrupt now. But you got to reconsider putting up one of your Kanemarts here. It's just not right."

Morgan pursed his lips, but remained silent. Nothing Harry Stetz could say was going to stop the bulldozers from coming on Monday.

"I don't know how to explain it," Harry began. "But a drive-in theater ain't like other places, Mr. Liddle. Drive-ins are special, they got life and energy. Especially The Cairo." Harry paused and glanced out of the projection opening to scan the empty parking lot. "I've never told anybody this, but sometimes when it's a real dark night and the movie's rolling, I'll look at all the cars, and it's like the years have all come together into one. Behind the minivans and Lexus's, I can see the shadows of older cars. You know, the kinds with the big fins and white-wall tires. Thunderbirds and Woodies. And these old V.W. microbuses, the kind the hippies all drove. I can see their shadows, Mr. Liddle. Just sitting out there like they never left."

"And sometimes when I'm showing one of the old movies, and the night's just right, all those cars and shadows come together. Three and four of them all sort of melt into one another like they're parked on the same spot, only at different times. Sounds crazy, doesn't it?"

It did sound crazy to Morgan, but the lawyer remained silent.

"It's like time don't matter at The Cairo," Harry said. "Like the past and the present are happening at the same time. All at once. And it's not just the cars. Sometimes I see people walking by. Couples and families laughing carrying on, only they shouldn't be out there. Not now, anyway. It's the way they're dressed, and how they look. I know they belong in the past. But they're still out there." Harry pointed to the parking lot and shook his head. "It's like The Cairo is holding on to a part them, and I'm the only one who can see it."

"Next, you're going to tell me The Cairo is haunted," Morgan said humorlessly.

Harry shook his head. "No, it ain't that. The Cairo don't have no ghosts. At least not like the kind in the movies I show. No, The Cairo's got something else. It's got folks' memories."

"I don't follow you."

"It's like this. People have been coming to The Cairo and making memories for forty years. Real important memories," Harry said. "The kind that are important enough that they tell their kids. And not too many places can say that, Mr. Liddle. Especially not a Kanemart."

Morgan snorted, peeved by the obvious reference to his parents. "And I'll bet most of those memories revolve around drinking and screwing."

Stetz didn't argue. "So? Kids drink and screw around at

drive-ins. What's so wrong about that? There's been a lot of folks who have met and fallen in love out there in that parking lot. But don't you see? That's the kind of stuff people remember all their lives, you know. Where they fell in love. Where the first did it."

Morgan rolled his eyes but Stetz continued.

"Mr. Liddle, people remember all the laughing and crying, and whatever that went on here. And in a way, The Cairo remembers it too. After forty years, I think The Cairo's been taking some of the memories folks have been making out there, and made them its own. And I don't think The Cairo's ready to give them up."

"Oh please." Morgan pushed his hands roughly into his jacket pockets. "I'm sorry, Mr. Stetz, but I really don't have time for this right now. So I'd appreciate it if you collected your tools and left."

Stetz nodded slowly, sadly, before turning to the tools left on the long counter that ran along the side of the projection booth. Morgan decided to wait outside. "Hurry it up, Harry," Morgan said.

As he left the blockhouse, Morgan's eyes widened as he looked out into the parking lot. "I'll be damned," he hissed. "Are you expecting somebody, Harry?" he called over his shoulder. "There's a car out here." Not waiting for a reply, Morgan stomped forward.

It was a faded green Dodge Dart, parked in the center of the otherwise empty parking lot. At first, Morgan thought it was unoccupied, but as he neared the car, Morgan saw two figures tussling in the back seat. *Son of a bitch!* he thought. *Some kids are making out.*

When he came within a dozen feet of the car, Morgan started shouting. "Hey you. Get the hell out of here, this is private property!"

When he got no response, Morgan came up along side the car and pounded on the trunk. "Get the hell out of here!" he shouted again. "Or I'm going to call the police."

Two shocked faces popped up and stared back through the windshield. For a second, they locked gazes with Morgan, then they ducked down, scrambling to slip back into their clothes. Morgan threw his hands up in disgust and wheeled about.

He stormed his way back up the gravel path intent on calling the cops from the cell phone in his car. Then he was going to tell Harry Stetz to get the hell off the property once and for all. The Cairo was dead; it would be a Kanemart within the year.

But as Morgan halved the distance between the Dodge Dart and his Lexus, a sharp beam of light split the darkness in front of him. Morgan stopped and stared at the white light, realizing after a few seconds, that it was coming from the projection booth. *That can't be*, he told himself. The 70 millimeter projector had been removed from the block house over a week ago. Slowly, Morgan turned and followed the path of the light from the projection room to the enormous screen.

On the thirty-foot screen, a youthful looking Michael Landon was turning into a werewolf.

His eyes fixed on the massive teenage werewolf, Morgan took two halting steps forward. *This isn't right. It can't be.*

Morgan's gaze fell from the screen to the parking lot. It was jammed with cars. Not the shells and shadows of vehicles like Stetz described, these were solid steel machines, all lined up in rows. Thunderbirds and Fieros. Hot-rods, Low Riders and just about everything else Detroit had to offer in the last four decades. And in those cars, the voices of hundreds of laughing teenagers spilled from their partially open windows.

Unable to comprehend what was happening, Morgan's gaze

242

fell on the Dodge Dart. The young couple he had interrupted was staring out of the rear window at him. The girl was buttoning the last button on her top.

But it was the scowl on the face of the young man that made Morgan freeze in terror. How many times in his thirty years had Morgan seen that scowl? How many times had it been directed at him?

A single word escaped Morgan's lips.

"Dad."

No sooner did the sound fall from his lips, a barrage of memories flooded Morgan's mind. Every story his parents had told him about The Cairo. Every story about their friends and the parties exploded in the recesses of his brain as if they were trying to get free. But behind the stories, another memory surfaced. An older memory of a story his parents never told him. It was his first memory, branded into his chromosomes and DNA at the first spark of life. And as it swam to the surface, Morgan understood for the first time the meaning behind the grins his parents wore whenever they talked about The Cairo.

His life had begun at The Cairo.

That's why the memory of the drive-in theater was always so important to Morgan's parents. Their only son had been conceived on a cool, September night while a teenage werewolf stalked the girl's locker room. He had been conceived in the back seat of a Dodge Dart that would later take a young married couple to Atlanta where Jack Liddle would start a job as a foreman in a tire plant, and Connie Liddle would raise their newborn son.

Morgan started for his parents' car but his legs refused to move. "Mom! Dad!" he cried, but the sound of his voice was swallowed by the night air as soon as it escaped his lips. "Please," he wailed, stretching out to the car. As his arms rose, they crossed the beam from the movie projector.

For a moment, Morgan could see millions of tiny red and white particles where his arm should have been floating in the light like dust before being were swept away by the beam. As he watched his arm dissolve, he heard Harry Stetz's words echo in his brain; *The Cairo ain't like other places.* Then Morgan felt a sharp tug as the rest of his body was pulled into the light. There was no pain as the light sliced through his body, breaking apart his flesh and scattering the collective protons and neutrons that comprised the substance of Morgan Liddle into the cool, night air. And before he melted into nothingness, the last spark of consciousness that remained of Morgan Liddle was propelled by the light onto an enormous field of white, and for a moment, it looked down from the top of The Cairo's massive screen at the hundreds of cars lined beneath him. It looked through the eyes of an eternally young werewolf. Then...

Then - 1970

Get the hell out of here or I'm going to call the police!

Jack Liddle snapped his neck up and glared at the man standing over his car. Connie also poked her head up to catch a glimpse of the man before he wheeled about and marched away. "Who the hell was that?" she asked.

Jack shook his head and cast a last angry look at the man. "Beats the hell out of me," he said. "But he's gone." Jack watched the figure stomp back toward the blockhouse before he turned in time to see Connie buttoning the last two buttons on her blouse. "Hey, what are you doing? We're not going to let some old hardass ruin our last night in town, are we?"

Connie laughed and brushed her finger across her husband's lower lip. "No, but I don't think we should be doing this now. Not here."

Jack looked surprised. "Why not? We've done it here lots of times before."

244

Connie reached beneath the back seat and pulled a warm beer out of a styrofoam cooler. "Yeah, but we weren't married then," she said, handing the beer to Jack.

"So," Jack said, taking the beer. "What's the difference?"

Connie giggled. "I don't know. It just doesn't seem like the right thing to do. Making out at the drive-in when we have our own apartment. And with that guy . . ." She shivered and cast a quick glance over her shoulder. "That just creeped me out."

Connie's husband of four weeks put his arm around her. "I guess you're right. We'll just go home and do it."

"Not until the movie's over," Connie said, lightly punching Jack in the arm. "You know this is one of my favorites."

Jack capitulated, content to sit in the backseat of his car and drink beer with his wife by his side. But instead of heading home at the conclusion of *I Was a Teenage Werewolf*, the Liddles stayed for the second feature, a b-movie called *Freaky Chickens*. When the two finally returned to their apartment, neither had the energy to fool around, so they took off their clothes and climbed into bed.

They snuggled for a while, and giggled.

And slept.

Now

"Memories," Harry Stetz said. He turned to his left but there was no one there. Confused, Harry removed his ballcap and wiped the back of his hand across his brow. He could have sworn someone had been in the booth with him. "Deja vu," he chuckled.

Popping the top off an Iron City beer, Harry scanned the

near-full lot. His mind did a quick calculation of the night's gate against what he owed the bank. If the concessions were good, he thought, and he dipped a bit into his saving, then he should have enough to fend off his creditors for another season.

Harry took a long swallow and closed his eyes. On the enormous screen, Michael Landon was changing into a werewolf. Even after thirty years, the kids still loved that movie. Harry smiled and listened to the voices of teenagers being carried in the night air. The sounds of laughter, passion, and a hundred different conversations melted together with the hum of the movie projector.

One more season of memories.

That's all Harry ever wanted.

The Urge

Joseph M. Nassise

Detective Simon Jackson awoke that morning with The Urge whispering darkly in his ears. It had been two months since the last time, five since the time before that, but in the last few days the voice had been getting stronger, more insistent, and he knew he couldn't hold out much longer.

It would have to be today, maybe tomorrow, at the latest.

He made a quick breakfast and dressed in his usual jacket and tie. Traffic was light; Jackson made it to the stationhouse a few moments before his tour of duty started and spent the extra time talking with some of the uniforms in the locker room before going upstairs to see what was on the day's agenda.

The Captain's briefing was short and sweet, which was a relief to all concerned. Jackson ended up with a stack of paperwork and a two day old mugging to investigate. Gino and Arthur got two grand larcenies and a suicide. Scofield still had the murder of the high school girl from last week. Marcy was out on vacation. Another typical day on the 8-4 shift in the 61st Precinct.

Jackson quickly grabbed a cup of coffee and returned to his desk. The paperwork was pure drudgery. It wasn't long before The Urge reared its ugly head.

It's time, you know.
Time to do another one.
You know you want to.
You'll like it, I promise.

He did his best to ignore it, knowing he couldn't escape it, but trying to keep it under control.

When he couldn't stand listening to it anymore, he went

out on the street and started hustling his contacts; doing what he could to track down anyone who might have seen the mugging. The trail was over 48 hours cold and in his business that meant it was as good as dead, but at least it gave him something to do and kept the voice in his head quiet for a couple of hours.

By lunch, however, The Urge was back, doing its best to force its way into his thoughts. He was sitting at a table in Mike's Diner, chewing resolutely on one of his famous rock-hard hamburgers, when he found himself staring at a couple of high school girls sitting a few tables away, the Urge whispering feverishly in the back of his mind.

The blonde one.
Yeah.
Her.
She's the one.
Remember how much fun we had last time?
You know you want to do it.
It's time, after all.

He must have been staring at them for some time, because he was getting funny looks not just from the girls but also from some of the other patrons. Even Mike was giving him a quizzical look from behind the bar.

He shook his head to clear it, paid hastily, and got the hell out of there before The Urge forced him to do something he didn't want to do.

He hadn't learned anything of any use while on the street and decided to head back over to the stationhouse to try and tackle the paperwork again. For the next few hours it became a battle of wills. The Urge would whisper in his ears, so he would slam it back down into the pit at the base of his skull. It would screech at him in a voice like nails on a chalkboard, so he would hum to himself to drown out its voice. But as the day wore on, he found himself listening to it for longer and longer each time it would make an attempt, until at last he couldn't stand it anymore.

"Okay, okay…" he said to it in a tired whisper. "You win. Tonight. We'll do another one tonight."

The yammering in the back of his skull quieted down as he gave in. That dark side of his subconscious, the one he called his Shadow, knew that he would keep his word; he always had before. Once he'd given in, his Shadow settled back down into the dark corner of his psyche and let him get on with the details.

He glanced around to find the squad room empty. It wasn't something that happened very often, so if he were going to do it, it would have to be now or never.

The filing cabinets were on the other side of the room, less than fifteen feet away from his desk. They were never kept locked, despite the Captain's repeat orders, which made what he had to do that much easier.

Five minutes later Jackson was on his way out the door, the files he needed tucked securely in his briefcase.

The rest of the afternoon seemed to limp past, now that he had made up his mind to make another retrieval. The last four had taught him how to go about doing things, so he didn't have many preparations to make. A simple check of his materials let him know that everything was ready. The stun gun was fully charged. The gag and the plastic restraints were in their usual places in the glove box. The hammer and butcher's knife were in the paper sack in the trunk. Jackson just needed to remember to add the fake ID and the badge. After that all that was left was to choose a target.

He moved into the living room and took a seat at his desk. Opening a drawer, Jackson pulled out a stack of files about potential targets and began to leaf through them. All of them were girls, between the ages of fifteen and twenty-one. Mostly brunettes, but there were a few blondes too.

Equal opportunity and all that, he thought to himself idly, remembering the girls in the restaurant earlier in the day.

He had his eye on one or two as potentials and set aside the others to make a decision between those few.

It took over an hour, but he finally had a target. Megan Jones. Blonde, as it turned out. Blue eyes. Small and petite, so there shouldn't be too much of a problem. She was from Riverside, about fifteen minutes outside the city, which was good because it was easily reachable yet reasonably secluded. Regular patrols would be at a minimum and he should be able to get in and out again without too much of a fuss.

Cleaning up the dinner dishes took another fifteen minutes, but after that he couldn't put things off any longer. The Urge was back now, raring to go, like a tiger suddenly faced with an open cage door and a big fat goat staked down before it. The Urge was getting out tonight, and it was gonna have some fun before the sun came up, that was for certain. He was just going along for the ride, like he always did.

Jackson went into the bedroom and dressed in the dark suit he had laid out for the occasion. His shoulder holster went on under the suit coat, and the badge went into the outside pocket for easy accessibility. A pair of well-shined shoes completed the disguise.

He grabbed the pilfered file off the table and headed out to the garage. Jackson had brought the Caprice home from work earlier and would be using it tonight just in case he was stopped. He might be able to talk his way out of trouble by pretending to be on official business and the car simply helped add to the disguise.

Picking up the skell was the part that he always worried about. If he was going to get caught, it would most likely be then. It was a question of choosing the right location, copping the right attitude, and getting out quickly enough before people started asking too many detailed questions.

For tonight's job he decided to head south, toward Lewiston. Jackson had been north for the last two and didn't want to show his face around there too soon. It was unlikely that anyone would remember him, but there was no sense in taking the chance. Halfway to Lewiston there was a county lockup. That was his destination.

The ride was quiet and uneventful. He used the time to try to plan his speech to the girl. Not that what he said mattered all the much; the shock of what they were going through was usually enough to keep anything he said from sinking in, but he always made the effort. He guessed it was just his way of trying to feel like he was doing the right thing.

Or maybe it was just to steady his nerves.

In any event, it helped to pass the time.

He reached the county lockup about an hour after he set out. He drove around back and parked by the rear security doors. He knew there were no windows back there and this would keep the chance of someone seeing something they shouldn't down to as bare a minimum as possible. Unless one of the officers inside decided to follow him out, Jackson knew he should be free and clear. He checked to be certain that he had the right set of credentials with him, placed the stun gun in the right-hand pocket of his suit, ready for easy access, picked up his clipboard, and got out of the car. Knowing the back door was locked, he walked around to the front and entered through the main entrance.

This facility was just like the hundred others he had been in, which was something Jackson had been counting on. A reception desk and a waiting room greeted him as he entered, and behind the desk was the duty sergeant. As Jackson approached, the sergeant put the magazine that he was reading down and cleared his throat, doing his best to look official. Jackson walked over and laid the federal badge he was carrying on the desktop in front of the sergeant.

"Michael Williams, FBI," he said. "I'm here to pick up," a quick glance at the clipboard and the official looking paperwork it carried . . . "Reggie Saunders." Before the other could say anything, Jackson passed him the paperwork.

Most government employees are cut from the same cloth. When faced with someone higher in authority, they will do what is asked of them with little or no resistance. Jackson was betting that since he looked official, carried official looking paperwork, and acted like he belonged, then the duty sergeant wouldn't be inclined to dig too deeply into the situation. As long as Jackson signed all the paperwork, the sergeant wouldn't bother calling his own superiors to verify Jackson's credentials or wonder why he had not heard of the transfer earlier in the day. It had worked the last two times Jackson had made retrieval and he was hoping it would work for him again tonight.

He wasn't disappointed. The duty sergeant looked over the paperwork, pulled some of his own out of a drawer, asked Jackson to sign here, here, and here, and then called down to lock-up to get the prisoner ready for transfer. Not a question asked. It couldn't have gone more perfectly if Jackson had scripted it.

Jackson stood in front of the desk talking sports with the sergeant until another officer came out with the prisoner in tow. Saunders was a typical low-life; all attitude and little intelligence. His rap sheet was as long as his arm and full of violence. He'd done time for armed robbery, rape, and was currently doing time for the murder of an elderly woman. He was at the county lockdown awaiting transportation in the morning to the new maximum-security facility in Sholton.

Unfortunately for him, he would never see the inside of another cell.

Saunders was dressed in the standard prison jumpsuit and the guard had him in cuffs but no shackles. That was fine with

Jackson. Saunders was a skinny little runt and Jackson
outweighed him by a good 75 pounds, so he didn't think the leg
shackles would be necessary. Saunders made a number of rude
comments as they turned him over, but Jackson just ignored
them. Taking him by the arm, Jackson led Saunders out the front
door and around the back to the car.

"Where we goin'?" Saunders asked, as Jackson opened the
rear door and bent Saunders' head to help him inside. Jackson
didn't answer him, just shut the door and opened his own. As he
climbed behind the wheel Saunders started in again. "I said,
'where we goin'? You deaf or somethin', cop?"

Again, the detective didn't answer.

At least not with words.

Instead, he calmly turned around and punched Saunders
straight in the mouth with a short, sharp backfist. Saunders'
head snapped backward and his nose suddenly gushed blood.

"Son-of-a-bitch!" he yelled, shaking his head to try and
keep the blood out of his mouth. "You stupid mothafuckin' son
of a..."

He never got any further. Jackson gave him his nicest,
biggest smile, drew his stun gun, and shocked the scumbag into
unconsciousness. *Nothing like sending 75,000 volts through a skell
to make your evening a nicer one*, he thought with a grin.

All it took was that little bit of violence to cause The Urge
to wake up and start jabbering again. This time Jackson didn't
mind. From here on out The Urge would be riding shotgun, if
not wholly in the driver's seat. And what it was saying sounded
like a whole lot of fun.

He giggled.

He couldn't help it.

Saunders twitched spasmodically for a moment or two even after Jackson removed the stun gun. He waited until Saunders had stopped moving, pulling on a pair of black leather gloves, then smacked him a few more times at The Urge's insistence. By the time Jackson turned back around and started the car, the rest of Saunders' face was a bloody mess to match his nose.

Heading back the way he had come, Jackson made it onto the highway and a few exits closer to Riverside before the scumbag woke up. He wasn't awake for more than a few minutes before he opened his mouth to speak.

Jackson caught his gaze in the rear view mirror before he could say anything, raised a finger, and shook it slowly back and forth.

"Uhhn uhhn uhn," he said.

The sight of his blood still drying on Jackson's gloves made Saunders' eyes widen in fear.

It also made him change his mind about protesting.

He stayed quiet for the rest of the ride.

It took a little over an hour to reach the Riverside city limits. Jackson cut west on Highway 202 and skirted the edge of town until he entered the warehouse district over by the train yards. This was a rough and tumble neighborhood, with more crack houses and street dealers per square city block than you would care to count. Life was cheap down here, often measured in hours instead of years.

His car was noticed within seconds of entering the area. The Caprice screamed cop, an effect he had counted on, and the street vermin disappeared into the darkness like quicksilver flowing downhill. Even the toughest street hood knows better than to call attention to himself by hanging around when the cops are on the prowl, which meant the chances of someone witnessing what

Jackson was about to do were slim to none.

It wasn't long before he reached his destination, a squat two-story warehouse set back from the road and surrounded by a chain-length fence. On either side similar buildings stretched, each abandoned and allowed to fall into a state of neglect years before. Jackson didn't need to check the address in the file on the seat beside him; a faded and torn yellow ribbon with the words "Police Line – Do Not Cross" emblazoned on it in thick black letters hung from either side of the open gate.

He pulled up against the gate and used the front of the car to nose it open far enough to drive on through, leaving it open behind him. Crossing the empty lot, he parked the car so it sat facing the gate, ready for a quick getaway should things go badly.

In the back seat, the skell's head was whipping back and forth as he frantically peered about at the surroundings. Jackson could guess what Saunders was thinking just from the expression on the man's face: *Psycho cop beats me up and drags me out to some deserted location. This is NOT good.*

Unluckily for Saunders, it was going to be a lot worse than he was currently imagining.

Jackson unlocked and opened the trunk. He opened the duffle bag and removed the cattle prod, making certain to keep it hidden below the level of the trunk and behind one leg so his passenger wouldn't see it. He left the trunk open, walked around to the back door, and unlocked it with his free hand.

Inside the car, Saunders squirmed in the seat, moving as far away from the door as he could get.

Jackson smiled at him.

Opening the door, he stuck the cattle prod against Saunders' body and set it off.

About ten times.

One after another.

Jackson was pretty sure his prisoner was unconscious by the third shock, but it never hurt to be certain.

The smell of burnt flesh wafted out of the car.

It was time to get to work.

It's all about balance, Jackson thought to himself. *Call it what you want: Ying and Yang, good and evil, the dark and the light. It's Nature's way to try to find a balance in all things. Usually there's not much we can do about it. People are born, people die, and that's all there is to life. But sometimes, when the conditions are right, we can change that balance. With a little nudge, we can tip it slightly to one side or the other. The opportunity only lasts for a few moments, and only a select few can make it work at all, but it can happen.*

When the conditions are right.

He left the skell lying unconscious in the back seat while he grabbed his equipment and carried it to the second floor.

The large open room was all but empty. When the body had been found three years ago, the police had followed standard procedure and removed everything that hadn't been bolted to the floor. In some cases, even things that had been bolted to the floor were removed, like the old boiler that contained the corpse.

The near emptiness didn't bother Jackson. He had brought along everything he needed.

The first thing he did was set up the small battery powered lantern he'd brought along. It cast a circle of light some ten feet in diameter, leaving most of the room shrouded in darkness. He slowly began to make an inspection of the floor, concentrating on the areas that were close to the vertical supports that honeycombed the warehouse floor.

It took some searching, but eventually he found the right location. No matter how hard they had tried the building's cleaning crew had been unable to completely eradicate the dark stains on the floor by one of the vertical columns.

Jackson placed the lantern on the floor beside the column. Next, he took the chains out of the bag and slung them over the rafter high overhead, then adjusted their height so that the meat hook on one end swung above the floor at chin level. He wrapped the other end around the column and secured the chain in place with a large padlock. He took out the electric drill, the hammer, and the combat knife. He put them in plain view close to the chain.

Trooping back down the stairs, he dragged the skell out of the back seat and dumped him on the ground beside the Caprice. Taking the leather straps out of the trunk, he used them to tightly secure Saunders' hands, feet, and knees before removing the handcuffs. Since Saunders was still unconscious, Jackson hauled him up and over one shoulder, then carried him up the stairs, where he slipped the meat hook through the straps securing Saunders' hands and left him dangling there with his feet scraping the floor. He took an extra moment to remove the man's shoes and socks.

Returning to the car, Jackson took the file off the front seat and locked everything up. Then he climbed back up the stairs.

The detective spent the time while waiting for Saunders to wake up going through the file. He paid particular attention to the crime scene photos and the autopsy report. He knew the suffering and pain had to be just right, the fear escalated to precisely the same level, or it would not work. He had learned that the hard way with the second retrieval he'd done and he still regretted the waste of a good subject with nothing in return. He was determined to do it right this time.

The Urge began whispering in the semi-darkness.

Use the hammer.
You know you want to.
Come on, it'll be fun.

"Not just yet," Jackson answered back firmly, knowing that the hammer was out of sequence. Using it when it wasn't called for would prevent any possibility of retrieval.

Which was, of course, just what the Urge wanted.

Jackson knew that he had reached the most critical juncture of the entire operation and he would have to be careful moving forward. He needed to guard against the Urge's excesses while at the same time use it to generate the pain and suffering required for what he needed to do.

He returned to where he had left the file and began to work through it, paying particular attention to the autopsy findings. He had most of it memorized from his research earlier in the afternoon, but wanted to be certain he had the sequence just right before he started.

He just hoped the coroner had been correct in his findings.

Memories of the time the coroner had been wrong stirred sluggishly in the depths of his mind, but the Urge's eager voice quickly dismissed them.

The knife.
Start with the knife.

This time, Jackson complied.

Turning back to his captive, he found Saunders watching him. The sweat was already pouring off his face and the stink of urine in the air told the detective all he needed to know about the man's mental state.

"Hi," Jackson said, brightly.

Saunders watched him warily, but still didn't say anything.

"Any idea why you're here?" Jackson asked.

Ignoring Jackson's question, Saunders said, "You can't do this. I got rights. This is police brutality." He jerked his arms and legs, sending his body bouncing about on the chains as he struggled to get free.

While Saunders struggled Jackson picked up the knife, stepped closer, then very casually slashed him across the chest through the prison uniform he wore.

"Jesus Christ!" Saunders swore. "You can't do this!"

Jackson laughed. "Yes I can. And I will," he said. "We're not even close to being done yet. Now you have five seconds to answer my question, or I'll cut you again."

"I don't know," Saunders replied.

"Then let me explain. Three years ago, a young girl was murdered in this room." Jackson kept his voice pitched low, forcing his prisoner to listen closely to what was being said. "She was raped, tortured, and murdered. And, as far as the coroner could make out, not in that order."

Saunders had stopped watching Jackson's face; his entire being seemed focused on the large knife that the detective was holding loosely in one hand.

"The girl, Megan Jones, was only fifteen. A young, innocent victim. Judging from the police file, the pain and fear she felt before dying must have been tremendous."

Saunders watched the knife as it turned over and over again in the palm of Jackson's hand, the light glinting off the blade in rhythmic cadences.

"The perpetrator, whomever it was, started with the girl's feet."

Here it comessssssssssssss, whispered the Urge in anticipation.

Without another word, Jackson stepped forward, trapped the other man's bound legs securely under one arm, and used the knife to savagely slash the underside of Saunders' right foot.

Just as quickly, he did the left.

It took a moment for the pain to hit, but when it did, Saunders began screaming.

The cuts were not deep, intended more to illicit a reaction than to cause any real damage. Jackson waited until the shock of the initial pain had passed and for Saunders to calm down.

Again, cut him again.

Jackson held off. There would be time enough for cutting very soon. Right now, he had to make Saunders understand just what was happening to him. And more importantly, why it was happening.

Jackson moved behind his prisoner and grabbed the man's left hand in his own. Saunders tried to squeeze his hand up into a fist, intent on protecting his fingers, but Jackson used the tip of the knife to keep the pinkie finger extended.

"You see Saunders, the world works in its own balanced way. Entire ecosystems are built around the concept of balance. Remove the wolf and the rabbit and deer overpopulate. Remove the rabbit and deer and you end up killing the wolf. Everything has a duty to fulfill. Everything has its own place in the chain."

Saunders whimpered beneath the tape as Jackson place the sharp edge of the knife at the base of Saunders' pinkie so that its long edge rose between that finger and the next.

"Only Man breaks this chain. Men like you, Saunders, who decide that it is okay to prey upon the young and the weak without giving anything in return. In your pride and your self-centered search for pleasure you use pain and death like servants instead of the masters of entropy that they truly are. When an innocent victim dies at the hands of a monster like you, that balance is disrupted, the cycle thrown off."

"Sometimes though, things can be set to right. Errors can be corrected. The cycle can be restored. Things can be put back into balance."

He tightened his grip on his knife.

"But there is a price. There's always a price. In order to balance the scales, you have to offer up something of equal value in return. Right now, you're all I've got to trade."

That said, Jackson began to saw off Saunders' left pinkie.

Saunders began screaming and didn't stop for a long time.

For the next three hours, Jackson worked his prisoner over. Slowly and carefully, he tortured the man in the same fashion that Megan Jones had been tortured in this exact same spot three years before.

First he used the knife.

Then he used the hammer.

Then he switched to the electric drill.

He used his hands intermittently throughout the process, until his knuckles were raw from the blows. His and his prisoner's blood mingled freely across their damaged surface.

Throughout it all, The Urge whispered fervently in the back of his mind.

Finally, as Saunders hung limp and bloody in the harness, his fear pushed to a fever pitch, Jackson stopped and rested.

As he worked to catch his breath, Jackson realized they were no longer alone.

The room around them was filled with a greasy black mist. Out of the corner of his eye, Jackson could see things moving in that mist; a cheekbone gleamed wetly here, a clawed hand covered in a gray, decomposing flesh reached out toward them there, white eyes with no pupil flashed into view and were gone just as quickly on the far side of the room. Like will-o-wisps in the night, each vision was there and gone before Jackson could focus on them, a situation he did not object to.

He knew that Saunders had also seen them when he heard a high-pitched keening noise floating across the room.

The mist seemed to twist and curl with greater frequency as the man's fear spread like a wildfire through the room.

Jackson sighed in relief.

He had done his job.

They had arrived.

The first time Jackson had encountered them had been entirely by accident. He'd lost control after catching a fleeing suspect, beating the man to within an inch of his life in anger over the senseless killing of an elderly man in a mini-mart. When he regained his senses, he'd found the alley in which he stood filled with the same greasy black smoke. Voices had spoken from the depths of the mist, asking him what he'd wanted.

Unthinkingly, he'd answered the first thing that had come to mind.

Surprisingly, they'd given it to him.

It wasn't until the Urge had started whispering to him that he'd figured out how to summon them on his own.

This time, he did not wait for their question.

"I've come to trade again."

A sibilant whispering filled the room, causing the hairs on the back of Jackson's arms and neck to stand at attention.

"I want the girl. Megan Jones, in return for this one," Jackson told the mist, indicating Saunders with one bloody hand.

The mist stood still for a moment, as if in indecision. Then with a banshee's shriek it swept forward, crashing around the two men like a wave breaking at its crest.

Jackson stood stock still, his eyes closed and his arms wrapped tightly about himself to guard against the chill he knew was about to envelope him. He felt phantom hands caress him and heard voices whisper in his ears. The hot fetid breath of something foul splashed across his face, inviting a reaction, but Jackson refused to give them one. He kept himself rigidly in control, somehow knowing instinctively that to do anything else would give them free reign to do what they would with him as well.

Saunders' terrified cries mixed with those coming from inside the mist, rising in volume until Jackson ached to cover his ears to drown them both out.

Then, as abruptly as it had begun, it was over.

Silence descended.

Jackson remained where he was for a long moment, being certain, then cautiously opened his eyes.

The mist, and Saunders with it, was gone.

At his feet lay the sleeping form of a young, blonde teenager dressed in a private school uniform.

Her name, Jackson knew, was Megan Jones.

Only a fading purple bruise remained, marring the left side of her face, testimony to what she had once endured at the hands of another animal much like Saunders. Even that would fade with time.

They were just getting off the highway when the girl regained consciousness in the front seat of the Caprice. She awoke confused, lacking memory of anything that she had experienced since the morning of the day she disappeared.

In his gentlest tone, Jackson informed her that he was a police officer and that he was taking her home. She'd been struck by a car, he told her, and had suffered a mild concussion but was otherwise okay.

She was still dazed by her experience and accepted the explanation, never even bothering to ask his name. When he pulled up in front of her house, she thanked him and got out of the car. He watched as she walked up to the front door and rang the bell. A face appeared at the window and a light went on over Megan's head, illuminating her where she stood on the front steps.

Jackson sped off just as the front door opened, disappearing into the darkness before he or the car could be recognized. From past experience he knew Megan would have no memory of the brutality to which she been subjected, but he knew that her parents would remember every heartbreaking moment from the second she had disappeared until now. They would want to know what had happened to her. They would want to know how she had come back.

Those were not questions Jackson wanted to answer.

With the rising sun Jackson headed for home, content with the night's events.

As he drove, a small voice began whispering in the back of his mind.

It's time, you know.
Time to do another one.
You'll like it.
I promise.

About The Authors

Joseph Nassise

A successfully published author of horror and Christian fiction. Nassise's debut novel, Riverwatch, was released in 2001 as the lead work in the newly created Spectral Visions horror imprint from Barclay Books of St. Petersburg, Florida.

Riverwatch has been favorably reviewed in such national newspapers as the Rocky Mountain News and the Scottsdale Tribune, as well as in industry publications such as Cemetery Dance Magazine, Hellnotes, and the Midwest Book Review. Critics have called his horror writing "hauntingly evocative" and "guaranteed to scare the socks off of readers."

Riverwatch was recently optioned to become a major motion picture from Media Entertainment of Tampa, Florida.

Joseph has been the guest speaker on various radio and cable television shows, including BookCrazy Radio. He has been a frequent panelist at conventions such as the North Eastern Writers Conference, the World Horror Convention, and Horrorfind. He recently completed an eight state signing tour for his debut novel.

Joseph is an active member of the Horror Writers Association and the Arizona Authors Association.

He can be reached via his website at www.josephnassise.com or by email at author@josephnassise.com.

Drew Williams

The youngest of five children, Drew Williams was born and raised in McKeesport, PA. Since earning his Ph.D. in Literature in 1993, Drew has been teaching English and Creative Writing in Durham, NC. Drew is the author of over a dozen articles and short stories including "Soon on Video," the winner of the Dark Moon Rising Halloween Fiction Contest for 2000. His novel, Night Terrors, has been named a Book of The Year by Inscriptions Magazine and is an EPPIE Finalist for Best Horror Novel of 2001. Check out his website at www.drewwilliams.com